PRAISE FOR LETA SERAFIM

FROM THE DEVIL'S FARM

"Set on the island of Sifnos, Serafim's timely third Greek Islands mystery (after 2015's *When the Devil's Idle*) centers on the murder of an unidentified boy who appears to be seven or eight. Lydia Pappas, a Greek-American ceramicist, found the blood-drained, trussed body of the likely refugee suspended over a fire pit near the shrine ruins of Thanatos. The crime scene offers few clues, and the inhabitants of the island's refugee camp, who live in tents and hovels, are mistrustful of the police and handicapped by the language barrier. Chief Officer Yiannis Patronas interviews Lydia (with whom he becomes smitten), as well as maverick American professor Richard Svenson and his three students from the U.S. Partonas also visits the refugee camp, where he meets a Syrian woman who says she's the victim's aunt. Serafim grounds her tale in Greek history, ancient and present, and provides a brutal and effective resolution to the case that will surprise most readers."
—*Publishers Weekly*

TO LOOK ON DEATH NO MORE

"A painful but engrossing story.... What saves the novel from a feeling of complete despair is O'Malley's love for Danae and his growing love of her country. This aspect of the war was unknown to me before this book. It's as important as the Blitz and the occupation of Paris, and Serafim makes me want to learn more."
—*Historical Novel Society*

"An impressively crafted read from beginning to end and clearly establishes author Leta Serafim as an exceptionally gifted novelist. Very highly recommended for community library General Fiction collections."
—*The Midwest Book Review,* Wisconsin Bookwatch

WHEN THE DEVIL'S IDLE

(Starred Review) "This classic fair-play whodunit, the excellent sequel to 2014's *The Devil Takes Half* (Serafim's first Greek Island mystery), takes Yiannis Patronas, the endearing chief police officer on the island of Chios, to Patmos, where someone has bashed in the skull of Walter Bechtel, a 90-year-old German, in the garden of his foster son Gunther's holiday residence—and carved a swastika on the victim's forehead. When Patronas asks Gunther about his foster father's past, Gunther becomes defensive and claims that his papa was 'just an ordinary man' and did not commit any atrocities during WWII. Serafim does an especially good job of integrating Greece's

current financial struggles into the story line, and Patronas's colleagues, especially an eccentric priest with a taste for seafood, lighten what otherwise could have been a very grim tale without minimizing the underlying horror of the background to the crime."
—*Publishers Weekly*

4 Stars: "The pairing of cynical Patronas and optimistic Michalis injects some humor in an otherwise moderately paced procedural. Serafim expertly creates the beauty of Greece. However, the real draws of this book are the fully developed, complex characters, and the facts on Greek culture and history. Book two in the Greek Islands Mystery series is sure to satisfy."
—*RT Book Reviews*

THE DEVIL TAKES HALF

(Starred Review–Featured as a Best Summer Debut) "Serafim's dense prose is perfect for lovers of literary and scholarly mysteries. Her plotting is methodical and traditional, with subtle nods to Sherlock Holmes, Greek mythology, and historical events."
—*Library Journal*

"[An] impressive debut…. Serafim has a good eye for people and places, and sheds light on the centuries of violent passion that have created an oppressive atmosphere hanging over the sunny Greek landscape."
—*Publishers Weekly*

"The Greeks have a word for it, and in this fast-paced, delightful mystery, that word is murder…. The real buried treasure is pure pleasure in Serafim's debut novel."
—Mary Daheim, *New York Times* and *USA Today* bestselling author of the Alpine and Bed & Breakfast mystery series

"Whether it's police procedural genre convention, the exotic island landscape, or the passionate Greek character, Serafim knows the lay of the land, and she confidently guides the reader. Armchair adventurers will get a solid grounding in Greece's violent and tumultuous past. The quirky pairing of Patronas and Michalis has the makings of an unorthodox investigative team and the beginnings of a beautiful friendship. This immersive escapist mystery should put Serafim on the map."
—*Kirkus Indie Reviews*

"The Greek setting gives this book not only an exotic locale but also characters that have a different way of looking at life and often, motives that wouldn't exist if this happened in… Cleveland. Take a literary visit to Greece. You won't regret it!"
—Jodi Webb

FROM THE DEVIL'S FARM

FROM THE DEVIL'S FARM

A GREEK ISLANDS MYSTERY

LETA SERAFIM

coffeetownpress

Seattle, WA

coffeetownpress

Coffeetown Press
PO Box 70515
Seattle, WA 98127

For more information go to: www.coffeetownpress.com
www.letaserafim.com

Cover design by Sabrina Sun

From the Devil's Farm
Copyright © 2016 by Leta Serafim

ISBN: 978-1-60381-244-3 (Trade Paper)
ISBN: 978-1-60381-245-0 (eBook)

Library of Congress Control Number: 2016951004

Printed in the United States of America

For Philip

Also by the author

The Devil Takes Half
When the Devil's Idle

To Look on Death No More

ACKNOWLEDGMENTS

I WISH TO THANK the following people: my husband, Philip E. Serafim, and my cherished friends and first readers, Nancy Nickles-Dawson, Margaret P. Carayannopolous, and Thalia Papageorgiou. Without their encouragement and support, I never would have finished this book.

I would also like to thank my colleagues and dear friends at Coffeetown Press, Catherine Treadgold and Jennifer McCord.

And last, but not least, my beloved grandchildren, Zoe, Grace, and George, who mean the world to me.

CHAPTER ONE

———◆———

Despise evil.
—The Delphic Oracle

BENEATH THE SHADOW of the old church, the woman paused to catch her breath and take a sip of water. She'd woken before dawn to make the long trek to the ruins, but in the end they had disappointed her. Part of a pagan citadel dating back to 1400 BC, the site had been ransacked for its marble over the centuries. It was mostly rubble now, the shapes of the Bronze Age buildings barely discernible in the stony earth. She'd explored every inch of it, seeking what, she did not know. Helen of Troy maybe? In the end, she had found nothing, only a grid of low-lying walls that went on forever.

The site occupied a hilltop behind the church of Aghios Andreas, one of the highest points of land on the Greek island of Sifnos. And if her guidebook was to be believed, it had been built by the Mycenaeans, the same race of warriors Homer had championed in *The Iliad*. But she'd seen no trace of those men today, little evidence of anything save for rocks and dust.

The museum didn't open until eight, so she'd had the place to herself, the only sound the relentless drone of the wind. Her hair had come loose and she pinned it back, irritated by the way it kept whipping across her face.

A goat path led away from the museum, and she decided to follow it to see where it led. Little more than a set of footprints in the brush, it disappeared a few minutes later, only a few broken branches in the undergrowth indicating the way.

She passed through a sheltered valley surrounded by bare hills and continued on.

She'd been walking about twenty minutes when she spied a second set of ruins high on a shaft of rock. Curious, she headed toward them and began to climb. The site was in even worse condition than the one by the museum.

Dark in color, it consisted of a single platform carved out of basalt, the blocks of roughly dressed stones positioned at a right angle against the steep slope.

The air smelled rank and there were flies everywhere, thick clouds of them, noisy in the silence. Nervous, she hesitated for a moment and looked back over her shoulder, then stepped up onto the platform.

The dead boy was trussed like a goat at Easter, bound by a chain at the wrists and ankles and hung over a pit at the center of the space. He had a gaping wound in his throat, and someone had built a fire, now cold, beneath him.

The woman staggered back and began to scream, growing more and more hysterical. She fumbled for her cellphone. Not knowing how to summon the police, what the emergency number was in Greece, she called her hotel and asked the man at the front desk to do it. There was no longer a police station on Sifnos, the man informed her; it would take him some time to notify the proper authorities and get them there. He begged her to return to the parking lot, to wait there, and not to speak to anyone except the police about what she'd seen. Greece was hanging by a thread. No need for people to know that children were being murdered here.

CHIEF OFFICER YIANNIS Patronas was fast asleep in the police station on the island of Chios when the phone on his desk began to ring. He was sprawled on a cot in his office with a sheet drawn up to his chin—his temporary bedroom since leaving his wife. He'd been dreaming of his mother with her apron on in the kitchen of their old house—a happy dream—and he kept his eyes resolutely closed, hoping to hang on to a fragment of it.

But then his cellphone started up. The ringtone from Wagner's "Ride of the Valkyries," the signal he kept for his boss, Haralambos Stathis, in Athens.

Cursing, he checked his watch: 5:45 a.m.

Never one for pleasantries, Stathis started right in. "A child has been murdered on Sifnos. I need you to round up your team and get there as fast as you can. Head up the investigation."

"Team?" Patronas repeated, confused. *Team? What team?* He had no team he knew of.

"Yes, those men you work with: Giorgos Tembelos, Evangelos Demos, and that priest, the old fellow who thinks he's Sherlock Holmes. What's his name? Papa Michalis."

Patronas sighed. "Oh … them."

Although the three men had been his colleagues for years, and he numbered them among his closest friends, they were hardly superheroes when it came to police work, especially Evangelos Demos, who squealed like a pig at the sight of blood and mostly just got in the way.

"But I'm on Chios," Patronas complained. "I'm nowhere near Sifnos."

"There's a flight from Chios to Athens at 6:30 a.m.," Stathis said. "I want you on it."

After Patronas hung up, he began sorting through his belongings in preparation for the journey. His old-fashioned tape recorder was the first thing he put in his briefcase, followed by a forensic kit of his own devising. Finally he opened the bottom drawer in his desk and extracted his razor and toothbrush.

Though freshly laundered, his uniform was hopelessly wrinkled. He'd have to buy an iron one of these days and learn how to use it. Stuffing it between the frame and the mattress and sleeping on it wasn't working. He couldn't keep living like this—storing his toiletries in the file cabinet, spending his nights on a fold-up cot. It would kill him.

His ex-wife, Dimitra, had seen to the details of their domestic life. Now she was gone, living happily ever after in Italy, the last he'd heard. She'd gotten the house in the divorce settlement—it was hers by rights, part of her dowry when they'd married—which had left Patronas out in the street with a suitcase and no place to go, adrift in every sense of the word. Given the current state of the Greek economy, he could barely feed himself, let alone rent an apartment.

Dimitra had always said police work was his life, the only thing that mattered to him—not her, never her. And so it had come to pass. The office had become not just his life but his physical home, too. The place where he ate, slept, and on occasion when the washroom was empty, bathed. He'd even decorated his little cubicle for Christmas, stringing up tinsel and purchasing an inflatable tree. Twenty-four hours a day, seven days a week, he was there. Not from dedication—God, no—but because he had nowhere else to go. There had been B.D. (before divorce), and A.D. (after divorce). But unlike time, his life wasn't marching forward.

He went into the bathroom and splashed cold water on his face. Turning his head from side to side, he checked his ears. His mother had told him they increased in size as you aged and he inspected his apprehensively. They were the same as always, as was the rest of him—swarthy and bewhiskered. He drew himself up and smoothed down his hair. *Not bad*, he concluded, giving himself a last once-over. *I might be the size of a pygmy, but by God I'm handsome. A Greek god ... Adonis, maybe.* He studied himself a few more minutes and sighed. *Adonis who'd been put in the dryer and shrunk.*

The trip to Sifnos would take five hours if he was lucky. Chios was in the Northern Aegean, within a stone's throw of Turkey, and Sifnos was one of the Cyclades islands, far to the south of it. Might take even longer, depending on the schedule of the boats. Although Patronas had argued against it, saying it would waste precious time, his boss had insisted they all fly first to Athens—

'it's only an hour by plane'—then take the ferry to Sifnos—'it's short trip, less than three hours'—saying he couldn't justify the expense of flying them there by helicopter. According to Stathis, a man Patronas had worked with for over twenty-two years, dead was dead. Corpses didn't wander off while you were getting there; they stayed where they were.

To make matters worse, his boss had insisted that Patronas 'bring the body out undetected.' Those were his exact words—an impossibility in Patronas' mind. Mid-summer, Sifnos would be crawling with tourists, and thanks to television, everyone would know what a body bag looked like. Chances are, news of the murder would be all over the Internet before he and his men had finished processing the scene.

The case already grieved him. A child ... God Almighty. What was the world coming to? Not only was his country financially bankrupt, it appeared at least one of its inhabitants was morally depraved as well.

Grabbing a pen, he wrote a note for a staff member, a self-styled computer expert named Nikos Zannaras, and told him to check for similar crimes when he came to work that morning. Patronas doubted there'd be any other murders like the one Stathis had described, at least not in Greece, so he instructed Zannaras to contact Interpol and scour the world.

Then he called Tembelos and the others, instructing them to meet him in front of the station in fifteen minutes and be prepared to travel.

He wished Stathis hadn't insisted he take Evangelos. A *paidovouvalos*, a fat man with a kid's face, he'd caused Patronas nothing but trouble since rejoining the Chios Police Force. The latest incident had been the theft of a valuable mosaic from *Nea Moni*, an eleventh-century monastery, which the perpetrators, a group of professionals from France, had chiseled off the wall and walked away with right under Evangelos' substantial nose. It hadn't helped his assistant's reputation that he'd been seen exchanging pleasantries with the thieves in the parking lot and had wished them '*bon voyage*' upon their departure.

Consequently, Patronas had taken him off active patrol and set him to work reorganizing the archives in the back of the station, instructing him to start at 1945 and work his way forward. A lifetime of paperwork, in other words. Nicely contained, Evangelos was, and Patronas was reluctant to turn him loose again.

"The murdered child was seven or eight years old," Stathis had said. "A little boy of indeterminate nationality. The woman who found him thought he might be Pakistani or Indian, given his slight build and coloring. Frankly, I don't care what he was. A child is a child. She said he's dark enough to be a gypsy, but he could well have been one of ours."

"You said he was killed on Sifnos?"

"Yes, in an area called Thanatos."

Patronas felt a twinge of unease. *Thanatos* meant death in Greek.

"It was brutal. Whoever did it set him on fire."

"They burned him alive?"

"Maybe afterwards, to cover their tracks. We won't know until the coroner takes a look.

"The government closed the police station on Sifnos and moved all the personnel to the regional unit on the island of Milos in the former Cyclades Prefecture. There's only one man left there now, Petros Nikolaidis. He's talking to the woman now and taking her statement."

"I know Petros. We were students together at the police academy. He's been on Sifnos for years, hasn't he?"

"Yup. He knows the island and you know murder. You'll make a great team, the two of you—Batman and Robin."

Patronas reached for his little spiral notebook, thinking that his boss was in a mood so he'd better tread lightly. He wrote, 'No cops on Sifnos.' Possibly, the absence of a police presence was the reason the killer had chosen the island.

"Was this woman the only witness?" he asked.

"As far as I know. Seems odd that she walked up to Thanatos, given the nature of the place. It's some kind of old shrine, dating back to the time of Christ. Falling down, apparently. Not much of a tourist draw. There's a well-known excavation nearby. I spoke to the director of the museum there. A group of Americans were in the area earlier this week, he said, not far from where the body was found. But aside from them, no one else went near it. Like I said, it's not a place people seek out."

"Any locals in the vicinity?" Patronas hated dealing with foreigners. Different languages, different cultures, it always made a case harder to manage.

"According to the museum director, the locals don't go there," Stathis said. "Woman's name is Lydia Pappas. Born and educated here, but lives abroad. Boston, I think. After you process the crime scene, I want you to turn her inside out. See if her story holds up."

"But she's Greek, sir. Greeks don't kill kids."

"Already made up your mind, have you, Patronas? Decided on the nationality of the perpetrator?"

Patronas knew better than to argue. Defending himself would only make it worse.

His boss was pushy and ruthless, a bruising little bulldozer of a man, but tonight he was more irritable than usual. He had a son, Patronas remembered, a boy about the same age as the victim.

"The child was tied up and hung over a fire by his arms and legs," Stathis said. "I want you to catch the person who did this, Patronas, and find him fast. And if that person should suffer a fatal mishap while you have him in custody, so much the better."

Stolid and unemotional, Petros Nikolaidis chose his words carefully when Patronas called him. "I don't know much about Thanatos," he said. "No one does. There are a lot of stories, and the locals say it's inhabited by witches. Just today an old man approached me and warned me to be careful. A native of Sifnos, he said he wasn't surprised to hear a child had been killed up there. 'This means only one thing,' he said. 'They're back. The devils who worship in that place.'"

Patronas laughed uneasily. "Come on, Petros. Old people say a lot of things."

It was true. Greece abounded with such legends. Foreign archeologists loved them and would visit remote villages in the hinterlands and listen to the elders, thinking they'd discover the Cyclops asleep in a cave or the wings of Icarus on a distant beach. The Minotaur on Crete was a favorite of theirs. Supposedly it had played a part in a ritual of human sacrifice, its victims appeasing a wrathful god. Patronas' mother-in-law had been full of such tales and he, for one, had no use for them. *Let the archeologists look as much as they want. The Cyclops no longer walked this earth.*

"How'd the old man hear about the murder?" he asked.

"His nephew runs the museum at Aghios Andreas. Old man probably knew about the killing before we did."

After arranging for a place to meet on Sifnos, Patronas said goodbye to Nikolaidis and slipped the phone in his pocket. He took a last look around his office to see if there was anything else he needed. Then, stepping around the remnants of last night's supper—a half-eaten pepperoni pizza—he opened the door and headed out to meet the others. Giorgos Tembelos, a shambling man with white hair, was waiting for him on the front steps, suitcase in hand, next to Evangelos Demos and Papa Michalis.

"It's bad," Patronas told them. "Another murder. Victim's a little boy."

Papa Michalis let out strangled moan. "Where?"

"On Sifnos. A place called Thanatos."

CHAPTER TWO

———◆———

Venture into danger with prudence.
—The Delphic Oracle

THE PLANE DEPARTED Chios on schedule. After landing in Athens, they hurriedly flagged down a cab and roared to the port of Piraeus, where they boarded the first boat to Sifnos. Stathis had arranged for a member of the *Limeniko*, the Coast Guard, to meet them at Kamares, the port of Sifnos, and drive them from there to Aghios Andreas. There was no road to Thanatos, he'd informed Patronas. They'd have to shoulder their gear and hike up to the murder scene.

A man in a blue uniform was waiting for them on the quay, standing next to an unmarked white van. After introducing himself, he reached for Patronas' bag and stowed it inside.

A Coast Guard cruiser was tied up nearby, and Patronas looked it over as he fastened his seatbelt, thinking it might be useful. He could spirit the child's body onboard and transport it to Piraeus that way. Fewer people would be involved and it would get to Athens faster. He'd have to check with Stathis and see if it could be done.

Although the cruiser was small, it was well equipped, one of the modern vessels used to search for contraband and illegal immigrants on the uninhabited islands in the Greek archipelago. Greece had close to five thousand islands, and the recent onslaught of immigrants coming ashore from Turkey had strained the government's resources, leading to sporadic acts of violence against the invaders—men from Pakistan and Bangladesh originally, now Syria, Iraq, and Afghanistan.

Patronas didn't envy the Hellenic Coast Guard its mandate. Given the country's porous nature, it would be impossible to seal it off or stop any boatman from discharging his cargo, be it human or otherwise, on its shores. Over the last few weeks, the Coast Guard had intercepted thousands of migrants, crossing over from Turkey to the Greek islands of Lesvos and Kos, in multiple incidents. The government then announced the number of undocumented people expected to enter Greece would more than triple in the coming year. Close to a million people were on the move across the Middle East, officials had reported, all seeking to pass through Greece and enter Northern Europe.

Patronas wondered if the victim had been one of those immigrants, brought here by his family. If so, where were they now and why hadn't they reported him missing?

Three identical sailboats were anchored close to the cruiser, their rigging clanging in the wind. Foreign tourists, Patronas judged, part of a flotilla making its way through the Cyclades Islands—Mykonos to Santorini, Paros to Sifnos and back again.

The islands were justifiably famous and drew over twenty million visitors every summer. A journey through them was what foreigners dreamt about. The Greeks, their economy in ruins, didn't dream of such things anymore. They only dreamed of having enough money to feed their children. His people were being washed away in a storm of debt and misfortune, the future of their children forfeited perhaps forever. If things didn't change, one day all that would be left of his homeland would be its beauty.

The driver of the van, a small taciturn man with greasy hair, started the engine. "When did you want to be picked up?" he asked, turning to Patronas.

"Sunset," Patronas told him. "We should be finished by then."

"Athens said you'd be bringing out the body."

"That's right."

They drove through Apollonia, the capital of Sifnos, then turned onto another road and headed toward Vathi, a modern settlement on the southern coast. Stathis had said the entrance to Aghios Andreas was about halfway between the two towns.

Patronas rolled down his window and looked out. The island was lovely in the midday light, full of terraced hills thick with olive trees. The air was fragrant with the smell of oregano and thyme. Closing his eyes for a moment, he breathed deeply, savoring the scent. Beneath the trees, the earth glimmered faintly in the sun. In ancient times, Sifnos had been famous for its gold mines, he'd learned in school, and it was as if a residual gleam still lingered in the soil.

In the old days the inhabitants of Sifnos were well known for their deceitfulness and greed, his teacher had said, and tried to cheat Apollo, presenting him with a gilt egg at the Oracle of Delphi instead of their customary gold one. Angry, Apollo retaliated and flooded their mines. An object lesson, if ever there was one. The teacher had gone on to imply such would be the fate of any student he caught cheating. Maybe not divine retribution as in the case of Apollo and the flooded mines, but something equally dire.

Patronas smiled at the memory, remembering how he and his classmates had tossed an exam folded up like a paper airplane out a bathroom window to another group of students waiting below. Textbooks in hand, the latter had solved the problems and sent the exam flying back. Unfortunately, all the answers had been wrong; the teacher had gotten suspicious, and everyone in the class failed. A flood of sorts it had been, that deluge of zeroes.

The priest had bought a guidebook and was calling out the names of the churches as they passed. "According to what it says here, they are scattered all over," he said. "Three hundred sixty-five total, one for every day of the year."

Patronas smiled. Not greedy anymore, the natives were pious now.

The van climbed steadily, passing through the settlement of Katavati and slowly traversing the mountain that formed the core of the island.

The ancient citadel of Aghios Andreas proved to be far bigger than anyone had anticipated. "More than ten thousand square meters," the priest informed them. In addition to the extensive ruins, a modern museum had opened in 2010 to house the finds from the excavation.

Perhaps it was its location—they were very high—but the place felt like a world apart to Patronas. Almost as if he was suspended in the sky. The day was clear and he could see three islands in the distance—Antiparos and Paros to the east, and Kimolos to the south—little more than dark shadows against the horizon. The Aegean seemed to fill the visible world, the landfalls in the distance mere markers in its vast blue expanse.

Idly, he wondered what had driven the ancients to build so high—what manner of monsters they'd been fleeing. And what had drawn the murdered child to this place. It was unlikely the child had come here on foot. He'd either taken a bus or someone had driven him.

Getting out his notebook, he wrote 'access' and put a question mark next to it.

As arranged, Petros Nikolaidis was waiting for him in the parking lot.

"I took a preliminary statement from Lydia Pappas and drove her back to her hotel," he told Patronas. "She was a wreck, shaking and crying. Covered with vomit."

"And the boy?" Patronas asked impatiently. "The dead boy? What of him?"

"I left him where he was. He's been there awhile, so prepare yourself."

Patronas and the others followed Nikolaidis through the ruins and down a poorly marked trail. Equipment in hand, they walked for a long time, passing through an empty valley and moving on, deep into the interior of Sifnos. The area was desolate, arid and rock-bound. No trees, no shade whatsoever, only a thin scrim of thorny brush and patches of mustard-colored lichen on the stony ground.

Nikolaidis pointed to an outcropping in the distance. "That's Thanatos. There are stairs leading up to the top, but they're pretty treacherous, so watch your step. The gravel can shift underfoot, and it's a long way down."

Judging by its appearance, Thanatos' origins were volcanic, the result of some prehistoric lava flow. The area at the base had been smoothed down over time, sanded by the ebb and flow of some long vanished ocean, but higher up, the lava remained rough, so black it seemed to pull the light out of the sky. Although the flow was threaded in places with bright bands of ingenuous rock—quartz, mostly—the overwhelming impression it gave was of darkness. It was as bleak a place as he'd ever seen.

Patronas had seen photographs of Devil's Tower, the basalt shaft in Wyoming that featured prominently in the American movie *Close Encounters of the Third Kind*. Thanatos reminded him of that place. Looking up at it now, he felt again a sense of unease.

Well on in years, the priest, Papa Michalis, was too proud to ask for help, but the long hike in the sun had cost him and his face was beaded with sweat. "How much farther?" he asked Patronas, wiping his brow on his sleeve.

"Just a few more steps, Father," Patronas said. "We're almost there."

On a leave of absence from the church, the priest now worked in the police department on Chios. He had originally been hired as a counselor, to help the wayward—the drunks and wife beaters—mend their ways, but his role had evolved over time and now included assisting Patronas and his team on criminal investigations. He was especially good at ferreting out the truth, even from the worst offenders. Patronas had no idea how he did it—maybe it was the priestly regalia, the black robe and the cross, a reminder that there could indeed be a hereafter, and in the case of habitual criminals, it might well be bleak—but he was unequalled when it came to gaining their trust and eliciting confessions.

The two had become friends over the years, often eating dinner together on their native Chios, drinking ouzo and sparring about human nature and the role God played or didn't play—Patronas being an atheist—in the affairs of man. The priest had told him long ago that family was one of the keys to human life. Apparently, homicide also played a part, for this was the third time they'd been summoned to investigate a murder in the last eighteen months.

But never for the killing of a child, Patronas thought sadly. *No, this is a first for us.*

Greece had one of the lowest homicide rates in the world, and consequently, most local law enforcement officials had little experience dealing with it. They had no firsthand knowledge of forensics, no idea how to chart the trajectory of the blood spatter, for example, or assess the time of death. The places under their jurisdiction were peaceful, so they'd no cause to acquire these skills. For the most part, Greeks died of old age or in car accidents; they did not die at each other's hands.

Patronas, on the other hand, had learned far more about forensics than he wanted to know, having solved two previous killings, and was now considered an expert in the field. His colleagues called him 'Hercule' now after Agatha Christie's legendary detective, Hercule Poirot. A man, not unlike Patronas, of diminutive stature with a well-groomed moustache. The thought amused him. He'd been lucky; that was all. He hadn't known what he was doing then and he didn't know what he was doing now. Thankfully, his fellow officers had chosen Poirot and had not dubbed him Miss Marple.

The priest's lengthy robe was giving him trouble and he paused for a moment to tuck a portion of it up into his voluminous drawers, exposing his heavy orthopedic shoes and long black socks held in place around his spindly calves by hideous old-fashioned garters.

Patronas looked away, embarrassed for his friend. Normally, he would have made fun of him—the garters alone demanded it, and those drawers, Mother of God, were the size of bed sheets—but today his mind was elsewhere. "I'm worried about this one," he said.

"As am I," Papa Michalis said. "The killing of a child? It is an abomination. Who could have done such a thing?"

"A psychopath, maybe."

"Yes, yes. Someone like Ted Bundy." Papa Michalis continued in this vein for a few minutes, enumerating the sins of Ted Bundy, who if he was to be believed, had murdered at least fourteen young women and as many as a hundred.

Patronas was sorry he'd brought it up. His friend was fascinated by serial killers and could go on at length, recounting their misdeeds in grisly detail. The names of the men Jeffrey Dahmer had eaten, for example, and which limb he'd usually started with. Or the fact that Jack the Ripper had extracted a kidney from one of his victims and mailed it to a newspaper. While Patronas understood that such people were a challenge for a priest—it was a thorny theological question: how does one forgive the unforgiveable?—he wished his friend would find another hobby. Collecting stamps, maybe.

"However, Bundy didn't kill children," the priest was saying. "I fear what we're after is someone far worse, with the means to lure a child here and slaughter him."

Papa Michalis fancied himself a great crime stopper, the true heir to Sherlock Holmes, but he tended to get carried away. Today was no exception.

Patronas waved him off. "We will go where the evidence leads us, Father.

And I seriously doubt it will lead us to someone worse than Ted Bundy."

"Bah, that's what you think. There is evil alive in the universe, Yiannis, and you and I, I fear, are about to enter one of its lairs. To pass through a dark portal into hell itself. "

As inevitably happened once he got going, the priest continued to speculate—brevity was a concept Papa Michalis had no use for—about the nature of the evil. As was his wont, he thundered off in the wrong direction— that of fiction and fantasy and bad American television shows.

Later Patronas would recall the conversation. Papa Michalis had been onto something that morning in Sifnos; he just hadn't realized it at the time. Evil was indeed alive in the universe, and like fear, it was contagious and sometimes infected whole groups, spreading like a malignant virus, a contagion of violence and misery.

Ahead, the lava that formed Thanatos shone dully in the sun. A staircase had been cut into the rock, so steep it had been like climbing a ladder. Patronas paused to catch his breath. Nikolaidis and the other men had already reached the top and called down to him to hurry. The steps were deeply worn, cratered from centuries of use. Bending down, he touched one with his hand.

Swab it for DNA, you'd probably find Cain and Abel's.

CHAPTER THREE

———◆———

Be a seeker of wisdom.
—The Delphic Oracle

HIGH ON THE rocky crag, the ruins at first glance appeared to be part of the natural landscape. The shrine, what was left of it, had tumbled off the cliff at some point, chunks of squared-off stone littering the valley below. All was quiet, the air absolutely still.

"A lesser temple, it isn't featured in any guide books or maps," Nikolaidis said. "It's a secret place, well hidden. Tourists rarely make their way here."

"And now all these people in less than a week," Patronas said.

"I know."

Starting with the perimeter, Patronas circled the ruins at a deliberate pace, seeking to get a sense of the area before processing the body. The shrine didn't amount to much, consisting only of a long, rectangular platform with a circular pit at the center. The child's body was in the middle, hanging above the pit from a metal pole.

A shallow trench had been dug alongside the outer edge of the platform. Seeing the rawness of the disturbed soil, Patronas assumed it must be new. Whoever had done it hadn't made much progress; the rocky substrata must have given them trouble.

What undergrowth there was nearby had also been cleared away, a pile of yellowing weeds stacked neatly off to one side. Patronas made a note to ask the museum director at Aghios Andreas who was responsible for the upkeep of the site. That person might have seen something or possibly been involved himself.

Three columns had survived the earthquakes that plagued the region. They stood like sentinels on the far end of the platform. Crude things, the columns, unrecognizable as Greek, with scratchy symbols and drawings etched into the stone. Not modern graffiti, Patronas judged, running his hand up and down one of them. No, these were far older, probably dating from the dawn of recorded time.

The child's wrists and ankles had been bound with a chain and fastened to the pole with a lock. He hung there about half a meter above the fire, suspended over the pit. Greeks had once transported dead livestock that way, two men shouldering opposite ends of a pole.

Nearly as big as a man's hand, the lock was unlike any Patronas had seen, forged out of bronze and encrusted with some kind of white residue. It looked ancient, possibly centuries old. He could see where the clasp had come loose, the metal on either side worn thin. Had the child been bigger, he might have been able to break free.

Why hadn't the killer used a modern lock, a padlock made of steel? Could be he was afraid of being recognized, didn't want to risk buying one on Sifnos. *Strange.*

Patronas worked part-time on Chios, overseeing security for an excavation run by Harvard University. As soon as he got the chance, he intended to speak to the archeologist in charge there, Jonathan Alcott, and ask him about Thanatos—see if Alcott knew who'd built it and why. Could be he'd also know the provenance of the lock. If it was as rare as Patronas suspected, such information might well lead them to the killer.

'Source of lock?' he wrote in his notebook.

The platform was constructed out of chiseled blocks of gray basalt, a huge undertaking given its location and the intractable nature of the stone.

Korakia, crows, were circling the site, cawing raucously, their dark shadows passing back and forth, high above him. Their presence made him nervous. He picked up a fistful of gravel and threw it at them, hoping it wasn't the boy's body that had drawn them. The child still had his eyes and had been spared that at least.

Papa Michalis and Petros Nikolaidis were wrestling with the yellow crime scene tape, seeking to secure it in place. There'd been talk of erecting a tent above the victim, but Patronas vetoed it. Although it was standard operating procedure, he considered it pointless now. After they finished, they would move the body out. It couldn't stay here a minute longer, not in this heat.

"Suit up in your protective gear and start at the periphery of the crime scene," Patronas told the two. "Move in on your hands and knees. Make a grid. Go over every square centimeter. Bag all the evidence you find. Tembelos will record everything while I deal with the body."

Camera in hand, Tembelos was already hard at work photographing the murder scene, starting as Patronas had on the outside of the platform and working his way in. Stepping close to the body, he took a head shot, then moved down the length of the child's body, the flash going off at regular intervals.

Patronas took a photo of the lock with his phone and sent it on to Alcott, asking if he could identify it. He planned to call him later, once the child's body had been dealt with.

Evangelos Demos, true to form, had taken sick almost immediately upon arrival and been banished from the crime scene by Patronas, who feared he would vomit on the corpse and contaminate the evidence. They had been there for over an hour, and Patronas could hear his assistant still at it, retching loudly off the side of the mountain.

"*Eisai touvlo*," he muttered under his breath. You blockhead.

As a cop, Evangelos was hopeless. He should have been a grocer. He'd be good at sorting vegetables. They'd have a natural affinity—potatoes and cabbages and him. With a sigh, Patronas returned to his work.

Stepping into his tyvek coveralls and booties, he hastily zipped them up and pulled on a pair of latex gloves. It was already close to 40°C, 100°F. He'd have to work fast. They were running out of time.

Nikolaidis was right. The body had been there for some time. Rigor mortis was giving way and the limbs were somewhat pliable now, the flesh waxen. The child's eyes were open but cloudy. The heat might have rushed the process, he wasn't sure. The coroner had more resources. He'd leave the estimate of the time of death to him.

A handsome child, the victim had skin the color of honey and thick black hair. The soles of his feet were heavily callused, indicating he'd gone barefoot for much of his life. The palms of his hands were also blistered in places, work-worn like those of a day laborer.

Patronas was surprised to see the fire had done him no real harm, only singeing the back of his shirt and causing some blistering on the skin of his extremities, most probably after death. It was the wound in his neck that had killed him.

There were a few beads scattered around the edge of the pit in an orderly way. Patronas touched one with a gloved finger before bagging it. Faience, he guessed, of no intrinsic value. There were also coins and a tiny metal bell. A line of thick red powder had been dribbled around the platform. He stepped closer and lifted the child's blood-caked shirt with his pen. His ribs protruded and his belly was abnormally distended.

Hunger or the beginnings of decay? Perhaps the forensic people would know.

He was a small boy and very thin. His hair was dirty and had been dressed with some kind of oil, a cloying and sweet scent Patronas could not identify. In addition to his t-shirt, he was wearing cotton shorts, but no underwear.

Judging by his coloring and the poor quality of his clothing, Patronas thought the Greek-American woman, Lydia Pappas, was right. *The child's most likely a Pakistani or Indian immigrant, a throwaway no one would miss.*

Patronas filled his notebook with observations, drawing a picture of the place where the body lay and measuring the depth of the stone pit beneath. He continued to urge the others to search carefully, to gather and bag what they found.

"Anything, a hair, an eyelash. Use your tweezers."

He snipped a few strands of the victim's hair and tucked them into a plastic envelope, intending to send them to the lab in Athens for analysis. Perhaps the technicians there could give him an idea of the child's ethnic origins. Remembering his coursework in forensics, he duly swabbed beneath the child's fingernails, across the palms of his hands, and the wound in his neck. He carefully packed the swabs and sealed the evidence bags, labeling them as he went. He was more careless when fingerprinting the child. *An eight-year-old? The child wouldn't be in any database. Even DNA would probably be insufficient when it came to establishing his origins.* The human race being what it was, no one was pure anything, or so the coroner had said.

"Mongrels," the coroner had told him. "And if the child is indeed from the Indian subcontinent, so are close to two billion other people." No, he and his men would have to find another way to establish the boy's ethnicity. Hopefully, they'd get lucky and someone would come forward and identify him.

Next he gathered up the coins, beads, and the bell and slipped them into separate envelopes, noting the location and writing a one line description. He didn't expect to find much more. Aside from a thin trickle of blood, it seemed tidy for a crime scene, orderly. Whoever had done this had been careful. There was little of the purpling where blood usually pools after a heart ceases to pump, which surprised him. And the victim's skin, though deeply tanned, was radiant in death, almost translucent. On his right foot he wore a little woven anklet with a red zigzag pattern.

For some reason, the anklet made Patronas want to cry for the boy whose name he didn't know, whose parents he might never find. For the time being, he and his colleagues would have to fill in, be the chief mourners, and sing the Greek hymns for the dead, the *mirologia*, for him.

"Do you think someone interrupted them?" he asked Tembelos, pointing to the ashes of the fire.

Tembelos looked puzzled. "Here?"

It was a valid point. Aside from scavengers, the crows and the flies, Thanatos had been bereft of life, sterile and gritty. It was like standing on the surface of the moon.

"Take another close-up of his face," Patronas ordered Tembelos. "We'll print copies and distribute them. Someone has to know who he is."

He studied the remains of the fire. By all accounts, the site had been deserted at the time of the murder. Only poor Lydia Pappas had been in the vicinity, out on an early morning stroll. *So if no one was here, why didn't the killer keep the fire going? Incinerate the body and destroy the evidence?* Another puzzle.

Whoever had done this was clever. He'd lured the boy up here and killed him without leaving a trace of himself behind. It was quite an accomplishment.

The red powder had caught the eye of the priest. He was crouched down, rubbing it between his gloved fingers.

"Odd," he said, looking up at Patronas. "I believe it is red ocher. Primitive man used it in religious rituals."

Patronas duly logged this in his notebook.

If it was indeed red ocher, they'd need to determine if the substance was easy to come by, and if not, where the killer might have obtained it. One thing was sure: this was no random attack. The crime had been elaborately staged, almost ceremonial in execution. *But why?* "There has to be a reason the murderer chose this site," Patronas insisted. "As a crime scene, it's virtually immaculate, way too clean. Could be the child was killed someplace else, brought here, and the ritual staged."

The priest waved him off. "Unlikely. It would have been too risky. He would have had to pass by the museum. Chances are someone would have seen him."

Patronas got a large plastic tarp out of his briefcase, unfolded it, and spread it out on the platform. Then he and Tembelos lifted up the pole with the body, removed it from the pit, and laid it gently down on the tarp. They broke open the lock and removed the length of chain, taking care to touch them as little as possible. Then they bagged the hands, head, and feet of the child and placed him inside a body bag, zipping it closed. Designed for adults, the bag was far too big and made a crinkling noise as it settled around the body.

The sight grieved Patronas even more. Even in death, the child had no place.

He sealed up the pole, encased it in plastic, and handed it to Tembelos. "Maybe we'll get lucky and the killer left some prints behind."

Returning to the platform, he pulled on a fresh set of latex gloves. He slid down into the pit where the fire had been and began gathering up the ash, bagging it fistfuls at a time. Buried deep between the stones were chunks of broken glass, iridescent with a strange residue.

Patronas summoned Tembelos back, and together they pried the stones farther apart. Cautiously, he probed the area between them. His fingertips caught on something. Pulling a brush from the forensic kit in his pocket, he dusted the ash away, assuming it was another shard of glass.

His breath caught in his throat when he saw the cavities in the bone, the gaping eye sockets.

It was a fragment of a skull.

Tembelos had been looking over his shoulder. "*Panagia mou!*" he gasped when he saw what Patronas had unearthed. Mother of God.

Seeking to touch it as little as possible, Patronas pried the bone loose with a metal tool and gently bagged it, then returned to the fire pit and dug deeper still. Beneath the skull he discovered more bones—the remnants of a ribcage and a tiny pelvis—half-hidden between the rocks. The bones were very dark, fossil-like almost. He kept working, first with one tool, then another, before finally switching back to the brush. The dead child called out to him, begging for justice.

The sun was setting by the time he unearthed the rest of the skeleton, the femur and spine, the latter so fragile and delicate it might have belonged to a bird. It was softer than the rest.

"Could be an animal," Tembelos called out, watching him. "A spring lamb somebody butchered up here."

"Maybe," Patronas said. But somehow he didn't think so.

He studied the ribs carefully. Stub-like and uneven, they were like fragments of petrified wood.

"So small," he said.

Together, they packed up the bones in silence. Deeply uneasy, Patronas stared out at the gathering darkness.

Between them, they'd unearthed something unholy that day.

Although he hadn't said anything, he was sure the bones belonged to a child. A young one, less than a year old. The boy hadn't been the first to die here.

THEY CARRIED THE boy's body back to the van and laid him out in the back. It had taken them long to get down from the platform, edging along with the body bag, flashlights in hand. Tembelos and Patronas had been in the lead with the corpse, Evangelos Demos and Petros Nikolaidis bringing up the rear with the metal pole and chain and all the forensic gear. Last down had been Papa Michalis with the evidence bags. Night was fast approaching and Patronas was desperate to leave.

The museum was closed by the time they reached Aghios Andreas, the excavation hidden in shadows. The driver was waiting for them beside the white van, the only vehicle left in the parking lot. He opened the back doors and stepped aside as they laid the body bag down.

Shaking his head, he shut the doors behind them. *"Kakomoiro,"* he whispered. Poor kid.

Patronas immediately called Stathis on his cellphone and asked him to arrange for the police cruiser to meet them at Platys Gialos, a village on the eastern coast, and once there, to take the remains to Piraeus. Petros Nikolaidis had said a new marina had been constructed there and it would be deserted at this hour.

Stathis liked the idea, saying it would be better than transporting the corpse on a commercial ferry.

The men boarded the van and fastened their seatbelts. The driver started the engine and they got underway. No one spoke during the ride, their melancholy cargo depressing all of them.

It took less than thirty minutes to reach Platys Gialos. Occupying a far corner of the harbor, the marina was well suited for their purposes. The cement quay extended well out into the bay, far from the tourist traffic.

There was a chapel about midway up the hill, but little else of note. A row of yellow mercury lamps illuminated the area, making it as bright as day, but as Nikolaidis had predicted, Patronas saw no people. A high wall ran perpendicular to the quay, protecting the boats from the sea, and the police cruiser was anchored at the end.

Getting out of the van, Patronas flashed his flashlight twice at the cruiser, the pre-arranged signal he and Stathis had agreed upon to announce their arrival. The captain sent two crew members out to assist. Together, they hoisted the body bag up, carried it gently onboard, and placed it in the hold of the boat. They were equally diligent with the evidence, storing it in a special container the captain had prepared. They went about their work quietly, whispering, as if afraid to disturb the child.

Patronas documented the transfer and had the captain sign for it. Establishing custody and chain of evidence was a necessary procedure, should the case ever come to trial.

The cruiser left a few minutes later, its massive wake a white scar in the water. Once there, the boy's body would be taken off the boat and driven to the lab in Athens in another van. Stathis would meet the cruiser, he'd told Patronas, and accompany the child personally to the morgue. He'd see to it.

His boss had been calling continually throughout the afternoon to monitor their progress. "What was the motive for the crime?" he'd asked Patronas at one point. "Was the child sexually molested?"

"Not that I could see. No, this was something else, sir. Scene was elaborately staged, almost like theater."

There had been a lengthy silence after Patronas reported he'd found a partial skeleton in the ashes of the fire.

"A serial killer?" his boss said in a low voice, as if afraid of being overheard.

"I don't know, maybe. We'll have to let the forensic people sort it out. Personally, I think they won't know what to make of it. We'll probably have to consult a forensic archeologist at the university about the bones' origins."

"Old, you think?" Stathis sounded hopeful.

"I don't know. They could have been tainted by the soil. It's volcanic—maybe some chemical reaction occurred. But they were brown, sir, the color of tobacco. Also, they were deeply embedded, so it was hard to say how long they've been there. The archeologists have a formula—so many centimeters equals so many centuries. Like I said, they'll be able to give us a better idea. Could be the bones were original to the site—two, maybe even three thousand years old. All I know is there was a lot of them, and they were little."

"An animal?"

"I don't think so, sir."

"Human, then." Stathis swore softly. "What else?"

"A bunch of old beads and coins were laid out in a circle around the victim, almost like an offering. Whoever it was would have had to bring them with him, indicating premeditation. Also, there was this red powder everywhere. Whoever did the killing nicked the child's jugular, but there was very little blood on the body or under it, which was strange—only a trace in the wound and down the front of his shirt. So where did it go? Given the catastrophic nature of the injury, he would have bled out within minutes."

Patronas paused for a moment, searching for the right words. "I couldn't believe what I was seeing, so I asked Tembelos to take a look and tell me what he thought. 'Only a couple of spoonfuls,' he said. 'Not enough.' He couldn't believe it either. He was pretty shaken up."

Truth was, Thanatos had frightened all of them.

CHAPTER FOUR

———◆———

As an old man, be sensible.
—The Delphic Oracle

NOT WANTING TO overwhelm Lydia Pappas, Patronas sent Evangelos Demos and the priest back to Kamares in the van, instructing them to check into the cheapest hotel they could find. He and Tembelos would meet them after they finished talking to her.

"Two double rooms. We'll bunk in pairs," Patronas said. "Tembelos and me in one. You two in the other."

"How long we staying, boss?" Evangelos Demos asked.

"Until we catch him."

Lydia Pappas was in an apartment at Leandros Studios, about half a kilometer from the marina, and after the van left, Petros Nikolaidis, Tembelos, and Patronas started toward it on foot. Patronas had ordered Tembelos to bring his video camera, planning to record every word she said for posterity. He always found it useful to review the footage of interviews in case he'd missed anything the first time around.

Nikolaidis said that after taking Pappas' statement, he'd examined her thoroughly and found no blood on her clothes, face or hands. "In addition, I bagged up her outfit and shoes and sent them to Athens to be tested along with the rest of the evidence—a precautionary measure. I don't think she's involved."

"It's a wonder you didn't spray her with luminol," Patronas said, impressed.

Nikolaidis had been the best student at the police academy, far surpassing his own lackluster performance. Born and raised on Serifos, a nearby island, he'd been a cop on Sifnos for over twenty years.

"Not much to do," Nikolaidis admitted. "Locals' idea of a crime is breaking the fast during Lent. Once in a while, a tourist will get drunk and drive off a cliff, but that's about it."

They continued to talk about Sifnos, with Nikolaidis sharing what he knew of the island. "Roughly two thousand five hundred Greeks live here year-round, and most are decent, hard-working people. They're pretty old school. *Panighiria, c*hurch festivals, is a major form of entertainment."

"Any troublemakers?" Tembelos asked.

"A handful, especially now with the migrants. Their presence has stirred things up."

"You actually think one of them could have done this?"

Nikolaidis nodded. "It's possible. There have already been a couple of incidents involving the migrants. Two or three of those men are known to be pretty violent."

He pointed to a large white hotel in the distance, saying, "Simitis stayed there when he was prime minister. You'd see him in his swimsuit on the beach, talking to people. No bodyguards in sight. He didn't need them then. Now, I'm not so sure."

"Besides Simitis, who else comes to the island?" Patronas asked, mentally taking notes.

"We don't get the tourist traffic of Mykonos or Santorini. It's mostly Greeks who vacation here."

Although the beach at Platys Gialos was said to be the longest in the Cycladic Archipelago, Patronas found the village that surrounded it surprisingly modest. With the exception of two large hotels, the one Nikolaidis had pointed out and another called Alexandros, almost all the businesses were small and family-owned. Benakis' rooming house/patisserie was typical, as was the little souvlaki place down the street. Although it was the height of the tourist season, no one was eating in either establishment, nor was there anyone in a bar called Mostra, farther down. It was one of the cleanest places Patronas had ever seen. The buildings had all been freshly whitewashed, and the only trash in the street was bougainvillea blossoms borne by the wind.

Beyond the village proper, Patronas caught a glimpse of another, poorer community, a dense warren of collapsing shacks and dank byways. Every surface was covered with graffiti. It edged a dry riverbed far back from the beach. People *were* living there. Patronas could see hovels constructed of plastic sheeting half-hidden in the rushes and smell traces of a poorly dug latrine. Migrants maybe, or perhaps a gypsy encampment? Hopefully his people were not this poor, at least not yet.

Nikolaidis gestured to the shantytown. "It used to be a campground. Migrants seized it about six months ago, just took it over. There's been a lot of discussion on Sifnos about what to do about it. The locals aren't happy. They want them gone."

Patronas studied the hovels, thinking he'd visit them the next day, interview the residents and find out if any knew the boy. The situation with the migrants was becoming increasing volatile all over Greece. A Pakistani had recently raped and beaten a local girl half to death on Paros, a neighboring island, setting off a violent backlash, a rightwing firestorm that was still burning.

He didn't believe the child's death on Sifnos was related to the incident on Paros, but he'd have to check it out anyway. Interview the local rabble-rousers. *For all their church-going, it could happen here, a migrant child done to death by a local. Payback for Paros.*

Everyday there were pictures of the migrants on the news, crossing the channel between Greece and Turkey on flimsy rubber rafts. Some of these boats had capsized and all those onboard had drowned, many of them children. It was tragic, entire families dead, the Aegean awash with bodies. And turning their backs on them wasn't the answer, he believed, or building a wall to keep them out like diseased livestock the way Hungary had. He and the priest had discussed the situation repeatedly. But if there was an answer, they hadn't found it. All those people pouring into Europe, some of them jihadists, intent on inflicting misery and destroying everything in their path. And unlike their ancestors, who'd given non-Muslims a choice—convert or die—these men were human time bombs and only wanted to kill.

As expected, Papa Michalis had counseled compassion.

"What if there's a critical mass in human life?" Patronas had argued, "A point at which outsiders tip some invisible balance and the others rise up against them? It's happened already once in Europe, people dying by the millions because of what they were. It could happen again, I'm sure of it."

"Sufficient unto the day is the evil thereof, Yiannis," Papa Michalis said. "The evil unto the day."

Still Patronas remained uneasy, fearing Europe was in for another round of bloodshed, that it was just a matter of time. The previous year, Greek farm guards shot and wounded over thirty men from Bangladesh, fruit pickers who'd been laboring for months without pay in Neo Manolada, a village in western Peloponnese. Prior to that incident, the same guards had killed two of the migrants' dogs, warning them 'This is how we'll deal with *you*,' and one had tied an Egyptian migrant to his truck and dragged him some distance. Then in January, a Pakistani man was stabbed to death on the streets of Athens. The situation was spiraling out of control. On the island of Lesvos, the epicenter of the crisis, a couple of Greek women had been raped by migrants. Acts of retaliation were sure to follow.

He, for one, had no problem with the Syrians, who were fleeing the deadly chaos that had engulfed their country. It was the others, the so-called 'economic refugees,' he had no use for. With fifty percent unemployment, there were no jobs in Greece. No way could the government feed or house these men. So why had they come? To peddle crap in the street? To beg?

His colleagues on Chios felt even more strongly, spoke of preventing the migrants from disembarking on Greek shores, of forcefully turning their boats around. An explosive situation, no doubt about it.

Across the street from Leandros Studios was a large swimming pool with a luxurious bar. A beautiful place. The underwater lights in the pool made the blue-green water glow like a jewel in the night, a warm breeze rippling its bright surface. It, too, was completely deserted, the carefully arranged tables like scenery in a play, everything in readiness for a performance that would never take place.

What was it Nikolaidis had said? The island was a Greek tourist destination. And this year, the Greeks had no money and they hadn't come.

"I used to have an office in Apollonia, staff and everything," Nikolaidis said, nodding to the empty pool. "But it's gone now, part of the government's austerity program. Way things are these days, I'm lucky to be employed."

Patronas lit a cigarette and inhaled deeply. He didn't want to discuss the decline of Greece, not tonight, not after what he'd seen. He still felt sick about Thanatos.

He looked toward the sea, wishing he could wade into it and wash away the memory, the image of the little boy and what had been done to him. He was too old for this, too old to deal with murdered children.

"What kind of person does a thing like this?" he asked Nikolaidis. "Chains a kid to a pole and slits his throat?"

"*Ena teras,*" Petros Nikolaidis said quietly. A monster.

CHAPTER FIVE

———— ♦ ————

Exercise nobility of character.
—The Delphic Oracle

A BEAUTIFUL WOMAN, LYDIA Pappas appeared to be in her mid-thirties. She had a thick mane of reddish-brown hair braided and pinned at the nape of her neck, and was dressed casually in cargo pants and a photographer's vest with little zippered pouches down the front. Pockets seemed to be the theme, and she had many.

Patronas and Nikolaidis were sitting on the terrace outside her apartment with her. The units in the complex all faced the public beach, and Patronas could hear the waves—little ones, *kymatakia*—washing along the shore. Out in the harbor, a light shone on the mast of a sailboat, star-like in the darkness. Lydia Pappas had turned off the overhead light and lit a lantern, saying she preferred it to the other, which drew mosquitoes.

After introducing himself, Patronas gave a little speech thanking her in advance for her cooperation and asking if he had her permission to tape the interview.

"Of course," she said.

He began by asking, "How'd you get to Aghios Andreas this morning? There are no buses at that hour."

"I rode up on a moped," she replied. "I timed it so I'd be there just before dawn. I wanted to watch it, to see the light fill the sky. It was glorious and I was glad I'd come. Such beauty. And then," she shuddered, "that poor, poor child. I don't think I will ever get over it."

Her voice was deep and melodic, and she had an intense way of speaking, a hint of the theatrical in her choice of words. "I keep seeing him hanging there." She closed her eyes, seeking to block out the memory.

Patronas nodded, understanding what she meant about the contrast between the beauty of the dawn and the ugliness of murder. Like her, he had never been able to reconcile the two, believed he never would.

"Where's your moped now?"

"I parked out front."

He asked for the keys and sent Nikolaidis out to take a look.

The child wasn't bleeding when she'd discovered him, Pappas went on to say. He had obviously been dead for some time. She had seen no one either going or coming and nearly fallen down the stairs in her haste to get away.

Patronas was curious about what had drawn her, a single woman, from Boston to Sifnos, and finally, earlier that day to Thanatos. Was she running away from something? A divorce perhaps, the death of a family member? Or had she come to Greece like so many others in search of something she lacked at home? He didn't know what brought them here, but they turned up every summer, those women, the sad ones like Shirley Valentine, who had affairs with Greek men and thought they'd discovered the meaning of life.

She sounded highly educated; her Greek was impeccable. Seeing her amphibious-looking footwear, olive drab sandals she'd chosen to wear with socks, he thought she might be a scientist, an academic of some sort. When it came to fashion, they were a nation unto themselves, the academics. Ralph Lauren himself wouldn't know what to do with them. His friend, Alcott, always wore a hat with flaps that covered his ears like a French Legionnaire's. It was a preposterous thing, that hat, justly ridiculed by the local Greeks. And socks. Alcott, too, was fond of socks. Woolly white socks that reached halfway up his legs.

It turned out Lydia Pappas was an artist, a potter. A 'ceramicist,' she said, who taught at a university in Boston in the winter and participated in a six-week educational program on Sifnos during the summer.

"Most of our coursework focuses on Greece—the ancient sites and history, the culture then and now," she said when Patronas quizzed her about it. "Regardless, the program is not affiliated with any academic institution, and the students don't get credit for attending." She laughed. "You want my honest opinion? It's a very pretentious and expensive summer camp. Costs upwards of seventy-five hundred dollars per student."

She fingered the zipper on her vest. "They pay me pretty well, and room and board are included. I wouldn't have been able to come here otherwise. I wanted to see the *tsoukaladika*, the ceramic workshops, on the island and learn how to make *skepastaria*, the pots the locals use for *revithia*, chickpea soup. Learn the technique and go back and teach it to my students in Boston. Sifnos has been justifiably famous for its potters since ancient times. At one time, the word 'Sifnian' was synonymous with the profession. It actually meant 'potter' to Greeks in the old days."

Patronas knew things were strange in America, but this was the first he'd heard you could study pot-making in a university. Pay good money to get a degree in *laspi,* mud. He shook his head. *Such frivolity. No wonder the Chinese are taking over.*

"I am an artist, Chief Officer," she said as if sensing his skepticism. "Clay is my medium. I am very good at what I do."

"Now about this morning?" Patronas said, seeking to return to the matter at hand. "Try and remember what you saw up there on that rock. The slightest detail could be important."

"The fire was out when I got there and the little boy was dead. I checked for a pulse, but that was all I did. I didn't touch anything. There were flies all over him. Flies crawling on his face, in his eyes." She shook her head as if trying to block out the image. "Flies everywhere."

"Did you see anyone else in the vicinity?"

"No. No one."

"Again, why did you go there? There are more convenient places to watch the sun come up."

"There's an American here and he said it was worth the trip."

Nikolaidis and Patronas looked at each other.

"How well do you know him?" Patronas asked carefully.

"I met him this summer. Leandros is not a big place—there are only three apartments—and I kept bumping into him. You know how it is when you work abroad? You make friends with people you'd never speak to at home. A man named Richard Svenson is in charge. Like me, he teaches in Boston during the winter and Sifnos in the summer."

"How did you both end up here?"

"The program rents apartments in Leandros and in a couple of the other buildings in Platys Gialos as dormitories for the kids."

She pointed out at the harbor. "He has a boat, a big inflatable Zodiac, and he and his students are always out on it. Sometimes he invites me along and I go, or we all have meals together. I'm here alone and it breaks up the solitude, keeps me from forgetting my English. He dives, too."

"So you're both professors in Boston?"

"Yes."

"And he's the one who suggested you visit Thanatos, that rock where you found the body?"

"No. Richard only recommended I visit Aghios Andreas. He didn't say anything about that other place. He'd gone to the museum earlier and said that I shouldn't miss it. That it was an impressive facility."

"And the summer study found this apartment for you?"

"That's right. The kids have to stay in one of the buildings the program leases and part of our job is to supervise them while they're here. Greece doesn't have the same liability and safety concerns as in the states, so there are no residential advisers or rent-a-cops. It's pretty lax actually, just us. We teach them, have a meal or two together, and make sure everybody's back in their rooms by midnight."

"You have any problems with them?"

Tired now, she fidgeted in her seat. "Not really. The study screens them pretty well. It's my first summer, but the program has been around for a long time. It's run by a consortium of Greek academics in the United States."

Patronas had no doubt the summer study had been devised by a group of his countrymen, wanting free airfare to Greece, an expense-free summer vacation. Many schools offered such things. Even the church ran one, Ionian Village in Peloponnese. His homeland called and the diaspora answered.

"So no problems?" he asked.

"None that I am aware of."

After asking her permission, he took her hand and gently rolled the tip of each finger back and forth on an inkpad. He pressed it onto the official fingerprinting card, one in each of the labeled boxes, first the left index finger, then the right. Her nails were blunt, cut straight across like a man's, and her skin was abraded in places, chapped from her days working with water and clay.

"Now if you'd be so good as to open your mouth," he said.

Lydia Pappas quickly complied and he swabbed the inside of her cheek. "Sorry I have to do this, but we need to eliminate you as a suspect. It's just a formality, nothing to worry about."

She gave him a bleak smile. "A clear sky has no fear of lightning."

It was an old proverb, meaning the innocent have nothing to fear. A strand of her hair had come loose and she brushed it back. Flame-colored, it caught the light of the lantern for an instant.

"Would you be willing to go back to Thanatos with me at dawn tomorrow?" Patronas asked. "Reenact how you found the body? You might have seen something at the time, but not realized it."

"Yes, yes, of course. I'll do anything I can."

"Very well then. I'll pick you at four thirty a.m."

She stood in the doorway when they left. Raising a tentative hand in farewell, she called out 'good night' and kept waving, the ink still smudged on her fingers. Patronas waved back.

Chapter Six

———— ◆ ————

What you learn as a child, you cannot forget.
—Greek Proverb

Judging by his expression, Richard Svenson wasn't happy to see Patronas and the other two policemen. He occupied an apartment on the second floor of the Leandros complex and was hard at work on his computer, a pile of books stacked up on the table next to him.

"Yes, what is it?" he snapped.

A narrow-faced man with thinning hair, he was dressed in jeans and a white oxford shirt and wore wire-rimmed glasses like John Lennon's. He had a fussy, slightly pompous air about him and spoke as if he expected to be listened to.

"May we come in?" Patronas asked. "We're police officers and we need to speak with you."

Svenson studied him for a long moment. "Tonight?" He made no effort to hide his annoyance.

"Yes. It's important."

While Tembelos set up the camcorder, Patronas and Nikolaidis hastily inspected Svenson's apartment. Without a warrant, they'd been forced to improvise, Nikolaidis engaging Svenson in conversation while Patronas pretended to use the bathroom. He hastily sprayed the sink and shower stall with luminol and checked the drains, finding no trace of blood. He then moved on to the bedroom, opening and closing drawers and rummaging around in the closet. He lifted his eyebrows when he emerged, signaling Tembelos and Nikolaidis he hadn't found anything. It was the Greek equivalent of shaking one's head.

"Why do you need to tape this?" Svenson nodded to the camcorder.

"I don't know what the protocol is in America, but it's customary in Greece."

"You people and your bureaucracy. No wonder your country is such a mess."

Ignoring the gibe, Patronas requested Svenson's permission to tape the interview.

Svenson nodded, saying he'd be happy to speak Greek if that would speed things up; he was fluent in both languages.

Relieved, Patronas slid his little Divry's English-Greek dictionary back in his briefcase. A tiny thing, it always took too long to find the word he was seeking, derailing an interrogation. The suspect would sit there yawning while he searched and searched, momentum hopelessly lost.

Alas, five minutes into the interview, Patronas found himself reaching for the Divry's; Svenson's Greek was simply incomprehensible. Endings gave him trouble. He was talking about an upcoming trip he was planning to Turkey and the marvelous food there, but instead of saying *yaourtoulou,* a goat dish prepared with yogurt, he said, *katroulou,* which meant 'baby girl pissing herself.' Worse, the American was unaware of his inadequacies and chatting up a storm.

Tembelos found Svenson's garbled Greek hysterical and was bent down over the camcorder, guffawing so loudly Patronas suspected his friend, too, must be pissing himself.

"Let's speak English," Patronas said in a tired voice.

He then gave his name and recited the date and the time of the interview as he had with Lydia Pappas. "First, please, what brought you to Sifnos this summer?"

"Where to start …. Well, to begin with, I'm a full professor at Boston University and I'm here running a summer study."

A talker, he went on to say that he had majored in religion in college—specifically obscure and ancient ones. Then he discussed the life events that had led him in that direction—a disappointment in love, the death of a brother. In the latter case he'd been quick to add, "from heart disease," not drugs or suicide or AIDs. He insisted that Patronas call him 'Richard,' saying he didn't believe in titles.

First names and best friends from the very start, even a foreign police officer he had never laid eyes on, a cop, who unbeknownst to him, was investigating a murder. A foolish man, Richard Svenson. *He should be more careful.*

In Patronas' experience, Americans only wanted two things in life: to get this party started and to stay forever young. Hence, Viagra and Grecian Formula. To shop was also on the list, but mainly with women.

Once, he'd preferred them to all other tourists, but since his country's economic collapse, his affection had waned, given way to resentment and envy. Greece was broke, yet here they came with their sunscreen and naiveté. And what they worried about enraged him. *Gluten, for God's sakes, when half the world is starving.* He started doodling furiously in his notebook, drawing Svenson with horns and a tail, waving an American flag.

"A few of the students are studying ancient religions under my tutelage," Svenson was saying, unaware of Patronas' dark thoughts. "They'll write a paper on what they've learned, get credit for their time. Initially, I wanted to take them to Ephesus and the cave churches in Cappadocia in Turkey, but the people who run the program ruled it out. I was hoping to visit Azize Barbara as well with its famous fresco of St. George and St. Theodore, struggling against the dragon and the snake. Much of our coursework this summer has been devoted to pagan and Christian symbolism—a great example of the synergy. I don't know if you're aware of the origins of the legend. Supposedly the dragon poisoned the countryside around Cappadocia, and to appease it, the people there fed it their children."

He kept pausing as if the policemen weren't clever enough to follow what he was saying and he had to wait for them to catch up. Patronas found him tedious, a little repellent.

Other men flexed their muscles, this one his erudition. Leaning over his notebook, Patronas drew another devil, this time wearing a mortarboard.

Svenson droned on and on. He seemed a little confused and used idiomatic expressions Patronas was unfamiliar with—'my mains,' was one, 'YOLO' another, which Svenson explained was shorthand for 'you only live once.' He liked talking about himself and seemed a little confused, one minute the youthful party animal, the next, a serious scientist. What you'd get if you crossed Mick Jagger with Albert Einstein.

"My latest research has been on one specific group," Svenson said. "I call them 'the people of the rock,' similar to the 'people of the sea,' the intruders who wreaked havoc throughout the area at the end of the Bronze Age. Mine was a far more enigmatic group, very small. No one knows where they came from or where they went. There were a number of individual subsets within the larger whole, rather like the Protestants during the Reformation, when everything began to splinter and come apart. The Anabaptists, if you will, of ancient times. If I can learn more about them, the specifics of their belief system, it will be a monumental discovery."

Small group? Monumental discovery? The two statements didn't add up.

Coming up for air, Svenson continued. "Little is known about these people. The few sites that have been discovered echo the religious practices of the Phoenicians, so the sect must have either originated with them or been the result of close contact."

"Any of these sites on Sifnos?" Patronas said. *Why am I bothering with this?* he asked himself, but something kept drawing him back to it, nagging at him. Could be it was what the priest had said about ritual murder, the idea that there might be a continuum between the past and the present and a child had died as a result.

"None that I'm aware of," Svenson said. "What's this all about?"

"That trench of yours …. The museum director told you it was illegal, but you dug it anyway. Why?"

"One of the students in the program, Charles Bowdoin, is debating whether or not to major in archeology and I wanted to give him a taste of what was involved. I thought we might get lucky and find some shards and send them out for carbon dating, establish how long the area had been in use. Some sacred places along the Mediterranean were occupied off and on for four thousand years, through the rise and fall of countless civilizations. A few even date as far back as the Paleolithic Age. You never know what you'll find."

"How did you know the ruins were there?" Patronas asked.

"I didn't. We just happened upon them. It was serendipitous."

Serendipitous? Jesus.

Svenson gave him a penetrating glance. "You didn't come here tonight to talk about that trench, Chief Officer. What's going on?"

Patronas laid the photo of the dead child down in front of him. "He was killed up there."

The color drained from Svenson's face. "Surely you don't think I had anything to do with it."

"Truthfully, I don't know what to think. Right now, I'm speaking to anyone who was in the vicinity."

"I wasn't the only one up there. Lydia Pappas was there, too." The professor's voice had gone shrill.

Not very chivalrous either, Professor Svenson. "I've already spoken to her," Patronas offered. "She's from Boston, too, isn't she? Is she a colleague at the university?"

"Heavens, no! Lydia's an assistant professor at a community college."

It was all there in that one sentence: Lydia Pappas' inferior rank and place of employment. Unfamiliar with the term 'assistant,' Patronas wrote down 'half.' Stood to reason, Svenson was a full professor. Hence, Pappas must be a half.

"When exactly did you dig that trench?" Patronas asked.

"Three days ago. We were only there a couple of hours. It was an inferno—well over a hundred degrees. Why? When did it happen?"

"Early yesterday morning, perhaps the night before."

"I was nowhere in the vicinity," Svenson said, visibly relieved. "I was in Platys Gialos. I spent the whole day there, never left."

"Anyone see you?"

"Oh, yes. Many people. I'm well-known in Platys Gialos. I ate at a taverna called Steki. I chatted with the wife of the owner, Flora. She'll remember me."

Patronas and Tembelos exchanged glances. Svenson was taking great care to provide himself with an alibi.

Seeking to establish a timeline, Patronas asked him how he spent his time on Sifnos, what he did on an average day. Did he and the students always travel together or were they allowed to wander off on their own?

He wanted to get a sense of the group's comings and goings, thinking their whereabouts at the time of the killing might prove significant. One could have been responsible. The site was too isolated, otherwise. No one else would have known it was there.

"The program gives the students a great deal of latitude," Svenson admitted, echoing Lydia Pappas' words. "I teach a class in the morning and one after lunch. Then, for the most part, they are free to do what they please until curfew. Once or twice, I've scheduled group activities—the trip to Aghios Andreas you're going on about was one—and then there was an evening in Castro. I try to have at least one meal with them, and sometimes we meet up at the beach and take the boat out." Svenson paused. "I'm not really their supervisor. I'm more of a friend."

More American foolishness in Patronas' mind. Kids needed supervision, not buddies. Otherwise, they went to hell. He'd once ridden his bicycle into his mother's freshly laundered sheets, pulling them off the clothesline and running over them with his tires. It had been an accident, but his mother didn't care. No, she'd picked up a fly swatter and let him have it, breaking it in half on his seven-year-old backside. That was how youth should be dealt with. *Smack, smack.*

As far as Svenson knew, none of the students in the program had ever journeyed to Thanatos on their own or spent the night there. "The idea is simply preposterous. Why would they?"

His demeanor changed after he saw the photo; he was far more cautious. "Do I need a lawyer?" he asked at one point. He also balked when Patronas wanted to fingerprint him.

"I'm fingerprinting everyone who was up there," Patronas explained, seeking to placate him. "I'm sorry, but it is necessary to eliminate you as a suspect."

That seemed to mollify him and he held out his hand. "I don't know what the university will say when they find out about this. Normally, teaching is a pretty staid profession. It isn't a blood sport." He laughed nervously.

Patronas stopped what he was doing and stared at him. A child was dead and here this man was making jokes. His dislike for the American grew, hardened into loathing.

The professor continued in this vein for a few minutes, mouthing inanities about himself and his academic career. "I'm renowned in my area."

It all seemed a little desperate. A reflex, Patronas concluded, as Svenson went on and on—that pathetic show of ego a nervous tic. When cornered, the man came out swinging the books he'd authored and the conferences he'd chaired.

"Lydia is an assistant professor, not a half professor," Svenson declared when Patronas read his notes back to him, the professor's voice arch and superior. "There is no such thing as a 'half professor.' Nor is there a quarter or a third. We have all our limbs, Chief Officer. In case you haven't noticed, none of us is an amputee."

CHAPTER SEVEN

———◆———

Make your own nature, not the advice of others,
your guide in life.
—The Delphic Oracle

S VENSON'S WARDS, THE three American students, were sprawled on their beds in the next apartment. A young man named Charles Bowdoin did most of the talking, laughing, and making a show as he welcomed Patronas into the room, apparently amused by the prospect of a police interview.

More than two meters tall with artfully tousled hair, Bowdoin towered over Patronas. Enjoying the advantage this gave him, he stepped closer, forcing the Greek policeman to peer up at him.

Patronas studied him. Bowdoin wasn't as handsome as he obviously thought he was—his features, especially his jaw, were too coarse and fleshy—but it was clear from his attitude that he thought he was something special. Patronas wondered what the American's background was, where his sense of entitlement came from. Money would have been his guess. Lots and lots of freshly minted money.

There were two other boys in the apartment with Bowdoin: Benjamin Gilbert, short and fair-haired with glasses, and Michael Nielsen, whippet-thin and muscular, whose cheeks and forehead bore a trace of acne. Both held back, giving them a cursory nod when Bowdoin introduced them; then they continued to fiddle with their iPads, content to let their friend speak for them.

Bowdoin quickly verified that all three had gone to Aghios Andreas and walked beyond it to a second set of ruins. Under Svenson's direction, they had dug a shallow trench, but the heat had overwhelmed them and they'd retreated, never to return. "End of story," he said with a shrug.

Patronas continued to probe. He kept the reason vague, saying only that it had to do with the trench, letting them think it was a matter of bureaucracy—Svenson's failure to secure the necessary permit.

Unshaven, the three students were dressed in flip flops, t-shirts, and jeans. Their manner bordered on insolent.

"Sure, dude," Bowdoin said when Patronas told him he needed to ask them a few questions. "Ask and we shall tell."

Since then, they'd made no effort to hide their boredom. Slouched down, they'd been furtively checking their electronic devices for the last ten minutes.

Patronas handed Charles Bowdoin the photo of the victim. "Recognize him?"

"Shit!" Bowdoin dropped the photo as if it burned his fingers.

"Someone murdered him near the place where you dug the trench." Patronas was watching the students carefully, but he saw nothing, no so-called 'tell.' Only shock and bewilderment.

Again, he asked what they remembered about their trip to Thanatos, if anything had seemed out of place, strange.

As always, Bowdoin spoke first. "It wasn't *Raiders of the Lost Ark*, if that's what you mean—just a bunch of rocks, same as everywhere else we've been. I wanted to be an archeologist before this summer, but not anymore. Man, am I over it."

"What about you?" Patronas asked Michael Nielsen.

"Svenson gave us trowels and we dug for a while. At first it was kind of fun, but then it got hot and we ran out of water and I wanted to leave."

Benjamin Gilbert nodded. "Svenson's big on reenacting things, 'making history come alive,' he calls it. He told us to pretend we were Indiana Jones. As if. The whole thing was stupid, just another of his little games. The only good part of being here is diving off his boat. There's a woman from Boston, Lydia Pappas. She comes with us sometimes."

There was a hint of yearning in his voice in the way he said Lydia Pappas' name.

Bowdoin had heard it, too, and he nudged Nielsen. "You should see Benjie when she's around," he said. "He's got it bad, been mooning around after her all summer."

Embarrassed, Gilbert grinned sheepishly. "Can't blame a fellow for trying."

"Anything come of it?" Patronas asked.

"Not yet." Gilbert laughed.

"We all wanted to hook up with her, didn't we, Charlie?" Gilbert added, looking to Bowdoin for support. "I wasn't the only one."

Patronas was unfamiliar with the term. "Hook up?"

Bowdoin smirked. "You know ... score, sleep with, *fuck*."

An old-fashioned Greek, Patronas recoiled at the vulgarity.

The students continued to make lewd jokes, each seeking to outdo the other two, chiding one another about their sexual conquests, the 'dogs' they'd bedded. A discussion that had horrified Patronas at first, until he realized 'dogs' was an American euphemism for ugly girls, not the real thing. Listening to them, you'd think that's all they did. If they were indeed students, they were majoring in sex.

Nikos Katzanzakis had written someplace that life was trouble; only death was not. To be a man, to be alive was to undo your belt and go looking for trouble.

Patronas fingered his belt buckle, wishing he had more of what Katzanzakis had been talking about, more of what these young men mistakenly believed they had. Felt a twinge of envy. Oh, to be bold and flashy and unafraid. But he was none of those things. No, when it came to women, he was pathetic. A sad little pigeon-toed man who was running out of time.

As a precaution, Patronas seized the students' passports, telling them he only needed to make copies and would return them the following day. Svenson's he intended to hold onto indefinitely.

"Got it," Bowdoin sang out and closed the door behind him.

A moment later, Patronas heard music coming from the room. He and Tembelos looked at each other. "Youth," Patronas said.

"Assholes," Tembelos said.

Svenson was waiting for them in the hallway, then followed them back down the stairs, rambling nervously about the three students. Nielsen was a runner—a champion, apparently, while the other two were something called 'legacies,' sons of noted alumni at 'prestigious Ivy League universities.'

Patronas didn't know what the Ivy League was and he didn't care. As far as he was concerned, character defined a person and those kids came up short.

Oblivious, Svenson continued to proclaim the group's innocence. "None of us would be involved in anything as sordid as this."

Listening, Patronas was inclined to believe him. Svenson was too much of a classroom Napoleon to pull this off—a man who fought in academic journals, not with his hands. And the kids were hopeless. They made Evangelos Demos look like a genius.

CHAPTER EIGHT

———◆———

Restrain your tongue.
—The Delphic Oracle

U NLIKE PLATYS GIALOS, Kamares was swarming with tourists—
Scandinavians mostly, a smattering of French and Germans. A ferryboat
had just arrived, and ahead the road was crowded with people. Taxis were
lined up along the quay, waiting with their trunks open for customers, and a
general sense of anticipation hung in the air.

Patronas pushed his way through the mob and entered a car rental agency.
Nikolaidis had requested that he rent a car, saying they couldn't keep using
the white van, that they needed to return it to the Coast Guard. Also it was
too conspicuous on an island as small as Sifnos. People would know they were
cops.

Seeking to save money, Patronas had argued against it. "Jesus, have you
seen the four of us? Even in a patrol car with 'police' painted on the side and
the siren going, nobody's going to mistake us for cops. Certainly not Evangelos
Demos, who is shaped like a bowling pin and has brains of the same material.
Nor Giorgos Tembelos, who can sleep standing up and frequently does. And
especially not Papa Michalis, who's almost eighty years old and looks like
Father Time."

His geriatric swat team. The three stooges in uniform.

But Nikolaidis insisted, saying that if they were going to interview
migrants they couldn't go in the van. The migrants would think they were
from immigration and run for the hills. He had also counseled against visiting
the camp at night, saying it would be better if they waited until morning. "It's
a dangerous place."

Flashing his identification card, Patronas requested a mid-sized SUV
from the clerk at the car rental agency. Stathis would scream, but it had to be

done. Both Tembelos and Evangelos Demos were big men, the latter alone weighing in at one hundred forty kilos, well over three hundred pounds. Petros Nikolaidis might have his own car, but it didn't matter. He and his men would suffocate in one of those little rental Fiats. The tires would splay, and when the rubber hit the road, it was apt to stay there.

The clerk said he had a red Toyota Rav, a big car for Greece, and handed Patronas the keys. "Fill it up before you bring it back. Otherwise, we'll have to charge you."

Standing next to him, a Greek woman was arguing about her bill. The disputed amount was small, less than eighteen euros, but she was almost in tears. Patronas listened sympathetically. His country was in trouble, no doubt about it. Even the Albanians, who'd poured into Greece by the thousands years ago, were fleeing. So many, there'd been a traffic jam at the border.

And now a new wave of immigrants was coming in to take the Albanians' place, a tsunami of newcomers. Muslim men for the most part. Strangers in every sense.

When he was growing up, it hadn't been like that. He remembered the Swedish woman who'd passed through his village when he was a child. Such a rarity, everyone had come out to take a look, pointing and whispering, 'xeni, xeni'—stranger, stranger—the old crones cleaning their glasses in order to see her better. And the placid Japanese woman who had married a local seaman and come to Chios to stay. The natives discussed her openly, as if she were a giraffe who had turned up in their midst, laughing and mocking her Greek. Not maliciously, more in fun, entertained by her Japanese accent. And now, xenoi were camping out in the squares of Athens.

Although it was after ten, the shops in Kamares were still open, and up the street, a bar called Captain George's was throbbing, people standing outside on the sand, drinks in hand. Waiters were hard at work filling pitchers from wooden wine barrels. It was a real tourist watering hole—there were over twenty barrels.

Patronas decided to leave the car until tomorrow and rejoined his men standing out in the street. In spite of the lateness of the hour, a group of kids were swimming in the harbor, splashing water and yelling at one another in Greek.

He remembered the dead boy, and with a heavy heart he watched the Greek children play, wondering if the victim had ever swum with his friends in the dark, laughed with them on a summer's evening.

"I wonder what his name was?" he said out loud.

The priest understood instantly who Patronas meant. "We may never learn it," he said softly. "All he'll ever be is 'child.' Child of our horror, child of our grief. Hopefully, one day, child, too, of our justice."

"I don't know if we'll get justice for him, Father. I don't know if we'll ever find out who did this."

"We have to. We have to seal off this evil, Yiannis. It cannot be allowed to spread. We must do everything in our power to contain it."

AFTER INSPECTING ALL seventeen of the restaurants in Kamares, with much discussion—eating being a serious business—they selected a midsized taverna named Stella's and sat down at a table next to the water.

Since Stathis was paying, they ordered extravagantly, lobsters and shrimp, an immense *fagri*, the fish alone weighing in at well over three and a half kilos. In addition, they told the waiter to bring them *revithokeftedes*, a local specialty made of chickpeas, and *tiganates karavides*, fried crawfish, an expensive delicacy. And to drink, ouzo to start, to be followed by two bottles of his finest wine.

The policemen sat there morosely, discussing the case in fits and starts, while they waited for their food. Each of them had been deeply affected, the priest moved to tears more than once when he spoke of it.

"Means, motive, and opportunity," Patronas said. "Until we learn more, opportunity is paramount. Access to the site is all we have at this point."

"Maybe it was political," Tembelos said. "Revenge for what that Pakistani did on Paros."

"Let's say you're right and the killer or killers wanted revenge," Patronas said. "Why there? Why Thanatos? If they wanted to send a message to the migrants, wouldn't they have chosen a more public place?"

Tembelos rubbed his eyes. "Personal then? A stepfather, maybe, or the mother's boyfriend?"

"Those kinds of killings are impulsive and usually directed at younger children—babies and toddlers mostly," Patronas shot back. "A man gets irritated, loses his temper, and beats the child to death. This was different."

"He's right," Papa Michalis agreed. "My feeling is this murder was carefully planned, steeped in ritual. The way they cut him … that wound on his neck. I've been thinking about it all day. Whoever did it knew what they were doing. For one thing, the incision was less than an inch long, straight across the jugular, and yet there was no pooling of blood under the body, very little blood anywhere."

"Maybe he was killed somewhere else and brought to Thanatos," Evangelos offered.

"Unlikely," Patronas said. "It was nearly impossible for the five of us to get him down from there. Carrying him up would have been exceedingly difficult."

"Maybe the murderer had help," Papa Michalis said. "Maybe it wasn't one killer, but two."

"Any other thoughts?" Patronas asked, reluctant to get caught up again in the priest's dark fantasy life.

The five men looked at one another.

"Could be the killer collected the blood," the priest said after a moment. "They used to do that in the old days."

He hesitated for a moment before continuing, "It was common practice at pagan temples. The priest or priestess—I'm not sure which—would nick the jugular of the animal, be it a lamb or a goat or a bull, and collect its blood. It was a way of securing the favor of the gods, a rite of sacrifice. Occasionally they killed human beings, too. There's evidence the Minoans took the life of a young man on Crete, shortly before the eruption of Thera. He was bound hand and foot and his blood was collected in amphorae."

He turned toward Patronas. "I know you have little use for the church, Yiannis. but it *has* brought us forward. As a general rule, we don't do such things anymore. But, oh how we used to …. Oh my, yes, from Abraham onward."

Arranging his robe primly, he continued to espouse his theory, "All I am saying is we should not exclude the possibility that the boy was killed as part of a religious ritual. The temple was Phoenician, and they were among the worst in this respect in human history, not Satanists, per se, but equally evil. Their god, Moloch, demanded children be sacrificed to him, and the Phoenicians in Carthage gladly obliged, burning their own babies alive. They placed them in the arms of a statue over a fire pit and incinerated them." His voice grew louder. "This child on Thanatos was burned, was he not? The absence of blood is extraordinary. There was no blood at the scene, correct? Ergo, someone had to have collected it. That is the only reasonable explanation."

"The Phoenicians have been gone for a long time, Father. It is unlikely one *of them* did this."

Evangelos Demos bit into a breadstick. "Maybe the killer drank it."

Patronas poured himself a shot of ouzo and gulped it down. It was going to be a long night.

They continued to argue. No one ate much when the waiter brought their food, the lobster and the shrimp growing cold in front of them, untouched. The ghost of the dead boy seemed to hover above the table.

"Ritual murder, human sacrifice, call it what you will," the priest said, pushing his plate away.

"Human sacrifice?" Patronas said. Just saying the words aloud frightened him—all that ancient darkness closing in, a vision of a god who required human blood. Although his teachers in school had glossed over the fact, he knew his forefathers had been murderous, bloodthirsty people and that Greek history was full of death, ritualized death. Look at Agamemnon, who sacrificed his daughter, Iphigenia, on the eve of the Trojan War. He killed his own child to fill the sails of his ships with wind.

As if there was ever any point to murder.

"Also the platform itself," the priest said. "I don't know if any of you noticed, but it had a greasy feel. Someone had burned things on top of it before, flesh of some kind; the rock was blackened and stained in places. The only time I've ever seen anything like it was on Samos at the Temple of Hera." He looked over at Patronas, his face tormented. "You're going to have to tear that place apart."

"Why?"

"Because it isn't just a pit, Yiannis. It's an altar."

CHAPTER NINE

———◆———

Practice what is just.
—The Delphic Oracle

Not yet ready to sleep, Patronas and Tembelos went for a walk after dinner, hiking deep into the countryside. They climbed to the top of a rise and started down, ending up in a wide flood plain about a half kilometer from Kamares. The area was full of gravel washed down from the highlands, the remnants of some ancient cataclysm. Mountains surrounded them, steep walls of rock reminiscent of Thanatos, pockmarked and full of shadows.

A donkey was tethered to a tree at the edge of the plain, a wooden saddle still in place on its back.

"Aren't you a fine beast," Patronas said, pulling up a fistful of grass and offering it to the animal.

In truth, the donkey was no more than a shape in the night, its breathing deep and regular, a series of poignant sighs. Still Patronas felt a kinship with it. It seemed melancholy standing there, suited up and ready for work, in need of comfort.

"Hee haw," he said softly, hoping the animal would respond and they might have a conversation. The donkey ignored him and stayed where it was, silent and implacable.

Despite all the tourists and migrants, Sifnos had kept its Greek character, he told Tembelos on the way back to Kamares. The donkey was proof of it. Foreigners hadn't yet made their presence felt.

"You see a jackass and you rejoice," Tembelos said. "You know each other, the two of you? Is this creature a long lost family member? A brother perhaps?"

They went on like this for a few minutes, sparring and trading insults. Patronas had been seeking to purge his speech of non-Greek words, and Tembelos, for one, had been highly critical. "What convoluted horseshit are you talking?" he asked him. "What the hell do you mean, *'filonikia'*?"

"It means 'victory over a friend.' It's a better way to say 'we had a fight.'"

Tembelos just rolled his eyes. "Why can't you just talk like the rest of us? Why do you have to pretend you're Demosthenes?"

Reaching down, he gathered up a handful of pebbles. It was said that the ancient Greek orator, Demosthenes, had used them to conquer a speech defect, and his friend suggested Patronas might want to do the same. "Here," he said. "Gargle with these."

They had rented two rooms at Morpheus Pension, a family-owned hotel on the outskirts of town. Evangelos Demos and Papa Michalis were already upstairs in their room. Patronas had banished them after dinner, unwilling to listen to them any longer, especially the priest, who'd been thoroughly keyed up and apt to talk all night.

The pension was well cared for, with a pretty, arched entranceway. Pots of geraniums lined the walkway that led inside, and the grounds were planted with jasmine and *nyxtoloulouda,* a fragrant plant that only blossomed at night.

The balcony off their room was small, but the view was pleasant, overlooking a densely wooded area, and beyond that, the sea. Rising from the garden below, the scent of flowers filled the air.

Stathis called as Patronas was getting ready for bed. "I did some research on those Americans. Richard Svenson is a real scholar, apparently. Pretty high profile. I doubt if he's your man."

'Your,' not *'our,'* Patronas noted angrily. Stathis was signing off on a case. As always, his boss never failed to disappoint.

"What about Lydia Pappas?" Patronas asked.

"I didn't see much under her name."

After he hung up, Patronas sat there on his bed, pondering what Stathis had said. So what if Svenson was a 'high-profile' professor? Being a celebrity didn't equal innocence; often it was exactly the opposite. Those movie stars in Hollywood were a case in point. And on occasion advanced university degrees did not preclude evil. Josef Mengele, the so-called 'doctor of death' at Auschwitz, had plenty of education, and look what he'd done with it? Performed bogus medical experiments and tortured people.

Let Stathis say what he wanted. He would keep Svenson on the list of suspects.

He was pretty sure Lydia Pappas was what she said she was—a clear sky. But one never really knew with women. Just look at Dimitra, whose metamorphosis after they got married had been worthy of Kafka. One minute, the docile little bride, the next—abracadabra—the evil sorceress. She might not have eaten children like the hag in "Hansel and Gretel," but she sure had done her best to devour him.

He needed to remember that tomorrow, when he took Pappas to Thanatos. Keep his guard up.

Tembelos was taking a shower in the bathroom, singing a song about Crete at the top of his lungs. The lyrics were beautiful, describing how a mermaid, the sister of Alexander the Great, would ask after her brother and stir the sea if the answer displeased her. Unfortunately, there were a lot of high notes, and Tembelos couldn't reach them.

Tone deaf. Maybe entirely deaf—it sure sounds like it. "Quiet," Patronas shouted, banging his fist on the wall.

Oblivious, Tembelos sang on, coming to an end in a terrible crescendo and starting back up again.

There were two twin beds in the room, and Patronas shoved them apart, giving a wide berth to Tembelos, who in addition to his lack of musical ability, tended to be active in his sleep, punching the pillow and boxing with people in his dreams. He also called out to women in a lascivious manner and smacked his lips, made fondling gestures with his hands. Patronas had shared a bed with him on a previous case, and it had almost ended their friendship.

After carefully laying his uniform over the back of a chair, he got into bed and pulled the sheet up over him. It smelled of soap and was pleasantly rough against his skin. He'd left the door to the balcony open, and he lay there for a few minutes listening to the sea. The waves sounded louder in Kamares than they had in Platys Gialos, booming and crashing along the shore. A cruise ship must be passing, its wake generating the onslaught.

Still humming, Tembelos emerged from the bathroom a few minutes later. Not wanting to talk, Patronas closed his eyes and pretended to be asleep. The hotel was named after the god of sleep in ancient Greece—Morpheus—and that's what he intended to do, by god, sleep.

Tembelos wasn't fooled. "How's it going with Calliope?" he asked, sitting down on Patronas' bed. "I've been meaning to ask."

Patronas had floundered after his divorce. Tembelos, sensing his friend's loneliness, had fixed him up with a cousin, a thirty-five-year-old school teacher named Calliope.

"When you fall off a horse, you get back up and ride it," Tembelos had said. "Same thing with women."

Seeing the broad flanks of Tembelos' cousin, Patronas had thought the advice fitting. Horse-like in the extreme, she was, this Calliope. A veritable Clydesdale. She also lived to instruct, never let up for a minute. Every date had been a lesson. What to eat and how to eat it, where the napkin went and the proper way to hold a knife. A fountain of wisdom. No, she was more than a fountain. She was a river, Calliope. Goddamned Niagara Falls.

His ex-wife had a similar personality. What was the expression? The wounded old horse sees the saddle and trembles. That was him, trembling all over.

"I think I'm too old for her," Patronas said, feeling charitable. "I'm fifty-five and she's thirty-five. Twenty years is a big difference."

"You can't keep sleeping in the office, Yiannis. It's no good. You're a wreck. You need a wife. "

"Maybe just an iron, Giorgos. Let's start with an iron."

A BRANCH KEPT BANGING against the outside wall, scratching like an animal seeking to get in. The sound awoke Patronas and he was unable to get back to sleep. Thanatos kept crowding into his mind—the suffering the boy had endured in his final hours.

He got out of bed and stepped out onto the balcony, fighting his way past the billowing curtains. He closed the door behind him, intending to smoke a cigarette and go back to bed. He needed to get a grip on himself and get some rest, to focus on the job and stop acting like the dead child was his son. The waves continued to pound the quay, foamy water spilling up onto the cement. In the distance, he could see the red and green buoys that marked the entrance to the harbor, a small lighthouse blinking just beyond. Outside, the wind was an even greater presence, sweeping through the garden and bending the trees almost double, gusts making rippling patterns across the surface of the harbor.

It was very dark and stars filled the sky. Leaning against the railing, Patronas picked out the constellations he knew. He had a telescope on Chios and he often took it up on the roof of the station at night when he couldn't sleep, solitary hours he cherished. Seeking to educate himself, he had even bought a book on astronomy. He didn't understand most of it. Novas? Black holes? The only black holes he knew were in people, in their diseased and troubled hearts. Stars were different, each one a miracle.

Sometimes they even made him think of God, that there might actually be one, the mystery of their light coming from so far away—proof of His existence.

Patronas had been six years old when he lost his father. To comfort him, his mother had told him that stars were the souls of the dead and that his father was up there now, that he had taken his place among them. 'He will always be there,' she'd said. 'You will always be able to find him in the night sky. His light will never leave us. It will last longer than all our imaginings— longer than the earth itself.'

He saw a star fall, and he wondered what she would make of it. A disgraced angel, maybe, one who'd violated one of the Almighty's many rules. She'd been like that, his mother, always with an explanation for everything, one the priests would approve of. A biblical verse for every occasion.

He shook off the memory. Another time, another life.

The door creaked and Tembelos slipped out to join him. "You all right?"

"No. Every time I close my eyes, I see him hanging there."

"I know. It was awful."

They stayed out on the balcony for a long time, watching the sea and smoking in silence.

"You ever go to that monastery in Athens, Kaisariani?" Tembelos asked, his voice so low Patronas could barely hear him. "That place where the Germans killed those people?"

Patronas flicked his cigarette off the balcony, a shower of sparks briefly lighting the night. "Sure," he answered, "a long time ago. Why?"

"You could tell something bad happened there, couldn't you? Sense it as you walked around. I thought at first it was the wind I was hearing, but it wasn't. It was them—the people who died in that place. Battlefields, too; they are like that."

Patronas had known Tembelos a long time. Taciturn and calm, his friend was not given to hyperbole or excessive emotion. He'd never once seen him cry. Yet tonight, he sounded awash with anguish. "What are you saying, Giorgos?"

"I'm saying Thanatos was the same. You could feel it in the air there, feel something bad had happened. You could almost hear that kid screaming."

CHAPTER TEN

———— ♦ ————

Take care to recognize opportunity.
—The Delphic Oracle

LYDIA PAPPAS WAS standing at the entrance of Leandros, waiting for Patronas. She was wearing jeans and a blue tunic with white embroidery down the front, and her shoes were the same amphibious ones she'd had on before. Her hair was loose, reaching almost to her waist, held back from her face by a faded cotton bandanna. In spite of the hour, she was wide awake and hurried out to meet him.

Patronas didn't expect their expedition to reveal much. All that was left on Thanatos were those muted screams Tembelos had spoken of. But Stathis had insisted on it, saying it was always a good idea to revisit a crime scene with a witness. Something might jump out them. Patronas had reluctantly agreed.

After greeting him cordially, Pappas got in the car and fastened her seatbelt. They drove in silence to Aghios Andreas.

Her expression was troubled. "I'm not looking forward to this."

"Neither am I."

That seemed to surprise her. "But you're a policeman. I thought you would have gotten used to these things."

"You never get used to it. Especially not in a case like this one, where the victim's a child."

Patronas parked the car in the empty lot below the museum and they got out. "Just do as you did on the day in question," he instructed her. "If you stopped on the way to Thanatos, I want you to stop now. Retrace your steps. Everything exactly the same."

The parking lot was full of shadows, the silhouettes of the distant hills strangely menacing in the dark. Having brought a propane lantern, Patronas lit it before starting off to Thanatos. It was like a spotlight on the darkened floor of the valley, the hissing gas loud in the quiet. He and Lydia Pappas walked side by side through the tall grass. The arc of light enclosed them.

A single barn swallow, awakened by the sound of their footsteps, was the only sign of life, soaring back and forth, high above them. Another swallow joined it a moment later, and the two flew off in perfect harmony, rising and falling in unison, the white tips of their wings like arrows against the night sky. For some reason, the birds reminded Patronas of his parents. They'd been the same, his mother and father, one completing the other. Their love carried them forward, transporting them until like the little birds, they, too, seemed airborne.

Pappas had moved on ahead and was striding quickly through the weeds. "This is where I first saw the ruins," she said, pointing to Thanatos. The rock was a stark black shadow against the horizon, far more sinister-looking than Patronas remembered.

Raising the lantern, he studied it carefully. "You can't see the temple from here."

"Sure you can. Look closely. It's there."

A moment later he saw it—the angularity that didn't belong, the succession of square blocks jutting out at the summit.

"You asked me what I remembered," Pappas said. "It was weird, but once or twice, I had the sense someone was watching me, that I wasn't alone that morning. At the time, I thought it was just my imagination, but now I'm not so sure."

"Do you think whoever it was followed you here?"

"No. I'm pretty sure they were already up here, spying on me from above. At least that is the sense I had."

Patronas studied her, dumbfounded. "But you kept going?"

She laughed. "I'm a Greek woman, Chief Officer, a force to be reckoned with. Nothing stops me. Fear least of all."

"I guess not," he said.

They climbed up the stairs to the temple and paused at the top to catch their breaths. To the east, the sun was rising and the sky was growing light.

Banded in pink, a thin scrim of clouds lay along the horizon. The color deepened as they stood there, the pink slowly giving way to gold. The sun broke through the clouds a moment later, bathing them in fiery red light.

"There's your dawn," Patronas said.

She laughed again, pleased that he'd remembered. "I always loved the legend of Orpheus, how the ancients said his music brought the dawn, that he awakened the sun with his songs. You can almost hear him now, can't you, hear his lyre?"

Patronas didn't hear anything, but he dutifully cocked his head and pretended to listen. No point in antagonizing a witness.

Lydia Pappas hesitated when they reached the platform. "The boy was there. Hanging right there in the middle … in the middle of that hole."

Moving timidly, she inched a little closer to the edge of the pit. "I was standing back here …. I leaned forward and checked his pulse, just in case, you know, even though I was sure he was dead. Then I got my phone out and tried to call the police, but I couldn't get a signal. I was a wreck by then, screaming and crying. I just wanted to get away."

"What drew you inside here?"

"The birds. There were *so many*, far too many for that hour of the morning."

"Did you hear anything while you were up here, a rock shifting underfoot, anything that would indicate there was someone nearby?"

"No, nothing. Only the creaking of the chain that held the boy. And of course, the cawing of the birds. Like I said, there were hundreds, and they were making a huge commotion."

Although Patronas and his team had thoroughly investigated the immediate murder scene, dusting the temple and the platform for trace, they had neglected the area beyond it, the wild hawthorn bushes that surrounded the platform. A serious omission, if what she said about being watched was true.

"Let's go take a look," he told her.

A few minutes later, they discovered an area where the brush had been tamped down. It was about five meters back from the temple and well hidden. A ledge of rock shielded it almost completely from view.

Pulling on latex gloves, he knelt down and parted the leaves, seeking evidence he could swab for DNA. It was a lucky find. Without her help, he would have missed the area—so faint was the evidence, the disturbed brush, the intruder had left behind. Judging from the barely matted leaves, whoever it was had only been there a short time.

Patronas also discovered a leather cord caught on some thistles and bagged it, as well as a charm lying on the ground beneath. A cheap souvenir, it depicted Pegasus ascending on one side and a classic profile of a man's face on the other. The latter was probably copied from an ancient coin.

"Do you think he was watching me the whole time?" Pappas asked.

"Maybe."

She wrapped her arms around herself. "I hate this."

They wandered around a few more minutes, reentering the temple and lingering by the pit. To his surprise, Patronas found himself discussing the details of the case with her, even going so far as to demonstrate how he'd jumped down and pried the stones apart at the bottom. How horrified he'd been to discover what looked like the bones of a baby, that little femur.

"I don't know if those bones are related to the case. This is an old place. They could possibly predate it by two, maybe three thousand years. A priest I work with said certain sects used to sacrifice babies before the coming of Christ."

"Why would anyone want to kill a baby?" she asked. "They're so small and defenseless, innocent. My God, what I wouldn't have given ...."

Her story came out in bits and pieces. She had no children, no family to speak of. "I had one miscarriage after another; then my marriage collapsed and I lost all hope of ever having children of my own."

Impressed by her candor, Patronas shared his own troubled history—his misspent years with Dimitra. The sons and daughters he'd longed for but never had. "My life went completely to hell after the divorce. I've got no home anymore. I sleep on a cot in my office and live on gyros and pizza."

Pappas touched his arm. "I'm no better. I microwave something and eat it standing up. I never thought I'd end up this way. I always thought there'd be a big table in my future with me at one end and my husband at the other, and all our children spread out in between, laughing and sneaking food to the dog." She threw up her hands in a gesture of resignation. "You know what they say? 'You want to make God laugh, tell him your plans.' "

Patronas nodded. "Funny how things work out."

"Funny isn't the word I'd use."

Convinced there was nothing left to see, they turned and started back down from the temple. No longer needing the lantern, Patronas turned it off. The sun had risen and morning was now upon them, cicadas beginning to stir in the undergrowth.

He was about halfway down the stairs when he caught sight of something shiny far below, a reflection of some sort. He made a mental note of the location, and when they got to the bottom, he told Pappas to stay where she was and he walked in that direction, searching for the source.

Embedded in a clump of juniper bushes was a knife, lying on its side. The metal blade had acted as a mirror and that was what he'd seen. It was about nine centimeters long and made of carbonized steel, a type very common in Greece. There were probably a thousand knives like it on Sifnos alone. Fishermen used them to gut fish.

The end of the blade was encrusted with blood.

After Patronas took a picture of the knife's location with his cellphone, he pulled on a fresh pair of gloves and carefully placed it in an evidence bag. He then walked back to where Lydia Pappas was waiting and showed it to her.

Crying out, she buried a fist in her mouth and staggered back, and a moment later, vomited down the front of her tunic. Patronas rushed to help her, holding her hair back and dabbing at the thin fabric with his handkerchief.

It took her a long time to recover. Stepping away from him, she took a long, hiccupping breath and wiped her mouth with the back of her hand.

She nodded to the bagged knife. "You think that's the one he used?"

"Yes. He probably threw it off the rock after he finished." *Stathis will be pleased with the find,* Patronas thought. *He likes to be right.*

Patronas took Lydia Pappas by the arm and helped her walk back to the parking lot. Hoping to distract her, he described his colleagues in the Chios Police Department, Evangelos Demos in particular, even going so far as to describe how he'd massacred a flock of goats during a stakeout.

"Worst night of my career. He just kept blasting away, and the goats kept falling over. *Chamos,* it was." Utter chaos.

"And yet he still works for you."

"Yes. What can you do? His son, Nikos, is handicapped. I got him into a special school on Chios. Truth is, I dearly love that boy. He's a sweet kid, calls me 'Sir Yiannis.' "

She laughed, the long curtain of her hair moving, glossy in the sunlight.

Hoping to make her laugh again, Patronas continued to talk, only aware of her nearness.

His mother had always said the devil had blue eyes and red hair. Yet this woman had both, a woman with a laugh like music, glorious.

"Way I'm talking, you must think I've eaten *glistrida,*" he said. *Glistrida* was a plant Greek villagers said loosened the tongue and made people babble like idiots.

"When you're not busy shooting up livestock, what else do you do?"

"I have a telescope and I look at the stars."

The smile she gave him seemed to warm the air. "Really?"

"Every night."

"Would you wish on one for me?" she asked.

"Sure. What should I wish for?"

She looked away from him, embarrassed. "An end to my loneliness. Someone to watch over me."

After Patronas dropped her off at Leandros, he touched the seat where she'd been sitting, kept his hand on it for a long time.

A horse was beckoning, and it wasn't Calliope.

CHAPTER ELEVEN

———◆———

Treat everyone with kindness.
—The Delphic Oracle

THE MIGRANT CAMP in Platys Gialos was far worse than Patronas had anticipated—a vast slum. Sand fleas were omnipresent, and the air reeked of excrement and rotting garbage. Sullen groups of people were watching him, backing away when he approached. He could sense their distrust and abiding rage. It was a palpable presence, as much a part of the landscape as the miserable hovels they inhabited.

Underfoot, the ground was knee-deep in plastic water bottles. Whatever euphoria he'd felt in Lydia Pappas' presence earlier that day had long since dissipated.

Enterprising, the migrants had constructed shelters out of a variety of materials. Nylon sheeting was the most common, but everything from sheet rock to tree branches had been used. A few had even carved out caves in the riverbank, burrowing into the soil like animals. Those without shelter were lying out in the open on flattened pieces of cardboard. One little boy was asleep in a wooden box, his shoes next to him; another was rolled up like a snail in a sheet of brown wrapping paper. A lucky handful were living in brightly colored tents—a great luxury given the surrounding squalor—but even these were overcrowded, ten or more people crammed into spaces meant for half that number.

Evangelos Demos was walking beside him. "How can people live like this?" he asked.

"They're refugees, Evangelos, not vagrants," Patronas said. "They don't have a choice."

"You smell that?" Evangelos made a show of sniffing the air. "That's raw sewage. And where there's raw sewage, there's cholera and typhus. It's not safe for us here, Yiannis. We should leave."

"I must commend you, Evangelos," Patronas said, feigning astonishment. "I knew you were a glutton and a fool, but you've added a whole new dimension to your character this morning. Carrying on about your health when you should be worrying about theirs." He indicated the migrants asleep on the ground. "What kind of person are you? Where's your compassion?"

"You can say what you want," Evangelos said, sulky now. "We should leave."

"Not an option."

Still grumbling, Evangelos followed him farther into the camp. The two of them started with the people living in the hovels closest to the village of Platys Gialos. Patronas did all the talking, worried Evangelos would alienate the migrants and mess up the interview.

Hell, the man would mess up tying his shoes.

"No need for this, Yiannis," Evangelos complained when Patronas motioned for him to be quiet. "I went to the police academy. I know how it's done."

Initially, Papa Michalis had also wanted to come with them. Pointing a gnarled finger at the sky, he'd quoted Deuteronomy in an effort to persuade Patronas. " 'Thou shalt open thine hand wide unto thy brother, to thy poor and to thy needy in thy land.' If those words apply to anyone now, it is to the migrants."

But Patronas had ruled it out. Working with Evangelos Demos would be punishment enough. He couldn't deal with the priest, too, who'd probably quote the New Testament to the Muslims and get them all killed.

Unlike Evangelos, Patronas for the most part enjoyed the company of the priest. Above all else, he valued the old man's wisdom, his compassion and profound understanding of the darkest aspects of the human soul. Evangelos was the real thorn in his side.

Even though he couldn't help it—intelligence wasn't something a person chose to have, it was preordained, or in Evangelos' case, not—Patronas always found working with him exhausting. Such stupidity was draining, made him feel like he had a kind of mental mononucleosis, like his brains had turned to mush.

ESTABLISHING WHO LIVED where in the camp proved to be a daunting task, as was figuring out what language to speak once they found someone willing to talk to them. Both sides just spoke louder in their efforts to be understood.

Patronas had checked; there were no official statistics as to the number of residents in the camp. He guessed it was close to four hundred. Everywhere he looked there were people. Exhausted by the journey, most were asleep on the ground. A few were cooking over open fires, smoke spiraling upward between the trees. One man was bathing from a spigot, completely naked, the water turning the ground beneath him to mud.

Judging from the smell, the ditch that ran alongside the camp was serving as a communal latrine.

Raw sewage, in other words, just as Evangelos said.

There'd been demonstrations on the Greek islands of Lesvos and Kos, refugees protesting their living conditions. "We are human," one of the signs had read. "SOS," said another.

"SOS," Patronas repeated to himself. It was an understatement.

According to news accounts, the migrants were entering Greece from Turkey, traveling to nearby islands—Lesvos, Kos, Samos—and from there on to Athens and Northern Europe. Sifnos was well out of the way, and Patronas wondered what had drawn them here, an island with little industry to speak of.

He and Evangelos had brought a stack of flyers, and they hammered them up throughout the camp. Sheets of white paper, they featured a black and white photo of the dead child and his age with the words 'missing' and 'reward,' along with Patronas' cellphone number. The reward had been his idea. He would gladly pay it himself, if it produced results. So far it hadn't.

Most of people in the camp couldn't read English, and judging by their reactions, the flyer scared them. Probably they had seen similar ones in the countries they were from. Desperados wanted by Interpol, terrorists and human traffickers, criminals of every description.

Patronas was pretty sure he'd seen a flicker of recognition in the faces of one or two of the migrants, but when he pressed them, they quickly retreated, holding up their hands in a gesture of surrender and backing away.

The vast majority were men, dark-skinned with features reminiscent of sculptures from ancient Babylon and Assyria, although there were fifty to sixty Syrian families mixed in as well.

A woman in a headscarf was hanging laundry on a rope strung up between two trees when he approached her with the photo. "You know him?" he asked in English.

She didn't understand and backed away, shielding her face with her arm.

"Speak to the men," Evangelos whispered to Patronas. "The women are afraid of you."

Over the course of five hours, they interviewed nearly every male in the encampment. Patronas even questioned the ones in the tents, getting down on his hands and knees, pulling the flaps back and crawling inside. A blast of hot air always welcomed him, the nylon cloth trapping the noonday heat.

Inside, the inhabitants appeared dazed, the children nearly comatose, fast asleep in their mothers' arms.

But the answer was always the same: no one knew who the dead boy was.

For the most part, Patronas found the Syrians to be the most helpful. Sitting together, they studied the photo carefully—men and women alike—before handing it back and shaking their heads. The others—the war-hardened Afghans, primarily—shied away, as did the Pakistanis and Somalians, but to a much lesser extent. A few of the Afghans were so openly hostile, spitting on the ground at Patronas' feet, that he feared for his safety. He would have arrested them if he could, but didn't dare, fearing he'd set off a riot.

One group of teenagers had an especially predatory attitude. They followed Patronas and Evangelos Demos throughout the camp, jeering loudly and making threatening gestures.

Frightened, Evangelos Demos again begged Patronas to leave. "*Tha mas sfaksoune*." They'll cut our throats. "In Calais, the men in the camp outnumbered the police two hundred to one," he went on, "and the authorities had to use stun grenades to subdue them."

"We don't have stun grenades," Patronas said. "Just keep walking."

As they were leaving, a middle-aged woman followed them out of the camp. One of the migrants, she was wearing a white *hijab*, headscarf, and a tunic, a long denim skirt and pristine white sneakers.

Dark-eyed and sorrowful, she could have posed for an icon of the Virgin Mary. She had that kind of face.

Hesitating, she reached for the photo and took it from him. "Sami," she said in English, caressing the image with her fingers. "Is Sami, little Sami." She began to sob, quietly at first and then louder.

"Was he your son?" Patronas asked gently.

"No, no. Is my sister's boy. Sami Alnasseri. He is ten, older than you say on the paper. He is a small boy, small for ten."

Patronas could hear people nearby, angry voices yelling behind him in Arabic. But whether they were seeking to silence her or someone else, he couldn't tell.

"Is it safe for you to be talking to me?" he asked.

"For a little, no more," she said. "We come from Aleppo in Syria, all of us. Sami's father, he has gone to Athens, and maybe after to Germany."

"Where's his mother?"

"She is dead in Syria. Long time dead. Many days it took for us to come and much money. Sami's father says Sami must stay here with me. They cannot go to Germany together. I am a woman, he say, no good for me to be alone in the camp. Too many men. Sami, he must protect me."

"Is his father coming back?"

"Yes. In one month's time." Choking back tears, she spoke very quickly, stumbling over the words. "Sami, he is with me many days. Works sometimes and gives me money. But then I don't see him, and people in camp say he is dead."

Patronas didn't know how to comfort her—a Muslim woman. Embracing her might well give offense. He didn't want that, nor did he want to use the translation app on his phone, seeking words of condolence in Arabic while she stood there and wept.

"He was a good boy," she said, wiping her eyes. "He clean the cars ... buy food for us."

A carwash maybe, or a gas station. "Is your name Alnasseri, too?" Patronas asked.

Something closed down in her face. "Noor," she said in a low voice. "To you, I am only ... Noor."

Patronas was familiar with the name. A common one in Arabic, it meant 'light.' There were probably fifty women called 'Noor' in the camp.

"What's your last name?" he asked.

Looking over her shoulder, she shook her head. "Noor," she said again.

Pretending to play with his phone, Patronas hurriedly took her picture. "Did your nephew have any friends?" he asked, leaving the issue of her name for the time being. "People who knew him we could speak to?"

"Yes. Sami, he had two friends."

"Do they live in the camp or outside? Can you describe them to me?"

Again, something passed over her face. Fear, grief, regret, Patronas couldn't say for sure. Perhaps it was a combination of all three.

"I must go," she said. "Is no good for me, this."

THE MUSEUM DIRECTOR at Aghios Andreas, Dimitris Papadopoulos, reported that the security camera at the entrance didn't work and that he had been waiting for funds to fix it for close to year. He didn't recognize Sami Alnasseri and said that as far as he knew, no migrant had ever visited the site.

Immaculately turned out, Papadopoulos wore a shirt that was beautifully ironed, Patronas noted sourly, as were his tight-fitting jeans. His hair was jet black and formed a natural pompadour, and he had an unctuous, self-important manner. He reported that as a student, he had labored with Varvana Philippaki, the Sifnian archeologist who'd excavated Aghios Andreas. "I've devoted my entire professional life to the site."

After much hemming and hawing, he verified that a group of Americans, an older man and three boys, had visited the museum earlier in the week then disappeared for long period of time. "I know, because I wanted to close early that day and I was waiting for them to come back and take their car out of the parking lot so I could put the chain up. I always like to be the last one off the hill."

"How long were they gone?"

"Two, three hours."

"When was this?"

He checked the calendar on his phone, scrolling up and down with a finger. "August nineteenth."

"You know anything about Thanatos?" Patronas asked.

"Not really. I do know that after we finished excavating here, we petitioned the Department of Culture for the funds to explore it, but the authorities wouldn't hear of it. I can't say as I blame them. The ruins there aren't even Greek. They're Phoenician." Papadopoulos said this last word with disdain, as if it dirtied his mouth.

"Phoenician?"

"Yes. You may not know this, but the Phoenicians were savages. Sacrificed children to their gods. Burned them in pits. Archeologists have found skeletons at other sites, skeletons of babies."

"Bones, huh?" Patronas recalled the little ribcage and femur he'd found on Thanatos, so old they were the color of rotting teeth, thinking they might date from that time. *Maybe Papa Michalis was right and a rite of human sacrifice did take place on that platform. Not recently, but three thousand years ago.*

Patronas planned to discuss both sites with Jonathan Alcott, an archeologist he had met during his first murder investigation, wanting to get his assessment of what Papadopoulos was saying. Could be the museum director was inflating the importance of Aghios Andreas for professional reasons, making it appear more significant than Thanatos for his own purposes.

Academics did that kind of thing, fought battles about places no one else cared about—a kind of wrestling, he supposed. Only instead of grappling and headlocks, they used paper, lots and lots of paper.

"The American was very learned," Papadopoulos said, returning to Svenson's visit. "He lectured the whole time, pointing to the artifacts on display and explaining their significance to the boys he was with."

"How did they get here?"

"In a Jeep. They'd brought excavating tools with them and were carrying them through the museum, sieves and trowels, that kind of thing. It worried me and I spoke to them about it."

"Did you ask what they planned to do with them?"

"Yes. I told them they couldn't dig here or anywhere else without a permit from the Ministry of Culture. 'If you do,' I said, 'you will be arrested and charged.'"

So Svenson had known his trench was illegal, but had chosen to proceed anyway. Patronas starred this information in his notebook.

"Do you know if they took the tools with them to Thanatos?" he asked.

"No," Papadopoulos said. "A tour bus arrived and I lost track of them."

"Did you speak to the Lydia Pappas, the woman who found the body?"

"No, it was too early, at least two hours before the museum opened. By the time I got here, the policeman had already taken her away."

"Had she been here before?"

Papadopoulos paused for a moment, thinking. "I don't know. Possibly. The path to Thanatos is not visible from the museum. Anyone might have gone there, and I wouldn't have known. I did see lights up there once. I'd stayed late and was on the way to my car. In the distance there were lights. Seemed strange at the time."

"When was this?"

"A week ago, maybe more. I'm not exactly sure."

CHAPTER TWELVE

———— ◆ ————

Be on your guard.
—The Delphic Oracle

PATRONAS CALLED STATHIS and asked if he could find an aide worker, someone who spoke Arabic and could translate for him. The boy's aunt and the other migrants might be more forthcoming if the conversation was in their own language.

"It was a mess in that camp," he said. "The migrants were suspicious of us and didn't understand what we were after. They saw the flyer of the child and thought we were there to arrest them."

"You identify him?"

"Yes. He was a ten-year-old Syrian named Sami Alnasseri. His aunt saw the flyer and identified him."

"Parents?"

"Mother's dead. Father's in the wind, on his way to Germany. Aunt was deeply traumatized. Wouldn't even give me her last name. Afraid would be my guess."

"Probably illegal."

"Maybe."

Patronas had followed her back into the camp after she'd left, calling, "Noor, Noor!" but she'd started to run, still crying, and the other migrants had blocked his way. They were so antagonistic, pushing and shoving him, he was forced to let her go.

Stathis was not sympathetic when Patronas described what had happened. "Forget about the translator. There's no money in the budget. You'll have to do the best you can without one. Muddle through."

Patronas couldn't believe his ears. "A child was murdered here!"

"Don't lecture me, Patronas. I was the one who brought you in, remember?

That said, I simply can't justify hiring a translator and paying, not just their salary, but their travel and lodging expenses, just to speak to a bunch of migrants. Not when our own people are starving. Speak to the Greeks in the neighborhood. Someone had to have seen something. At least with them, you'll understand what they say."

Bridging three hills, Apollonia was actually a collection of villages, the priest informed Patronas and the others in the Rav, thumbing through his guidebook in the front seat of the car. It merged with a second town, Artemonas, near the summit of the highest peak, and two smaller towns, Ano and Kato Petali, farther down the slope. It also included Exambela, which meant 'trouble in night,' in Turkish, a notorious place during the Ottoman occupation. Papa Michalis twittered as he said this. He always found sin to be great entertainment, Patronas had noticed, telling and retelling stories of human depravity and chuckling to himself. Perhaps it was all those years in the monastery, all that piety and prayer and denial. But there was no mistaking it, the old man had a prurient streak that rivaled Hugh Hefner's. Patronas had read somewhere that Quakers, restricted to non-violence by their religion, killed mosquitoes. Perhaps something similar was at work with his friend. Only with him, it wasn't bugs, but sex.

Although the road to Kamares bisected the town, effectively dividing it in half, there was very little traffic. And the area catering to tourists was limited; the majority of the bars and restaurants were confined to a single picturesque alley behind the square. A number of stores were selling locally made ceramics—Patronas had counted at least five on the way here from Kamares—so Lydia Pappas had been telling the truth, at least in that respect. Potters were indeed hard at work on Sifnos.

If the overall impression of the migrant camp was darkness, here in Apollonia it was light. There were churches everywhere, each one dedicated to a different saint or celebrating an aspect of the Virgin. The Virgin of the Mountain was one, high on a hill above Platys Gialos, the Virgin of the Life-Giving Spring in the seaside village of Chryssopigi was another. So many, it didn't seem possible. The priest had told him that Jews believed God only needed thirty-six righteous men and He would preserve the world. That number seemed about right to Patronas. He'd seen his share of evil over the years; and he doubted God Himself could find more than that.

Patronas sat down in a coffeehouse on the far side of the square and motioned for his men to join him. It was an elderly establishment full of rickety tables and chairs. Solitary pensioners were seated throughout, nursing Greek coffees and reading newspapers from across the political spectrum, smoking and arguing with one another other in a desultory fashion.

Patronas quickly brought his men up to date. "The victim's name was Sami Alnasseri, a Syrian refugee. I spoke with the boy's aunt. She claims her nephew had two friends on Sifnos, but balked when I asked her to describe them. She seemed very frightened."

"Someone threatened her, you think?" Petros Nikolaidis asked.

"Maybe. On Lesvos, the Syrians asked to be segregated from the rest of the migrants, claiming they'd brought money with them and the others were beating them up and stealing it. Could be something like that is going on in Platys Gialos. Some perceived danger."

Tembelos nodded. "Migrants we spoke to were afraid, too. Hard to get them to talk to us. Nothing doing."

"Listen, we might have caught a break," Patronas said. "I went back to Thanatos with Lydia Pappas early this morning and found a knife buried in some bushes at the base of the rock. It was covered with blood. I'm convinced it's the murder weapon. I also found a leather bracelet and a charm close to the pit where she found the body. I've sent both off to Athens to be processed for DNA."

"Coroner finished with him yet?" Tembelos asked.

"No. We're still waiting. We need to establish what drew the boy to Thanatos and find out who lured him there. The so-called 'friends' his aunt mentioned might have been responsible. This might also have been an internal affair, some form of internecine warfare, although I doubt it. The boy had a sad life. Mother dead, father in Germany."

"Easy prey," Tembelos said, nodding.

"Stathis wants me to speak to the Greeks who live around the camp. The rest of you continue what you're doing. See if you can get a fix on those two people. At the very least, we need to determine their nationality."

An old woman was working behind the counter, kneading dough and laying it out on a tray to be baked. She lingered after bringing them their order, eavesdropping on their conversation. "It's about that boy, isn't it?" she said. "The one who was killed?"

"Yes," Patronas said. "We're investigating his murder."

Reaching for one of the photos, she studied the child's face for a moment. "They live near Cheronissos, too, in a field out there, not just in Platys Gialos and Kamares. They're everywhere now, those people."

Judging from her tone, she didn't approve of the migrants' presence on her island. *"Lathrometanastes,"* she spat. Illegals.

She might as well have said 'vermin.'

DRIVING BACK DOWN the hill to Platys Gialos, Patronas noticed that the migrant camp was located almost directly below Aghios Andreas. He hadn't realized it before, but thought it might be significant. Marshy, the area around the camp was sparsely settled, clumps of reeds separating the small landholdings.

In spite of the economic downturn, vacation houses were being constructed along the shore, even a small two-story hotel, the old olive trees it had displaced uprooted and lying next to the new cement foundation. Once they'd been considered valuable—'a father plants olive trees for his sons,' it was said in Greece—and now they were dying, cast off and discarded.

Flyers in hand, he went from house to house, knocking on doors and asking the locals if they recognized Sami Alnasseri. While it was relief to speak Greek, he discovered nothing new. By and large, the people he spoke to were reluctant to get involved in the affairs of the migrants and politely shut the door in his face.

One young couple told him they were newcomers to Sifnos, having chosen to abandon their hectic lives in Athens and work the land the way their grandparents had. Brought here no doubt by the economic implosion, unemployment among Greeks their age being well over forty percent.

With their small plot, they could survive indefinitely, they boasted, obviously pleased with themselves. No need to pay for heating fuel; the climate was mild. They could grow fruit and vegetables, raise poultry or a flock of sheep, even fish if they had to. Survive.

"I grew up that way," Patronas said. "There are worse ways to live."

With their high-topped sneakers and rock star clothing, the two seemed unlikely peasants, however. The woman had purple streaks in her hair, a diamond stud in her nose—the man, a tattoo of a rearing stallion on his forearm. Neither appeared particularly energetic.

They should have stayed in Athens, he decided, remembering how hard his mother had worked. They'd never make it as farmers, here or in any other place, tilling the soil and spreading manure.

"You ever witness any incidents near the camp?" he asked, flipping to a clean page in his notebook. "People harassing the migrants?"

"Once," the woman said. "A couple of thugs were shouting at them and telling them to go back where they came from."

"Could you describe them for me?"

"They were skinheads. Greek from the sound of them."

A SMALL GROCERY STORE was located across the street from the couple's landholding. Patronas pushed open the door and went inside. A white-haired woman was shelving canned goods in the back, and she turned toward him, wiping her hands on her apron. "*Ti thelete?*" What do you want?

He gave her the child's picture. "You know him?"

She nodded. "Some of the kids from the camp steal from me. They come in, grab a can or two, and run out again. He was one of them."

"You report them?" If so, there'd be a police record, possibly the names of Sami Alnasseri's friends.

"No, never. How could I? Report a child for stealing food? You see how they live, worse than us during the war."

"You have any idea who might have killed him?"

"No. Everybody on Sifnos is talking about it. 'Not ours,' they say. 'The dead boy was one of *theirs.*' I don't like it. It's as if he doesn't matter."

"I heard two men were harassing the migrants. You know who they were, who might want to harm these people?"

"There've been a couple of incidents here and in Kamares," the woman said. "Fights, mostly. Nothing like this." She hesitated, "Some of them are my people. I know their families and we grew up together on Sifnos. One or two are from Athens."

"Please. I need their names. It might be important."

"The worst are Costas and Achilles Kourelas. Start with them and you'll find the rest."

Patronas gave her his phone number. "There's a reward," he said. "If this leads to anything, I'll see that you get it."

"I don't want a reward. He was a little boy. We should have made room for him and his people among us. We should have fed them and made them feel welcome."

After leaving the store, Patronas visited a few other houses, seeking to verify what he now knew; that a boy named Sami Alnasseri had once lived in the vicinity, a child who was hungry and stole food. But again, nothing came of it.

Seeing an elderly woman harvesting figs along the side of the road, he stopped and spoke to her. The air was thick with wasps, drawn by the rotting fruit, and she batted them away with her hand while they talked. An old-fashioned villager, she was dressed entirely in black, a kerchief on her head and *tsokara,* crude heavy sandals, on her feet.

"I might have seen him," she said. "Some boys play in the street here sometimes, running around shouting. He might have been with them. I don't pay much attention. Anyway, I wouldn't have understood what they were saying, not that jibber jabber of theirs."

She turned back to her work, plucking a fig from the tree and dropping it into the straw basket at her feet. "Not enough for us and now *they* come. We should sink those rafts."

CHAPTER THIRTEEN

———◆———

When crows sing, the righteous take flight.
—Greek Proverb

"COSTAS KOURELAS AND his son, Achilles, are pretty unsavory characters," Petros Nikolaidis told Patronas. "They're members of that right wing political party, *Chrisi Avgi*, the Golden Dawn. I've had numerous run-ins with them. They're violent men. You never know what they'll do."

"We'll take Tembelos and Evangelos Demos with us. If nothing else, we'll outnumber the renegades. And if there is a fight, Evangelos Demos' sheer bulk will ensure victory. All he'll have to do was sit on them."

"A tank would be better," Nikolaidis said. "They're enormous, those two, an army unto themselves."

"How many members of *Chrisi Avgi* are there on Sifnos?"

"Not many. Ten, fifteen at most. As in the rest of Greece, they've gotten more powerful over the last couple years, recruited more people into the party. Two members beat up a Pakistani man not too long ago. But the victim refused to testify, so I had to let them go. I'm pretty sure the son, Achilles Kourelas, was the instigator of the attack. He's pure poison, talks about exterminating the migrants like they were cockroaches."

"He from Sifnos?" Patronas asked.

"No. Athens, I think. Works odd jobs on the island with his father, picking fruit and helping out on the farms, repairing cars and motorcycles. Whatever he can find."

PATRONAS PARKED THE car alongside the road, and Nikolaidis guided them down a steep slope. They were far to the north of Apollonia in a rocky wasteland, high above the sea. There'd been mines in the area at some point; Patronas could see slag heaps glimmering on the hills, frozen streams made up of chips of metallic stone. Untended olive trees clung to the cliffs, their leaves rippling in the wind.

Costas Kourelas and his son lived in a small building about half a kilometer from the road. Patronas doubted they owned the property. Most probably the two were squatting there, the land being too poor to farm. Engine parts littered the yard, the soil greasy under them, and tattered shades hid the interior from view, the windows streaked with filth. Little more than a shed, it had probably housed animals at one time—chickens, would have been Patronas' guess. A pair of bucket seats from a sports car were sitting outside the house. Well-used, evidently they were Achilles and Costa Kourelas' idea of lawn furniture.

Patronas observed it all with a sinking heart. *This is what happens when men don't have wives or mothers to look after them*, he told himself, repelled by the junkyard feel of the place. *And here I am, going down that same road, no doubt about it.* He recalled the tottering pile of pizza boxes on the floor of his office, the sink where he shaved every morning, caked with gray whiskers and toothpaste. Tembelos was right. He needed to get back on that horse and ride it. *Giddy-up, giddy-up.*

Standing behind him, Tembelos whispered, "*Katapatoun*," squatters.

"*Meros gia gourounia*," Patronas whispered back. Pigs.

Costas Kourelas was kneeling next to a massive truck engine, tinkering with a screwdriver, his son standing beside him. Neither appeared happy to see them.

Both men had shaved heads and the physiques of bodybuilders, the muscles of the older man softening now in middle age and giving way to fat. Bare-chested, he was wearing a wide leather belt around his waist to support his back.

His son, Achilles, had shoulders like a Russian shot putter and looked like he weighed half a ton. As he stood there in the sun, his skull gleamed as if oiled.

Judging by their living conditions, they didn't have enough money to pay for a barber, Patronas concluded, looking them over. Probably took turns wielding a razor. Father would scalp the son, and then the son would return the favor. Not exactly Nazi Stormtroopers, they were more like strongmen in the circus.

"How do you do," he said politely, introducing himself. "I'm Chief Inspector Yiannis Patronas of the Chios Police Department, and these are my colleagues: Officers Evangelos Demos, Giorgos Tembelos, and Petros Nikolaidis."

Grunting, the older man got to his feet. His fingers were black with oil and he wiped them on a rag. "Costas Kourelas," he said gruffly and shook Patronas' hand. "You're here about that dead kid, aren't you? Anything happens to the migrants, it's on us."

His Greek was heavy, *poli vari,* his accent that of a *maggas,* a member of an urban underclass rarely seen anymore. In the old days, men who spoke like Kourelas were known for their combativeness, rough individuals who picked fights and knifed others in nightclubs. The reasons never amounted to much—the offender might have eyed a girlfriend or interrupted a song they liked—it was more a point of honor with them. A slight, be it perceived or actual, always had to be dealt with. It could not be allowed to pass.

Strange, a man like that taking up residence here.

His son, Achilles Kourelas, picked up a wrench and began banging it against the engine. Metal against metal, the sound was deafening, and there was menace in the gesture. "Go ahead, talk," he growled. "We're listening."

"I heard you two are members of the *Chrisi Avgi,*" Patronas said.

"So what if we are?" the father said. "It's a legitimate party. There's nothing criminal about it."

"A migrant child was killed two days ago—"

Kourelas interrupted him. "Murdering kids isn't part of *Chrisi Avgi's* agenda. All we want to do is to protect our homeland, to keep Greece for the Greeks."

"You beat up a man in Kamares. A migrant from Pakistan."

"Stories." He nodded to Petros Nikolaidis. "Your friend here has it in for me."

Wrench in hand, Achilles Kourelas continued to pound the engine. "The only language those people understand is violence. Car bombs and guns," he shouted. "They fucking *behead* people. You let them in, there'll be mosques on every corner, imams on loudspeakers five times a day."

"It's simple," his father said. "We don't want them here with their honor killings and crap, *Sharia. Halal.* Everybody hates them. The only difference is we have the guts to say it. As for that kid, someone in the camp did it. They're not like us, those people. They're backward. You heard what happened to that Greek girl on Paros. A Pakistani raped her and beat her half to death."

"That's what this was about?" Patronas asked. "Revenge?"

"We'd never lay a hand on a kid," Achilles Kourelas insisted. "Nobody in *Chrisi Avgi* would. It's like my father says—one of those men in Platys Gialos did that boy. Carved him up because he was a Kurd maybe. A Sunni instead of a Shiite."

"You ever been to Thanatos?" Patronas asked, watching them.

The older man answered without hesitation, "Yeah, we went there once when we first got here. We were out shooting birds and we stumbled across it. I climbed up to take a look and climbed back down again."

A complicated answer.

"When was this?" Patronas asked.

"A year ago."

Patronas and Nikolaidis looked at each other, both thinking the same thing: if they found their DNA on the platform, they'd have them. Both men were certainly strong enough to carry a ten-year-old boy up to the platform and kill him. Means, motive, and opportunity. Costas and Achilles Kourelas had all three.

"Tell me about the Pakistani you assaulted," Patronas said. "What did he do to you? Why'd you go after him?"

"Because he was fucking *here*," Achilles Kourelas shouted, pointing to the ground with the wrench.

He continued in this vein for more than ten minutes, actually using the word, cleanse, *katharisoume*, a couple of times when talking about the migrants. It was a poisonous speech, a litany of hate.

"Careful, Achilles," his father said.

Although Patronas and his men kept after them, they got little information, only a festering sense of grievance and rage.

Patronas was sure both had been arrested before, probably even done jail time. Hard as he tried, he found them impossible to intimidate. Costas Kourelas kept mocking him, asking which of them, he or Nikolaidis, was playing 'good cop' and which was playing 'bad.'

"I think it might be you, Chief Officer," he said at one point. "Short as you are, you're tough. A real *kolopetsomenos*." Leather ass.

Nor was there any physical evidence on them that Patronas could see, injuries that might warrant further investigation. Neither had any scratches on his hands or forearms, chest, or neck—wounds a child might inflict, seeking to fend them off. No visible bruises.

Achilles Kourelas went back to pounding the wrench. A steady, thunderous drumbeat in the late afternoon stillness.

Sounding the alarm, warning his fellow Greeks the barbarians were coming.

The Greek poet Cavavy had written a poem called "Waiting for the Barbarians." Patronas had always liked it and he could still recall a couple of lines. Something about how everyone was waiting for the barbarians, who never came and perhaps no longer existed, which was unfortunate because those people had been 'a kind of solution.'

The recent influx of migrants gave these two men a cause, gave meaning—however desperate and bleak—to their lives, as did their membership in the Golden Dawn, a political party that espoused racism and hate. As Cavavy had pointed out, it was a symbiotic relationship. *Without the migrants, Costas and Achilles Kourelas would be nothing.*

"Can you vouch for your whereabouts two days ago?" Patronas asked.

"Sure." Achilles Kourelas slammed the wrench down again. "We were both here, same as now. We didn't leave."

Saying they had nothing to hide, the two agreed to be fingerprinted and held out their hands. Patronas also swabbed them for DNA, inspected their Greek identification cards and handed them back.

"One last question: who else was involved in the beating of that Pakistani in Kamares?" he asked.

"You want us to sell out our friends?" Taking a step closer, Achilles threw the wrench at Patronas, striking him on the side of his head. "You filthy *baskinas!*" You miserable pig!

Crying out in pain, Patronas stumbled back and fell, blood streaming into his eyes. Achilles was on him in a second, shouting abuse and kicking him in the ribs. He was about to bring the wrench down again when Evangelos Demos sailed into him like an airborne whale, tackled him and threw him to the ground.

"You're under arrest!" he shouted.

Pulling Kourelas' arms behind his back, he handcuffed him and dragged him off in the direction of the car.

Costas Kourelas helped Patronas to his feet. Worried, he dabbed at his wounded brow with his oily rag and within minutes was able to staunch the bleeding.

Fearing the contaminants the rag contained, Patronas winced. From the look of it, it had served many purposes during its lifetime, perhaps even done duty as toilet paper.

"You're going to have a hell of a bruise," Kourelas said.

Tembelos put his arm around Patronas and together they limped up the hill to the car. Patronas' aching ribs weren't his only problem. He didn't know how they were going to get back to Apollonia. There wasn't enough room in the Rav for everyone, not with that ham-fisted monster, Achilles Kourelas, in tow. They'd probably have to make two trips.

CHAPTER FOURTEEN

———◆———

Too many opinions sink the boat.
—Greek Proverb

THE MUNICIPALITY BUILDING in Apollonia had once been a 'C class' hotel. And, like all the government offices Patronas had ever visited, it remained 'C class.' The musty, claustrophobic space had no air conditioning, and the rooms were stifling. Little fans whirled on the desks, ruffling piles of papers like decks of cards being shuffled. The entire place reeked of mildew and angst, a fitting summation in his mind for the current state of the Greek civil service.

Standing there in the lobby with Petros Nikolaidis and Evangelos Demos, he felt like he'd stepped back in time, to the era when cement had been the material of choice and Soviet architecture had been the inspiration.

Earlier he'd stopped off at the local medical center, a modern building near the center of Apollonia. The doctor in charge, a kindly young man doing his alternative military service, had assured him he had nothing to worry about—his wounds were minor. He didn't have a concussion, nor were his internal organs in danger. "Ice might help."

After much discussion with his boss in Athens, he had been forced to release the younger Kourelas on his own recognizance, pending a formal hearing. The prisoner had sworn in a written statement that Patronas had frightened him, causing him to lose his balance and drop the wrench on his head. The whole thing had been an unfortunate accident, and he was very, very sorry. *Chrisi Avgi* had a lawyer on its payroll, a slick operator from Athens who'd briefed Achilles by phone on what to say.

It was a preposterous situation, but Stathis had counseled Patronas not to get caught up in an assault case now. "Lawyers here are talking about going out on strike, and if they do, the judicial system will shut down. You could get hung up indefinitely. Focus on the murder instead. You can go after Kourelas later. As they say, 'Revenge is a dish best served cold.' "

"I don't want revenge, sir. He assaulted me. I want to enforce the law."

"Never mind the law," Stathis said.

"But that's my job. I'm a cop. I'm sworn to uphold it."

"Your job is to follow orders," Stathis yelled and slammed down the phone.

And that was that.

Worse for Patronas was the fact that he was now indebted to Evangelos Demos for saving his life. He'd have to tiptoe around that fathead until he retired. And knowing Evangelos, he'd remind him of the debt every chance he got.

After his associate shot the goats, Patronas meant to confiscate his service revolver, a worrisome lapse, given that Evangelos was perfectly capable of shooting up, not just goats, but any living thing, Patronas included. *Most probably in the back.*

On all sides, idiots: Stathis, Evangelos, Papa Michalis with his psalms and his prayers. Even Tembelos had been acting up.

His friend remained deeply uneasy about the case. "We should get out of here," he'd told Patronas on the ride back from the clinic. "Go back to Chios. Tell Stathis to fuck himself."

"Justice," Patronas reminded him. "Justice for the kid."

"I say we forget about justice this time. Just this once, we let it go."

"Why? You afraid?"

"Of course I'm afraid. I don't want this killer anywhere near me. I don't want to look into his eyes or breathe the same air. You saw what just happened. This case is going to kill you, Yiannis. Mark my words, it's going to break your heart."

A GLOOMY SPACE WITH dirty white walls, the so-called murder room was full of boxes and broken-down office equipment, non-functioning printers and computer monitors, listing chairs. The only light was a naked bulb hanging from the ceiling, which would have been fine except that it kept going out—an electric short of some kind—and leaving Patronas in total darkness.

He was sitting at a desk in the corner, painstakingly entering the day's events in the murder book. His men were off eating dinner and Nikolaidis had returned home for the night, so he had the place to himself. He'd bought a bag of *tyropitas,* cheese pies, at a snack bar in Apollonia and walked back here to the office. Something nagged at him, but he couldn't remember what it was. He thought if he reviewed his notes, it might come to him. So far, no luck.

Lighting a cigarette, he walked over to the window and looked out. A terraced ravine led downward, linking Apollonia to the next village. Street lights cast a lonely glow on the tarmac of the road. It was close to eleven and everything was quiet.

Earlier he'd called the archeologist on Chios, Jonathan Alcott, and asked him what he knew about Richard Svenson. "You've worked in Boston. Ever heard of him?"

"Lots of professors in Boston. I'll have to check him out and get back to you," Alcott said. "How soon do you need the information?"

"As soon as you can get it."

"Why? What's he done?"

"He's a suspect in a murder case. A ten-year-old Syrian boy was killed here two days ago. Crime was oddly staged. Some kind of ritual, it looked like. There was red ocher sprinkled around, and although the kid's throat was cut, there was very little blood."

"The way the ancients sacrificed bulls?"

"Exactly. Papa Michalis keeps insisting it was a human sacrifice."

"Seems unlikely an American professor would be involved. Do you have any other suspects?"

"Two thugs from *Chrisi Avgi*. You familiar with a place called Thanatos? That's where it was."

"Ah, Thanatos," Alcott said. "It's an anomaly, that one. Theory is it was built by a small, breakaway sect from the eastern Aegean. A rogue group with roots in Phoenicia, which evolved over time or degenerated—the vote's not in yet—into a separate and distinctive culture. Supposedly Thanatos was sacred to them in much the same way Delos was to the ancient Greeks, or so the story goes—a great shrine, a place of pilgrimage and worship, the very center of their universe." Alcott paused. "You need to bear in mind, this is all conjecture. I'm just passing on what was discussed at a conference I attended. If the site was used as extensively as it was thought, there would have been substantial traffic in the area. *And* there was talk of exploring the seabed off the coast of Sifnos, but nothing ever came of it."

Svenson had a Zodiac, Patronas remembered. Maybe he hadn't been using it for water sports as he claimed, but instead had been diving for artifacts.

Alcott never spoke, he lectured, and this time was no exception. "Phoenician cosmology is very interesting," he went on. "They worshipped a trinity. *El*, their primary god, was the protector of the universe. You might know him by his biblical name, *Baal*."

"The one Moses sacrificed the calf to?"

"Not Moses, his brother Aaron. But yes, the very same. Baal was around for a long time, his name evolving into *Ba'al Zabub*, a derogatory term in Hebrew, meaning 'Lord of the Flies.' Later still in the New Testament he became *Beelzebub*, or Satan, Lord of Darkness."

Writing this information down, Patronas underlined it. *Satan had once been worshipped on Thanatos.* The thought chilled him.

"His son, *Malgarth* or *Moloch* as he was sometimes called, was known as 'the rider of the clouds.' It was also said that he slew dragons."

"Dragons? You mean like Saint George?"

"Similar. I've long thought the martyrdom of St. George echoed the coming of Christianity, the dragon he supposedly killed being the old faith—paganism if you will—and the maiden he rescued, an aborted human sacrifice. The story originated in Asia Minor in the tenth century, but it might well be older."

"Is the legend from Phoenicia?" Patronas asked, remembering what the priest had said.

"No, no. Cappadocia and Georgia."

Suddenly, Alcott had Patronas' attention. Twice in forty-eight hours. It couldn't be a coincidence.

"Did this sect practice human sacrifice?"

"Hard to say. Like I said, we don't know much about it. Gods never die. They change form and are worshipped under different guises, but they endure. And our prayers to them don't die, either. What do you think the Minoans prayed for? For the earth to stop trembling, for it to leave them in peace."

"What do you pray for?" Patronas asked, curious.

"The health of my children. Good fortune. The usual things."

"You never pray for your enemies to suffer?"

Alcott gave a little laugh. "That's the problem with Christianity. There's no room for malice."

"I found other bones when I was processing the scene," Patronas said. "The skeleton of a baby. Could be the bones date from the time you're talking about."

News of the bones intrigued Alcott. He said he'd arrange for someone to excavate the site if they were indeed ancient. "They may well prove significant. At the very least, they will strengthen the belief that Thanatos was an important Phoenician religious center."

"Coroner's processing the bones now," Patronas said. "If he can't establish how old they are, he is to send them on to the University of Athens and have the Department of Archeology run radiocarbon testing on them."

"Aside from the Spartans, the only other people who killed babies were the Phoenicians, so that would fit. But that won't help you, not with the current case. They vanished more than twenty-five hundred years ago, long before the time of Christ."

Patronas' sense of foreboding deepened. 'They're back,' the old man had said, according to Nikolaidis, 'the devils who worship in that place.'

According to his mother, a pious woman, there was only one true faith, and it was Greek Orthodoxy. Everything else was bunkum. And to an extent, Patronas still subscribed to many of its tenets. Not in the Bible per se, but in the struggle between good and evil it depicted, the eternal struggle for mastery over the human soul.

Given what he'd seen on Thanatos, evil had just won a round.

CHAPTER FIFTEEN

———◆———

Live without sorrow.
—The Delphic Oracle

L EANING BACK IN his chair, Patronas closed his eyes and sat there, thinking.
Finally he picked up Svenson's passport and reviewed it, glad that he'd had
the foresight to hang on to it. Extraditing a man like Svenson from the United
States would take time, if it could be accomplished at all. He'd made copies of
the students' passports and returned them already, but something about the
professor still bothered him and he wanted to keep him in Greece.

Svenson's passport appeared to be authentic: the colored photograph
bearing the appropriate signature, the face staring back at him suitably neutral
as required by law. Richard Svenson, born in Marlboro, Massachusetts,
in 1964. The passports of the American students were equally innocuous:
Benjamin Gilbert, nineteen years old, McLean, Virginia; Charles Bowdoin,
also nineteen, Wellesley Hills, Massachusetts; and Michael Nielsen, the runner,
twenty years old, San Diego, California. Lydia Pappas had also surrendered
her passport, smiling as she did so, repeating what she'd told Patronas earlier,
"A clear sky has no fear of lightning." She was thirty-nine, according to the
document, born in Piraeus, Greece.

According to his notes, Costas and Achilles Kourelas were also from
Piraeus. He hadn't kept their Greek identification cards, only copied down the
information. Given their limited resources, they wouldn't get far if they fled.

Patronas laid the papers out on the table and shifted them around as if
playing solitaire. The day hadn't been a complete loss. Tembelos had caught
Achilles Kourelas on film attacking him with the wrench, so that monster
would eventually go to jail. The only question was when. The evidence was
irrefutable.

The table was littered with faxes from Athens detailing Costas and Achilles

Kourelas' sorry history and Richard Svenson's exalted one, the professor's curriculum vitae meticulously translated into Greek. Stathis had seen to that.

There was also a stack of documents from Interpol, along with the standard questions. Patronas had inquired about ritual killings and the response from the agency had been overwhelming, ten pages or more. 'Human sacrifice was not unknown in Europe,' the first sentence read. A satanic group, the Friends of Hekate, was believed to be responsible for a number of disappearances in England between 1960 and 1980, but no children had been taken during that time, only adults. Another group, The Sinister Calling, was known to perform ritual sacrifices in caves or on isolated hilltops. Following the rite, the priest would wash his hands in the victim's blood. But far more prevalent, according to Interpol, were acts of sacrifice by recent immigrants from the Indian subcontinent and sub-Saharan Africa. The cases were similar to the one Achilles Kourelas had spoken of. In 2005, three people from Africa were found guilty in England of torturing an eight-year-old girl they thought was a witch. Not long after, if Interpol was to be believed, there'd been a handful of slayings to appease the Indian god, Kali, a sword-wielding monster. The latter was an old tradition, evidently. According to what he'd read, a boy was killed every day at the Kali temple in Calcutta two hundred years ago, and the tradition remained alive to this day in backward parts of India.

Patronas shoved the papers off to one side. Not only did they depress him, but they would not help with the case. Calcutta was a long way off, as was the temple of Kali. And supposedly, the only god worshipped on Sifnos was a benevolent one.

He bit into one of the *tyropitas* and sat there, chewing. A stack of the victim's photos occupied the center of the table. He eyed them guiltily. Forty-eight hours gone and he'd accomplished nothing—found no clues, no motive, no killer.

Making a decision, he called the harbor police. "I have seven persons of interest in the killing of the child at Aghios Andreas," he told the dispatcher. "The first, Richard Svenson, is an American academic, a teacher at that summer study here. He's staying at Leandros in Platys Gialos with three of his students. I want someone on them day and night. Your man can sit in a chair outside their rooms if he wants. I don't care if the Americans see him. Might be good if they did, might trigger something. I also need to keep track of two local men, Costas and Achilles Kourelas."

"No need to tell me where they live," the dispatcher said. "Everybody on Sifnos knows those two. They're famous."

"Also a woman named Lydia Pappas. She's Greek, but works in the States. She's staying in the same place as Svenson."

"Sorry. Can't track her, too. I don't have enough people."

"Very well. Have the man monitoring Svenson keep an eye on her and I'll take over for him later tonight."

Like a faithful dog, he'd keep watch outside her door. Tell her he was there to protect her. Point out the constellations, if he got the chance, the vastness of space. Run his hands through her autumn-colored hair.

"Focus," he told himself.

Writing in his notebook, he worked out the surveillance schedule. They'd alternate with the harbor police and observe the suspects in eight-hour shifts. He'd nap in the afternoon and work the last one, sit outside and watch the apartments at Leandros until the sun came up.

A few minutes later, the dispatcher called back. All seven suspects were now being monitored. "I've got one officer at Leandros, another outside the house where Costas and Achilles live. That should do it until tomorrow."

Patronas then asked him to pull the registration on Svenson's Zodiac. Upon arrival in Greek waters, all boats were required by law to check in with the port authorities, customs, and health officials as well as immigration and currency control. The bureaucracy was onerous: a roster of passengers and crew members had to be presented, a radio license, and the boat's original registration form as well as insurance papers. In addition, if Richard Svenson was indeed scuba diving as Lydia Pappas had said, he would have had to secure written permission for that as well. Something else to check.

That said, they didn't stamp passports upon entry to Greece by boat. Patronas wasn't sure the rules even applied to Zodiacs, given that the inflatable boats were often used as tenders to larger vessels and as such, were virtually impossible to track. Still, it was a place to start.

Nikolaidis had phoned to say he'd checked around and found out that Sami Alnasseri had worked at a gas station on the road to Kato Petali.

"What's interesting is that Achilles Kourelas occasionally worked there, too," he said.

"So they knew each other."

"According to the owner, Kourelas kept to himself. He never spoke to Sami or any of the other migrants. 'Treated them like lepers,' the owner said."

PATRONAS WAS ON his third *tyropita* when his cellphone rang again. His uniform was flecked with filo, and he dusted himself off before answering, fearing it might be Stathis, calling to check up on him. Once his boss had called him in the middle of the day and insisted on 'face time,' only to discover Patronas was still at home in his pajamas—yellow silk pajamas that were far too big for him. Who knows what had possessed Dimitra to buy them? Seeing them, his boss had laughed his head off and docked him a full day's pay. This had been before the divorce. Now he no longer had a wife, yellow silk pajamas, or a place to lay his head.

"Police?" a woman asked. She sounded frightened.

Patronas recognized the caller's voice immediately. It was Noor from the camp, Sami Alnasseri's aunt.

"Yes, this is the police," he answered. "Where are you?"

"In the street," she said. "I call from the payphone."

Patronas knew exactly where she was standing. There was a yellow payphone on the sidewalk in the middle of the Platy Yialos. She might be far away from the migrant camp, but she was still exposed, a Muslim woman in a *hijab,* standing under a streetlamp in the middle of the night.

There was a long silence and Patronas assumed she'd run out of coins when suddenly she spoke again. "I have a box of Sami's things. Is not much, but I leave for you."

Before she hung up, he begged her once again to describe Sami's friends. "At least tell me what language they spoke."

"He only talk of these men. They never come to the camp."

So the friends were older and they were not migrants.

"I know this is hard for you," Patronas said, "but did Sami ever tell you where they were from, if they were Greek?"

"No. Sami, he never say."

"Are you sure? It's important. Otherwise, we may never find Sami's killer, never get justice for him."

"There is no justice," she said, starting to cry. "Not for us. We are lost. My country, my people, and now little Sami. All lost. Everybody lost."

Hating himself, Patronas continued to pressure her. "We'd like you to fly to Athens and identify your nephew's body, make the necessary arrangements for his funeral. I don't know what your customs are, but I will help in any way I can."

"I cannot," she said simply.

"We'll pay your way."

"It is not the money. I am a woman. I am forbidden."

"It's important. Without you, Sami will be buried in Athens and forgotten. Without mourners, with no one to cry for him."

"I will cry for him." Her voice was thick with tears. "I will cry for Sami."

A moment later the line went dead.

"Hello!" Patronas shouted. "Hello? Are you there?"

But all he heard was the sound of the receiver banging against the pole.

EXHAUSTED, PATRONAS STOWED his notebook in his briefcase, turned off the light, and left the murder room, his footsteps echoing down the empty corridor. He wondered what the woman, Noor, was so afraid of, if it was the killer or someone else in her life. She hadn't mentioned a husband, but maybe he was in the picture. Could be he didn't want her speaking to the police. Men dictated what women could do in those countries—how much they had to cover their faces, whether or not they could leave the house.

How he wished he'd had that power in his own marriage—the chance to veil his wife from head to toe and boss her around. He shook his head at the thought. As if anyone, least of all him, could have contained that woman. Dimitra was like a human blast furnace when she got going, Would singe the hair right off your head—other parts of you, too, if you weren't careful. Breathing fire, she'd unman the most stalwart male. He'd never stood a chance.

Overcome by melancholy, he remembered the night she'd told him the reason they had no children was because of him, that he was sterile, a mule in every sense. She'd been to a doctor in Athens, been tested, and she 'knew.' How she'd gloated as she said it.

He closed his eyes. *How did I ever endure all those years with her?*

Idly, he wondered if what she'd said was even true or if she'd just said it to hurt him. Dimitra did that. She used her tongue to maim. He'd never followed up with a doctor to verify what she'd told him. Maybe he should one of these days.

Pulling out his cellphone, he called Tembelos and told him to come and pick him up, then opened the door of the municipality building and walked out into the street to wait. Overhead, the stars were bright. He studied the night sky, dwarfed as always by its immensity, and picked out Orion and Pleiades. He wondered what his place was in the cosmos, the purpose of his time here on earth. Initially, like most Greeks, he'd thought it would be family—that he'd spend his days providing for a wife and children—but that was not to be.

Truth was, like Lydia Pappas, he had wanted children desperately. After his father died, it had been lonely in his mother's house. He'd yearned for sisters and brothers, for someone to play with. He'd married Dimitra partially for that reason, to have a companion and not be alone. And he'd always thought one day he'd have a house full of children, grow deaf from the sound of their laughter.

He shook his fist at the sky, cursed God for Sami, cursed God for all of it.

Tembelos arrived in the Rav a few minutes later and screeched to a halt in front of him. "Hey, boss, you ready?"

Patronas was dismayed to see the priest in the car, slumped over in the backseat, his head lolling on his chest. The old man was snoring peacefully, his beard rising and falling, wafting with each breath as if borne by a gentle breeze. His robe was in disarray and he looked more than a little drunk.

"What the hell is he doing here?"

"Had no choice," Tembelos said. "Old fellow consumed enough food to feed a small city and fell asleep in the car. I don't know if 'sleeping it off' applies to eating, but that's what he's doing."

"He make you pay?"

"Of course. No fish this time. Filet mignon and a bottle of French Bordeaux."

"Bordeaux?"

"Yes. You should have heard him. Chateau this and Chateau that. Waiter couldn't believe it. Austerity is not a word Father is familiar with."

"Or self-denial."

"That's two words."

Patronas recalled his dinner, that sad little bag of *tyropitas*. Unlike Papa Michalis, he was familiar with self-denial in all its guises, beginning with his wedding night and moving onward. Maybe in heaven he'd be rewarded, be able to drink Bordeaux at least. He doubted God would provide him with a woman, doubted sexual congress was part of heaven's plan.

Again, he thought of the Muslims, how the Jihadists were promised seventy-two virgins when they died. Far better than the Christians, who only got feathers and a halo.

Getting into the front seat of the car, he fastened his seatbelt. "Sami Alnasseri's aunt called from a payphone in Platys Gialos. She has a box of the boy's things she wants to give us."

"She say anything more about his two friends?" Tembelos asked.

"Only that they were 'men' and didn't live in the camp."

Tembelos hit the steering wheel with his hand. "It's them, I tell you, Costas and Achilles Kourelas."

Patronas shifted around in his seat, trying to get comfortable. His ribs hurt and he wished he'd let the doctor tape him up. "If it was indeed Kourelas, father and son, or some other member of *Chrisi Avgi*, it will be a catastrophe for Greece, Giorgos. You'd better pray it was a foreigner who killed that boy and not one of our own."

"Yiannis, all the evidence points to them."

"A Greek would never do something like that." Patronas was clutching at straws and he knew it. "Children are cherished in Greece."

"Not migrant children. You know what men like that are capable of. Look at Pavlos Fyssas, that rapper in Athens. Writes a couple of anti-fascist songs and they kill him. Prime Minister got it right that time: 'The descendants of the Nazis are poisoning the foundations of a country that gave rise to democracy.' "

"Things are worse in Athens."

"Yiannis, you're dreaming. Achilles Kourelas would have beaten you to death if Evangelos hadn't intervened. He hit you with a *wrench*, for God's sake. I don't know what's wrong with him. Steroids maybe, but he's a murderous bastard."

"But why kill a child?"

"For the same reason Hitler killed the Jews. There's something twisted in him. You know the saying: 'From the devil's farm, neither lambs nor kids.' In other words, from the devil's farm, nothing good ever comes. It's like that with Costas and Achilles Kourelas. The only thing they'll ever succeed at is inflicting pain."

It was a long speech for Tembelos, obviously one he'd thought about.

Patronas looked out at the darkened hills, suddenly afraid for Sami's aunt.

"*Ela grigora,*" he urged. Hurry.

CHAPTER SIXTEEN

———◆———

Pity those who have been beaten until the arrival of judges.
—The Delphic Oracle

PLATYS GIALOS WAS so quiet Patronas could hear the sea, the soft booming of the waves along the shore. The wind was up, and it made a mournful sound as it swept through the deserted village.

He saw no sign of Sami Alnasseri's aunt, but as promised, she'd left the box for him on the pavement by the payphone, painstakingly labeled 'for polic.' The box was small, about the size of an old-fashioned cigar box, and well worn. Something in Arabic was scrawled across the top. Sami Alnasseri's name, Patronas guessed, seeing the clumsy childishness of the writing.

The child's treasures had been modest: a leather dog collar, well-worn and chewed almost through, a blue spiral notebook, and a couple of modest toys. Patronas opened the notebook and flipped through the pages, then tipped it over and shook it out to make sure he hadn't missed anything. A few of the pages were written on in Arabic, and there was a drawing of an airplane on the inside cover. The tail had given the boy trouble and he'd erased and redrawn it a number of times. Patronas could see the marks clearly, the paper wrinkled and soiled from the child's efforts. The only other things in the box were a little figurine of a man made of straw, bound together with strips of cellophane, and a donkey carved out of wood. It was tethered to a little slatted cart piled high with crude facsimiles of fruit, misshapen watermelons and oranges, and a cluster of grapes. Patronas spun the wheels of the cart with a finger and put it back in the box.

Tears filled his eyes and he clutched the box to his chest. He knew who Sami Alnasseri was now, and he grieved for him.

Stepping under a streetlight, he opened the notebook again. What he'd mistaken for Arabic was actually Greek. A series of phrases the boy had copied over and over:

> *To onoma mou einai Sami.* My name is Sami.
> *Ti kaneis?* How are you?
> *Pos se lene?* What is your name?
> *Eimai apo tin Suria?* I am from Syria.

Either he'd been trying to teach himself Greek or someone had been instructing him. He stowed the box in an evidence bag, thinking he'd send it to Athens and have them dust it for prints. He wondered where Sami's passport was, the rest of the documentation he'd been issued upon his arrival in Greece. Perhaps the boy's aunt had held onto them.

He was opening the door of the Toyota when he heard a sudden tinkling of glass, followed by a huge explosion. Smoke started pouring out of the migrant camp and everywhere people were screaming.

"Holy Jesus, what was that?" Tembelos cried, jumping out of the car.

"A Molotov cocktail!" Patronas yelled. "Come on. Someone just firebombed the camp."

Spotting a man running away, they gave chase, but he was too fast and escaped, sprinting across the fields and vanishing into the night.

The Molotov cocktail had set the brush along the riverbed ablaze. It was almost the end of August and the vegetation was very dry. The fire spread quickly, growing in intensity as it advanced through the undergrowth. Little by little, the sheeting on the hovels began to burn, melting like wax and sending up clouds of acrid black smoke as it disintegrated, the ends of the plastic writhing and curling like living things.

Migrants were fleeing in all directions, their eyes wild with fear. A woman jumped into the sea with a young child in her arms, her long black robe floating up around her on surface of the water. Others soon followed. Late at night, the sea was very cold, and the children shrieked and cried.

Within minutes, the trees surrounding the camp began to burn, the pines seething and crackling as the resin ignited, going up on all sides like Roman candles. The air was so hot, Patronas could barely breathe, but he and Tembelos rescued as many people as they could, charging toward them through the smoky haze and leading them to safety.

Fearing the priest wouldn't survive, Patronas ordered him to stand back. "Console the victims. If they're injured, have a local person drive them to the clinic in Apollonia."

Tembelos was helping an arthritic old woman escape when there was a huge splintering crash behind him. Without thinking, he pushed the woman to the ground and threw himself down on top of her. The massive tree missed them by centimeters, but the shower of sparks set his clothes on fire, tendrils of flame burning his legs.

Terrified, he thrashed around, twitching and writhing as if having a seizure.

Patronas and the old woman grabbed him by the ankles and pulled him to safety. They rolled him back and forth on the ground and threw dirt on his clothes.

"How are you, Giorgos?" Patronas asked, kneeling beside him. "Are you all right?"

Tembelos gritted his teeth. "What can I say, Yiannis? *Eimai kalopsimenos.*" I got roasted.

Patronas helped him to his feet, and together they fled the camp, the old woman in tow. Holding her scarf across her face with one hand, she clutched Patronas' arm with the other. She was surprisingly strong and had a fierce grip, her nails digging into his flesh like talons.

Tembelos tried to embrace her when they got to the street, to thank her for saving his life, but she just bowed her head and muttered something in Arabic, a blessing it sounded like. Watching her hobble away, Patronas wondered what her history was, where she had learned to save men from burning to death. Like applying tourniquets, it was a terrible knowledge to possess.

Half the people in the neighborhood were now fighting the blaze. A local man in bedroom slippers and bathrobe was lugging a hose over his shoulder, seeking a spigot to screw it into. Others were filling buckets with a slurry of sand and seawater and dumping them out on the flames. A line quickly formed, people dunking their buckets into the sea and passing them on to the person standing next to them, the last one in the procession running up to the fires and emptying the water out. Even the hipster farmers had gotten involved, husband and wife beating back the flames with wet blankets.

Patronas was surprised to see that Lydia Pappas was one of the runners. Her auburn hair had come loose, her face surrounded by a flattened mass of sweaty curls, and her clothes were covered with ash. Catching sight of him, she gave him a weak smile. Then, picking up her bucket, she headed back into the inferno.

Svenson and his students were also in the vicinity, not laboring as intensely as the rest. They dabbled at it, leisurely, with their buckets. Patronas noticed Bowdoin was taking pictures with his cellphone, and he signaled for him to stop.

Shrugging, the boy slipped the phone back into his pocket. Gave Patronas a two-fingered salute.

The migrants were huddled together, watching the camp burn on the far side of the street, their faces stony. A few of the children were shrieking, clutching at their mothers' skirts for reassurance. Patronas ordered his men to speak to them, to ask them in English if they had seen the person who did this, if they recognized him.

"It was arson, no question about it. Someone deliberately firebombed the camp."

IT TOOK NEARLY two hours to put out the fire, and by the time it was over, at least half of the camp had been destroyed. A huge number of people had gathered by then, the entire population of Sifnos, it looked like. A group of priests were talking to Papa Michalis, looking across the street at the smoldering wreckage and shaking their heads.

Though in a great deal of pain, Tembelos insisted on waiting it out. "I told you we should leave. We're under siege here. First you, now me. Who's next? Evangelos?"

Evangelos was standing next to them, placidly eating a gyro, a big messy one in a pita, *tzatziki,* garlic sauce, dripping down his chin. Patronas had no idea where Evangelos had acquired it. Perhaps his associate had hidden talents.

As for Evangelos being the next victim, in Patronas' opinion, it couldn't happen soon enough.

"Not too many people got hurt," Papa Michalis reported. "I counted fewer than twenty. For the most part, they only had minor injuries."

Deeply shaken, the mayor announced he was opening up a local school for the people displaced by the fire. "You can live there until September," he told the migrants. "After that, I'll make other arrangements for you."

"You see, Yiannis," the priest said. "The fire changes everything. It's human nature, I guess. Mankind is always better at survival than success. It takes a crisis to bring out what's best in people."

Patronas could think of lots of occasions when a crisis gave rise to not what was 'best in people,' but to bloodletting and mayhem—the assassination of Archduke Ferdinand came to mind—but he kept those thoughts to himself. Let the old man think what he wanted. Such delusions were probably nutritional—fueled the priest's belief system and supported his faith. Unacquainted with faith himself, Patronas assumed it was a fragile thing, made of gossamer and starlight, and needed shoring up on a daily basis.

The local bus was idling in the street, waiting to ferry the migrants to the school. Greeks from the neighborhood began loading it with blankets they'd brought from their homes, bags of food and clothing. They helped the migrants climb onboard and handed their children up to them.

"*Ola kala*," they kept saying. Everything is fine.

A handful of Greeks had offered to take the victims of the fire into their homes, and Patronas watched them lead them away. The migrant children were holding their parents' hands and skipping along beside them, laughing together.

Seeing them, the priest smiled. " 'For I was hungry and you gave me food. I was thirsty and you gave me something to drink. I was a stranger and you welcomed me.' "

He continued on in this vein, quoting the Bible and commending the people of Sifnos for their generosity and goodness, their adherence to the word of Jesus. " 'Then Jesus looked up at his disciples and said, 'Blessed are you who are poor, for yours is the Kingdom of Heaven.' "

Patronas rolled his eyes. It was hard to believe someone could turn a firebombing into a testament of faith, but that was what Papa Michalis appeared to be doing, seeing signs of God's bounty even where it didn't exist. Satan's maybe—Beelzebar or whatever the hell Alcott had called him—but not God's, definitely not God's.

CHAPTER SEVENTEEN

———◆———

Tell me who your friend is and I will tell you who you are.
—Greek Proverb

CHAOTIC AND OVERCROWDED, the clinic in Apollonia was full of people, the burn victims and their relatives and friends. A few were sitting on chairs in the waiting area. Others were spread out on the floor. However, the great majority were standing in the hallway outside the examining room, clustered around the gurneys that held their loved ones, effectively blocking anyone else from getting by. A couple of older women in caftans were keening loudly, their voices rising and falling in a dirge-like chorus that set Patronas' teeth on edge.

He'd been waiting with Tembelos for more than an hour to see the doctor, and those women had been caterwauling the whole time. He didn't know where the noise they were making came from, the Sahara maybe, what he imagined a bunch of grieving Bedouins might sound like. All he knew was he hated it. Human agony, fresh from the desert.

A total of nineteen migrants had been hurt, Sami Alnasseri's aunt among them, but fortunately, no one had died that night. Patronas had caught sight of her when she was brought in, but after seeing her injuries, he quickly abandoned the idea of speaking to her. She'd been hooked up to a morphine drip, groggy and in pain. Questioning her now would be a violation of all he believed in, the equivalent of torture.

When Tembelos' turn came, Patronas helped him up onto the gurney. His friend cried out as he settled himself down on the thin mattress, adding his voice to the unholy chorus in the hallway, his eyes shiny with tears.

"Ach, Giorgos," Patronas whispered.

The doctor was the same one who'd treated Patronas earlier and he shook his head when he saw him. "You again?"

"What can I say? It's not easy being a cop these days."

"I know. I saw the demonstrations on television."

Recently there'd been huge protests in Athens, farmers driving their tractors into the city to protest the new wave of austerity measures and the searing cuts to their social security payments. They'd blocked the roads and occupied the center of the city. A number of policemen had been injured in the subsequent melee. Head injuries mostly—concussions and the like.

Until tonight, Patronas believed he'd been one of the lucky ones, assigned to Sifnos this summer when the rest of Greece was up in arms. But now after Tembelos got hurt, he felt cursed.

After clipping away Tembelos' clothing, the doctor examined him carefully. "The wounds aren't extensive," he said, "but they're deep. I'm afraid you might have some trouble with your left leg in the future. Scar tissue may limit your mobility."

The hair on one side of Tembelos' skull had also been burned. It didn't look terrible, only as if he had been badly barbered, little singled tufts interspersed with swaths of exposed and blistered skin. Moaning, Tembelos kept feeling it with his hand. "My hair, what happened to my hair?"

"It'll grow back," the doctor assured him. "It's your leg I'm worried about."

Before he left, the doctor handed Tembelos a bottle of painkillers and a cane. "Keep the weight off that leg. It will help promote healing."

Scowling, Tembelos held the cane at arm's length, as if it were a cobra. "You see this, Yiannis?" he told Patronas, shaking it at him. "It's a cane. A fucking cane. This case just keeps getting better and better."

AFTER LEAVING THE clinic, they drove back to Platys Gialos and camped out in front of Leandros. Patronas had promised the harbor patrolman he'd relieve him, and he wanted to keep his word.

He'd wanted to go alone, but Tembelos insisted on accompanying him. "Hurts no matter what I do, so I might as well work. Anyway, I want to get this done and go home. I'm sick of this place."

They parked the Rav across the street and took turns sleeping in the backseat. Tembelos was in a great deal of pain, and he kept moaning every few minutes. Neither of them got much rest.

"No offense, Yiannis," Tembelos said over breakfast the next morning, "but Florence Nightingale, you're not. When a person is suffering and cries out in pain, you're supposed to comfort them, not cover your ears."

"I'm sorry, Giorgos. I'm exhausted."

They were sitting in Narli's Café, drinking coffee and eating tyropitas. *Breakfast or dinner, it doesn't matter,* Patronas thought. *The menu is exactly the same.*

"Maybe I should warn Calliope off," Tembelos went on. "I'm not sure I want my cousin mixed up with a man like you." The words were harsh, but his friend grinned as he said them.

"Might not be a bad idea," Patronas said, rejoicing that he might be off the hook. "I'm not myself these days."

"Yiannis, Yiannis, I've known you a long time. No offense, but you were never a prize."

After finishing breakfast, they walked across the street to the migrant camp.

Pawing through the ashes searching for clues, they found chunks of glass spread over a large area and painstakingly collected them, hoping to obtain enough to gauge the size and shape of the bottle that had been thrown.

Wincing in pain, Tembelos leaned against the cane. "Timing was curious," he told Patronas. "Was the bomb aimed at us or at them?"

"Them, I think. If it had been us, they would have blown up the Toyota."

Patronas doubted they'd find fingerprints on the glass shards, but he planned to dust them anyway. Normally, he would have sent them on to Athens, but not this time. He was afraid more people would die if he didn't catch the person responsible, that whoever it was would continue to wreak havoc among the migrants on Sifnos.

Petros Nikolaidis was in Apollonia, taking statements from the people in the clinic who'd been injured in the fire, and Papa Michalis and Evangelos Demos were working their way through Platys Gialos, speaking to the local residents there.

"Ask them if they saw anything," Patronas instructed. "Height, weight, anything that would help us to identify the arsonist."

The priest had chosen to station himself outside the camp, saying a Christian clergyman would not be welcome in there today. For once he had chosen to do the sensible thing. "Much as I'd like to help you, Yiannis, my presence will only antagonize these poor people, serve to alienate them further."

Evangelos had held back for an entirely different set of reasons, Patronas believed—cowardice being the main one, indolence following close on its heels. He didn't pull his weight, substantial as it was.

If a suspect was shooting at them and he ordered Evangelos to return fire, he was pretty sure his subordinate's response would be 'huh?' The only help Evangelos would ever provide was as a shield.

The epicenter of the blaze had been a particular point along the riverbed. Judging by the burn pattern on the ground, the arsonist had tossed the Molotov cocktail into the foliage there and fled, running out to the road where Patronas and Tembelos had spotted him. Noticing how close the explosion was to the hovel where the woman, Noor, had been living, Patronas wondered if she, and not the camp itself, had been the real target.

The migrants still left in the camp were picking through their belongings and cleaning them off. A woman in jeans and a headscarf was shaking out a wet sheet and hanging it on a line, with a toddler playing at her feet. It was a poignant image. Surrounded by charred trees and ash, she stood there with a basket of clothes, going about her housework as if it were an ordinary day.

Technically savvy, Tembelos got out his cellphone and pressed the translation application. Then, looking down at the screen, he called out to her in broken Arabic. Smiling tentatively, the woman answered. They went on like this for a few minutes, call and response, each one answering in turn.

It was like watching time-lapse photography, so slow was the conversation. Still, it was a conversation, the woman obviously understanding what Tembelos was saying. It was a revelation to Patronas, so he pulled out his phone and looked for the application Tembelos had used.

'As-salam alaykum,' his friend had said. Obviously a greeting. He repeated the words slowly, working his tongue around them. He'd get Tembelos to show him how the application worked and would revisit Sami Alnasseri's aunt at the clinic.

Feeling more optimistic, he unearthed yet another sliver of glass and slipped it into an evidence bag.

Underfoot, the ground was blackened in a rough circle, the brush deeply charred where the bottle had exploded. A miasma of smoke still lingered, wisps like Spanish moss enshrouding the bottoms of the trees, and there was a distinct chemical smell in the air, gasoline or some other kind of accelerant.

The roof of the shack where Sami and his aunt had been living had been covered with rushes, which caught fire almost instantly, resulting in a wall of flames and trapping her inside. She'd barely escaped with her life. Her skirt had caught fire, and like Tembelos, she had sustained third-degree burns on her legs.

Panicking, she'd jumped down into the dry riverbed and buried herself in the sand. Her quick thinking had saved her. She was still in the clinic, and according to the doctor, would be there for some time.

As far as Patronas could determine, the fire had devoured everything she owned, but he painstakingly went through the remains of her hovel anyway. Three meters square, it appeared to have been one of the better ones. The dirt floor was swept clean, and the bedding, what was left of it, was rolled up neatly in the corner. A board, resting on a stack of bricks, had once served as a table. He spied a pot, its contents charred beyond all recognition, in a far corner of the hovel, and a battered backpack, lying on its side near the entrance, remnants of blackened cloth hanging in shreds from its metal frame.

Like an archeologist, Patronas inspected everything, seeking to determine what each item had been before being incinerated. Inside the backpack, he found two passports and a slim role of banknotes. Thoroughly burned, they disintegrated when he touched them, leaving behind a fistful of papery ash.

He would need to find another place for her to live when she was discharged from the clinic. Petros Nikolaidis had volunteered his house, saying there was plenty of room, but Patronas worried that her presence might put Nikolaidis and his family at risk. Better to install her in a room at Morpheus Hotel instead, preferably the one next to his. He'd station Tembelos outside and leave him there, sitting peacefully day and night with his leg propped up. Lots and lots of overtime , and that asshole, Stathis, would have to pay for it.

Wandering back from the riverbed, Patronas saw another chunk of glass and nudged it with his foot. He and Tembelos had separated and were making a wide sweep, working their way out from the point at which the Molotov cocktail had exploded. There were still hot spots everywhere. Patronas had trodden on a few already, secret places where the fire still smoldered, making him more cautious.

After they finished collecting the fragments of glass, they laid them out on the ground and shifted them around, fitting them together like pieces of a puzzle. Judging by the remnants they'd unearthed, the bomb had been a big one, several gallons of accelerant in one huge glass jug.

"Achilles Kourelas," Tembelos said, studying what was left of the bottle. "He's the one who did this."

Patronas nodded. Full, the glass jug would have been extremely heavy, and Achilles Kourelas was a big, strong man. He could probably lift a car, if he set his mind to it. Tossing the jug into the bushes would have been child's play. Tembelos' words made sense.

Still, it was just a hunch, and hunches were a bad idea when it came to police work—led to frame-ups and the convictions of innocent people.

The fact of the matter was they had no tangible proof Achilles Kourelas was involved—no DNA, no fingerprints, no nothing.

Palianthropos. The younger Kourelas was an awful human being, no question about it. A bully and a brawler. But an arsonist? Whoever had thrown the Molotov cocktail had to have planned the attack in advance, had bought the jug and gasoline. From what Patronas had seen, premeditation wasn't Achilles Kourelas' style. He might hate the migrants and espouse ridding Greece of them, but he wasn't alone in his bigotry. Lots of other people felt the same way, and any one of them might have thrown the bomb.

"I'm not convinced Kourelas is responsible," he told Tembelos. "A firebombing? He had to have known it would lead straight back to him."

"Hate rules him, Yiannis. Rules both father and son, and this was a hate crime."

Patronas and Tembelos continued to probe the ground, the area they tilled gradually growing bigger and bigger. A group of migrants were watching them collect the glass, their expressions hard to read. Patronas was glad they were there. He wanted them to see him laboring on their behalf, to be counted as one of the just.

Only about a hundred shanties remained standing, and the mayor was talking of closing the camp down altogether. The shelters that survived were sad places, full of the detritus of human life—plastic basins for washing clothes, unopened tins of food, and homemade diapers.

"You wanted a public message," Tembelos said, nodding to the camp. "I'd say you got one."

An elderly man standing outside one of the tents addressed them in halting English, "A cowardly act, to burn sleeping people."

"We'll catch whoever did this," Patronas said. "You have our word."

The man ignored him. "I thought Greece was better than this."

"So did I," Patronas said.

STATHIS WAS SKEPTICAL when Patronas called that evening to report in. "You think the two crimes are related, the killing and the fire?"

"It stands to reason," Patronas said, careful to keep his tone respectful. His boss sounded like he was irritated, and he didn't want to set him off.

"Two violent acts in less than a week?" Patronas said. "I can't believe it was a coincidence."

"You think one perpetrator is responsible?"

"My guess is more than one person is involved."

"A couple of vipers, then."

"Maybe more than a couple, sir. Could be there's a whole nest of them here."

"Question Costas and Achilles Kourelas again," Stathis ordered. "We need to put a stop to this."

"A waste of time, sir. We have no evidence that either was involved. Just being members of *Chrisi Avgi* doesn't make them criminals."

"In my mind, it does. Go talk to them, Yiannis. Do it and do it now, or I will fucking fire you."

"Sir, I cannot do it now. I cannot go visit those two men at this hour of the night. They are already hostile. It would be suicide."

"Very well, tomorrow morning then. Call me and tell me what you've learned. I'll be waiting."

CHAPTER EIGHTEEN

---◆---

She will put both his feet in one shoe.
—Greek Proverb

Patronas and his men ate dinner in the same taverna in Kamares, a proper meal with many courses, appetizers of every description.

"If the people of Sifnos are indeed greedy," the priest said, sticking his fork into a grilled sardine. "I'd say it works in their favor with respect to cooking. Greedy means you want more—more oil and butter, that extra tablespoon or two of sugar. The cooks here are generous with everything."

Nikolaidis nodded. "The cuisine of Sifnos is justifiably famous. One of the greatest chefs of Greece, Nikolaos Tselementes, was born and raised near Apollonia, and his legacy lives on to this day." He raised his fork in salute.

"I'll say it does," Papa Michalis said.

Smiling blissfully, he cut the little fish in half and popped a piece in his mouth.

"You always say human beings are better at survival than success." Patronas gestured to the wide assortment of dishes on the table. "No offense, Father, but this is hardly survival."

Tembelos laughed. "You're right," he said. "Survival would be the crap they ate during the war. Not fish like these."

"Believe me, I know about survival," the priest said, becoming serious. "When I was young, I was so hungry I would steal artichokes from a field on my way to school, cut them with my jackknife and eat them raw. The problem was the juice would stain my lips black and the teacher would know and beat me."

"An inauspicious beginning for a priest," Patronas said. "Stealing …."

"Artichokes only. Never anything else."

"Still, Father. I believe theft is mentioned in the Ten Commandments. It's expressly forbidden.

The old man had insisted on ordering *barbounia,* the most expensive fish in Greece, and for once, Patronas was glad he had. They'd also ordered a kilo of fresh sardines, basted in lemon, oregano, and olive oil, *mastelo,* lamb cooked in red wine until it practically melted, and a portion of *Sifnian myzithra,* a tangy local cheese, so tasty they'd ended up fighting over it. For dessert, they'd eaten *melopita,* a cake made of cheese and flavored with honey. They drank ouzo and over three liters of wine. After they finished, Tembelos staggered back to the hotel, saying the alcohol had sufficiently dulled the pain of his burns to let him sleep.

The others quickly dispersed, Patronas to Leandros, Nikolaidis, Evangelos Demos, and the priest near the home of Costas and Achilles Kourelas. Patronas had instructed them to observe only, to do absolutely nothing on their own. Evangelos and Nikolaidis were safe on that score. Papa Michalis, he wasn't so sure about. Greatly excited about the prospect of a stakeout, the old man was apt to do or say something stupid and give them away.

"Keep an eye on him," he told Nikolaidis. "The fact that he's a priest won't protect him from those two."

Patronas remained convinced Achilles Kourelas was innocent, at least of the arson, and that bringing him in would be a mistake, but he didn't know how to get out of it and still hang on to his job. Once Stathis got an idea in his head, it stayed there. And tonight, that idea had been Achilles Kourelas. Guilty until proven guilty.

"Cats wearing gloves never catch mice," Stathis had said, a proverb he recited often.

As usual, his boss didn't know what he was talking about.

He might be a cat, but given their relative size, only a fool would mistake Achilles and his father for mice.

AFTER NIKOLAIDIS DROPPED him off, Patronas walked around to the back of Leandros. He was very sleepy and thought he'd watch the apartments of the four suspects from a prone position, lying on a chaise lounge on the beach.

It was after midnight and a soft breeze was blowing, stirring the surface of the sea and ruffling the canvas umbrellas lined up along the shore. There was less ambient light in this area, and overhead, the stars were like sequins sewn across the sky.

Once, Patronas had collected a jarful of fireflies and used them as a nightlight, delighted by their flickering in his room. His mother had quickly put an end to it, repelled by the idea of bugs in her house, and dumped them out in the toilet, but he still remembered the little creatures' unsteady twinkling. *Would that I could harness starlight as easily, to contain it in a jar.*

Upstairs, Svenson and the students were all present. The doors to their rooms were open and he could hear them talking, rock music booming in the background.

He was in the process of dragging a chaise lounge from the apartment complex down to the beach when he caught sight of someone walking outside Lydia Pappas' apartment. There was no light on and he paused, not wanting to alert the intruder to his presence. Two people emerged from the apartment upstairs, and like him were silently watching whoever it was moving around in the dark. Bowdoin and Nielsen, Patronas guessed, judging by their silhouettes.

"Chief Officer, what are you doing here?" Lydia Pappas sang out.

Anticipating a night of solitude, Patronas had brought a thermos full of coffee with him. He was so startled, he dropped it, the liquid leeching out and darkening the sand. Her presence was unexpected, and it unnerved him.

"You're a witness in a murder case," he stammered, straightening up in an effort to appear taller. "I'm here to protect you."

A lie, but a small one. Far better than telling her she was a suspect in the boy's death. Not the most sophisticated man when it came to women, Patronas was sure such knowledge would not further his cause.

"So you're here to protect me?"

Patronas couldn't see her well in the dark, but it sounded like she was laughing. "That's right," he said.

"What makes you think I'm in need of protection?"

"Recent events would indicate there's a madman loose on the island."

"You better come up here then," she said, patting the seat beside her. "I'd hate to be attacked by a madman."

Patronas looked up at the balcony. Whoever had been there was gone. The boys' scrutiny made his skin crawl. He wondered if Lydia Pappas knew the students had been watching her.

"Come on," she coaxed.

Feeling foolish, he left the chaise lounge where it was and joined her on the terrace. He was surprised to see that she, too, had been injured in the fire, her left arm in a sling.

"What happened? You're hurt."

She nodded. "A burning branch fell on me."

"Is it bad? Your pottery ... will you be able to work again?"

"I'm fine." Hoisting her bandaged arm in the air, she turned it from side to side. "Actually, I'm proud of it. I only wish I'd been able to do more."

Dressed in a shapeless peach dress, she had just taken a shower, and the smell of soap still clung to her skin—a woodsy, herbal scent that reminded

Patronas of pine forests and rain. A detective, he suspected there was no bra under her garment. That led to other thoughts, the possibility of a thong and how one might go about removing it.

She began braiding her hair, working her fingers deftly through the wet strands. When she finished, she tied it back with a bandana, a red paisley one with tiny knots at the ends.

A lantern was on the table and the flame flickered now and then, illuminating only a small area of the terrace. Again, Patronas had the sense that he and Lydia were an island unto themselves, just as they'd been that morning on the way to Thanatos, the circle of light like a wall against the darkness.

"What are you doing up so late?" he asked.

"My arm was bothering me and I couldn't sleep. Anyway, it's a glorious night." She smiled at him. "You look exhausted. Every time I see you, you're working. Don't you ever stop?"

"It's been a rough week. A lot has happened."

They spoke again of the fire, the horror of the burning camp, and the dead child, the plight of the migrants and what their presence would mean to Greece.

"I know they are unwelcome here now," she said. "It's understandable, given the economic situation. But we *can't* permit people to use violence to *drive* them away." Leaning toward him, she recited a passage he was unfamiliar with:

> First they came for the Socialists, and I did not speak out—because I was not a Socialist.
> Then they came for the Trade Unionists, but I did not speak out—because I was not a Trade Unionist.
> Then they came for the Jews, and I did not speak out—because I was not a Jew.

"It's from Auschwitz, I think," she told him. "The point is you have to defend people who are defenseless. To put out the fires threatening to engulf them. Literally, in this case."

"Do you think it will come to that in Europe?"

"Judging by what happened here, I'd say it already has."

Continuing to talk, they slowly moved on to more personal topics: her struggle to make a place for herself in academia, his ongoing battle with Stathis and diminishing salary, how he planned to survive financially when he retired.

"I worked security at an archeological dig in Chios .... I suppose I could go back to it. I'll miss police work, though, catching villains and putting them in jail."

"Don't you find it depressing?"

"Sometimes. A priest I work with says, 'Murder disturbs the harmony of the world and we need to restore it, to reset the balance between good and evil.' I'm not a religious man, but I *do* believe in what I do, in obtaining justice for the victims, no matter who they are."

She nodded. "Especially when that victim's a child."

"Yes. He never had a chance, little Sami. His father took off and left him, and he never knew his mother. He didn't have much of anything, just a few toys and a beaten up old dog collar."

Feeling himself tear up, Patronas wiped his eyes. "I'm sorry," he said, humiliated to be crying in front of her. "The lack of sleep must be getting to me."

Lydia Pappas touched his face with her good hand. "It's rare to meet a man who cares as deeply as you do, who'd fight for a young refugee he never knew." She continued in this vein for a good five minutes, commending him for his decency. "I saw you rescuing those people from the fire, braving the flames and pulling that old woman out." She smiled. "At one point, I could swear your hair was smoking."

"That wasn't me," Patronas said, embarrassed. "That was my friend, Giorgos Tembelos."

Lydia Pappas continued to extol his virtues, singing his praises like he was Jesus and it was Easter.

Could be American hyperbole, Patronas thought. They did that, Americans. Used superlatives to describe the most mundane items—in this case, him.

Another possibility was that she found him attractive and she was flirting. Taking a deep breath, Patronas decided to go with flirting.

Having been with only one woman—his wife, Dimitra, who as a rule did all the talking—he had no idea how to flirt back. He supposed courtship was like chess: you made a move and she made a move, and hopefully, instead of shouting 'checkmate,' you ended up in bed. Still, he might be misreading the signals she was sending. In his opinion, the female sex was one of the great puzzles of the universe, right up there with the big bang, string theory, and the dark side of the moon. God knows he wasn't Stephen Hawking.

Upstairs, the light went out in Svenson's apartment. The students, however, were still at it. Rowdier than ever, they sounded like they were jumping up and down on the bed.

Svenson shouted, "Quiet!" and after that, someone closed the door and the noise died down.

At one point, Lydia Pappas asked Patronas to point out the constellations to her and he did, taking her by the hand and leading her out onto the sand. She lost her balance on the way there and fell against him, perhaps by design. She seemed disappointed when he righted her and stepped away.

"There's Orion, and to the west there, that's the Pleiades," he said. "See it? People have been aware of it for a very long time. Archeologists say the ancient Greeks oriented the Parthenon, based on the constellation's rising."

Returning to the terrace, she produced a bottle of wine and they drank it out of coffee mugs, the only dishware she could find in the rental apartment. She was surprised to learn Patronas liked poetry and could recite the works of Seferis and Cavavy by heart. They also discussed Greek music, agreeing that the composer, Manos Hadjidakis, was superior to all others.

"You like Kazantzakis?" he asked.

"Yes. Especially 'Report to Greco.' "

Patronas nodded, remembering how Kazantzakis had described his mother as a *neraida*, a mermaid, in "Report to Greco." Supposedly Katzanzakis' father had caught a glimpse of her dancing in the moonlight, caught hold of her magic kerchief, and made her his wife.

No one would ever have written those words about his mother, much as he loved her. She was not even remotely magical. Neither was his wife. They'd been rooted to the ground, those two. A tree, in his mother's case. Nettles and thorns in Dimitra's.

But Lydia Pappas? She was better than a mermaid. She was a goddess. Patronas wondered what would happen if he grabbed her kerchief tonight. If, like Kazantzakis had written, magic would ensue.

"You want to see the stars? You should go swimming at night," he said, sounding bolder than he felt. "That's the way to do it. I know a place not far from here. After I wrap up the case, you want to go with me?"

"Yes, I'd like that."

Suddenly, there was a commotion upstairs and a door banged open. "Hey, look who's here," Bowdoin shouted, peering over the balcony. "That cop's down there talking to Lydia."

Nielsen and Gilbert quickly joined Bowdoin; all three stood there whistling and catcalling. They eventually returned to their room, but by then it was too late. The mood was broken.

"Don't pay any attention to them," Lydia Pappas said. "Every time I turn around, they're there, leaning over the railing of the balcony, looking down at me. It's like living in a fishbowl. I wish Svenson would rein them in, but he can't be bothered. 'Boys will be boys,' he said when I complained about it. 'Boys will be boys.' "

"They make a pass at you?" Patronas asked, remembering what Bowdoin had said—that one of his roommates had a crush on her.

"No. No one's made a pass at me all summer."

"I beg your pardon," Patronas said, drawing himself up and pretending to be offended.

Laughing, she poured the rest of the wine and they drank it, Lydia Pappas resting her head on his shoulder. When he tried to kiss her, she whispered, "Not here," and pointed to the balcony.

Her tone was apologetic, as if seeking to justify her rejection to him.

Patronas felt the beginnings of hope.

Around three a.m., she departed, saying she had a class to teach in the morning and needed to get some sleep. "Good night, Chief Officer. I look forward to our swim."

Returning to the chaise lounge, Patronas stretched out, thinking he'd only close his eyes for a few minutes. His sleep was restless and filled with demons, people screaming and burning, tarantulas that transformed themselves into men.

Lydia Pappas must have returned at some point during the night, for when he awoke at dawn he was covered with a blanket and his thermos was once again full of coffee.

Chapter Nineteen

---◆---

Pity the brave man who is caught between two weaklings.
—Greek Proverb

BEFORE HEADING OFF to interrogate Costas and Achilles Kourelas, Patronas held a brief meeting with his men. "I don't care what Stathis says; we have no proof they're guilty of anything, save bigotry, which means we proceed cautiously. We politely announce we are taking them in for questioning and put them in the car. No handcuffs, no *fasaria*"—uproar.

The five of them were sitting around a table at Narli's, drinking coffee and eating, yet again, *tyropitas*, big square ones made of filo and feta cheese. The sun was bright against the water, and people were already sunbathing on the beach, a few taking shelter under the tamarisk trees at the water's edge. Patronas wished he could join them and linger there in the shade. He wasn't looking forward to the day ahead.

He paid the bill and stood up to go, brushing crumbs off his uniform. Filthy, it was like a collage of dust and debris from every place he'd been on Sifnos. He hoped Lydia Pappas hadn't noticed, the night before.

He had been speaking to her in front of Leandros that morning, thanking her for the coffee, when his team showed up. Save for the priest, they had all expressed their appreciation for her, rolling down the windows of the Toyota and sticking out their heads in order to catch an eyeful as she walked away.

"*Po, po,*" Tembelos said admiringly.

"For God's sake, Giorgos," Patronas said, "what would your wife say?"

An interesting question, considering that Tembelos' wife, Eleni, was a legend on Chios for her passionate and jealous temperament. She'd once caught her husband ogling a Swedish tourist on the beach—hardly Giorgos' fault as the woman had been topless—and threatened to unman him then and there, shouting and working her fingers like scissors. Tembelos had confided to Patronas that while he loved Eleni dearly, he was more than a little afraid of her.

And well he should be, Patronas thought. He could still see those long, manicured nails going up and down. They'd been painted red, he remembered—bright, arterial red.

It was easy to see where the ancients had gotten the idea of Medusa … they'd just looked across the table at their wives.

"Eleni? Na massas koukia kai na tin ftyneis," Tembelos said with a laugh. Eat beans and spit at her.

Patronas reflected on the situation. Maybe going swimming with Lydia Pappas wasn't such a good idea. A Greek woman who'd spent years in America might well embody the worst of both cultures, a potentially lethal combination. Medusa crossed with Hillary Clinton.

"You seem distracted. What happened with you and the potter last night?" Tembelos asked.

"Nothing happened between me and Lydia Pappas. I was on the job the whole night, working surveillance."

"So, no hanky-panky?"

"No, just old-fashioned police work."

"You keep saying 'work,' Yiannis. What you need is a little more 'play.' " He leered at him. "Take her and go off and make mud pies together. Make something."

"Love?" Patronas offered.

"As in 'to make' …. Sure, absolutely. It would do you a world of good."

THEY TOOK TWO cars to the house of Costas and Achilles Kourelas, Patronas riding shotgun next to Petros Nikolaidis in his Ford Fiesta, the other three following close behind them in the Rav. Far below, Patronas could see the Chapel of *Chryssopigi*—Virgin of the Golden Spring. With a sculpted bell tower, it occupied its own narrow peninsula and was the scene of numerous destination weddings. Picturesque and beautiful, it was the symbol of Sifnos and the most photographed site on the island.

They passed through the outskirts of Apollonia and Artemonas then followed the road to Herronissos, a distant fishing village. The landscape grew more and more forbidding as they journeyed north, the land falling away in a series of deep ravines that led straight down to the sea, olive trees gradually giving way to patches of dry brush and finally to nothing. Patronas spotted a sign to a ceramic workshop, another written in Byzantine script indicating there was a church nearby. There was little else of note, just one bare hill after another. Absolutely empty, they were like bruised shadows against the horizon.

"This is where they mined gold in ancient times," Nikolaidis said, nodding to the expanse of rock.

Patronas studied the area, "Any mines still working?" he asked.

"No. The gold gave out before the birth of Christ."

High on a distant mountain, Patronas caught a glimpse of Profitis Elias, the rectangular building crowning the highest peak, as was the custom in Greece. Although it was still early, the air was stifling.

Nikolaidis looked over at him. "You look worried. Are you sure you want to do this?"

"Stathis didn't give me much choice. He told me to load them up in the cars, take them back to Apollonia, and interview them, see what dusts out. Maybe take a look around while we're here, see if we find a jug like the one that was used for the Molotov cocktail."

"My money's on them for the firebombing."

"It would certainly be consistent with their politics. Maybe they killed the little boy, too. But we have no evidence in either case, and without evidence, we can't go forward."

"Dangerous game to be playing, cornering those two. They won't like our coming here today."

"We'll just have to brave it."

Lighting a cigarette, Patronas stared out at the landscape. It would be a lengthy process, the arrest—if it came to that. Most likely an all-day affair. After questioning Achilles Kourelas and his father in turn, reading them their rights and securing a confession, they'd have to drive them to Kamares and board a ferry to Milos where there was a proper jail—father and son undoubtedly protesting the whole way.

As before, they parked along the road and headed down the hill toward the house. Taking their cue from Patronas, no one spoke, all of them affected by his dark mood.

Their targets were sitting outside in the two car seats, drinking coffee and smoking cigarettes. As before, they'd been working on a motor and their clothes were stained with grease.

Costas Kourelas got to his feet when he saw them. "What the hell are you doing here?"

"We want you and your son Achilles to come with us," Patronas said.

The older man narrowed his eyes. "Why? Are we under arrest?"

"No. We just need to talk to you, nothing more."

Reluctantly, Costas Kourelas agreed. Achilles Kourelas said he wanted to use the bathroom first and started back toward the house. Patronas moved to accompany him, but Achilles waved him off, saying he'd only be a minute.

Letting Achilles Kourelas go, Patronas wandered around the yard while he waited. He saw no evidence that would indicate the two had been involved in the firebombing. The same discarded cans of motor oil still littered the yard, but there were no glass bottles to be seen. These men weren't stupid. *Chances are if they were guilty, they already disposed of the evidence.*

Patronas decided that after he'd settled Costas Kourelas and his son in the interview room in the municipal building, he'd call Stathis and have him secure a warrant, then send Tembelos and Nikolaidis back to search the place again, break open the door if they had to and inspect the rooms inside.

No matter how heinous their political beliefs, they were guaranteed a lawful search under the Greek constitution; they had the same rights as everyone else. Patronas believed in the rule of law and had dedicated his entire adult life to upholding it; he wasn't about to abandon it now.

As soon as Achilles Kourelas emerged from the house, the whole party started up the hill to the road—each suspect flanked by two policemen. They were doing fine until they got to the car and Evangelos Demos tried to push Achilles' head down in an effort to get him in the backseat, apparently the way he'd seen cops do it on American television shows. It was a stupid maneuver, for Achilles Kourelas wasn't handcuffed and could have gotten there fine on his own. Evangelos also went about it clumsily, shoving him down and knocking his head against the doorframe.

Letting out a mighty roar, Kourelas reared back and clobbered Evangelos Demos with his fist, then threw him to the ground, grabbed him by the hair, and began dragging him back and forth—wiping the earth with him, or so it seemed. He continued to pound him, cursing and calling him names, spittle flying.

Petros Nikolaidis tried pulling him off, but Kourelas head-butted him and from the sound of it, broke his nose. Within seconds, they were both covered with blood.

"Stop him before he kills somebody!" Patronas yelled.

Lurching and swinging his arms like a bear in a cloud of gnats, Achilles Kourelas continued to do battle. Tembelos was the next to fall, shrieking and clutching his knee where Kourelas had kicked him.

Patronas had drawn his gun by this point and was waving it at Kourelas, screaming at him to cease and desist or be shot. Laughing, Kourelas crouched down and began circling Patronas like a wrestler, stepping closer and retreating, jeering and baiting him. A moment later, he lunged, knife in hand, and stabbed him in the stomach.

Clutching his gut, Patronas collapsed on the ground, seeking to hold on to the knife as he fell, not wanting his weight to push it in deeper. He could feel blood spilling over his fingers, smell its metallic tang.

Achilles Kourelas took a step back and stood there, looking down at him, his expression hard to read. Rage was there, but also bewilderment, as if he hadn't expected this to happen, to have a cop lying at his feet, bleeding. Stooping down, he pulled the knife out of Patronas, and drawing back, moved to stab him again. It was a big knife, nearly identical to the one Patronas had found at Thanatos, and Patronas closed his eyes, wondering if his mother would really be there to welcome him on the other side.

Suddenly, a shot rang out and Achilles Kourelas looked up in surprise, blood gushing from his shoulder and darkening the front of his shirt. He dropped to his knees with arms outstretched, then fell face forward into the dirt. He scratched the ground feebly with his fingers once or twice as he tried to raise himself up, a bubble of blood forming on his lips, then collapsed and was still.

His father ran to his side. "Achilles! Oh, my God ... Achilles!"

CHAPTER TWENTY

⸺•⸻

Praise the good.
—The Delphic Oracle

PATRONAS HAD NO memory of the trip to the clinic or the first twenty-four hours he spent there. When he finally awoke, he was lying in bed, hooked up to a variety of machines and desperately thirsty. Evangelos Demos was sitting on a plastic chair next to the bed, staring off into space. His forehead and chin were scraped raw where Achilles had dragged him across the gravelly earth, and he looked like he'd been crying.

"Water," Patronas said weakly.

Jumping up, Evangelos filled a cup from a pitcher on the nightstand and held it to his lips. "You need anything else? Should I get the doctor?"

"No, no." Waving the glass away, Patronas collapsed back on the pillow.

"You were in the operating room for a long time," Evangelos reported. "More than four hours. At first, we wanted to airlift you to Athens, but the doctor said there wasn't time. You'd bleed out before the helicopter arrived. Nikolaidis drove like a maniac, a hundred kilometers an hour, honking and screaming at people. Giorgos was in the backseat, holding you in his arms, trying to keep you warm so you wouldn't go into shock, pressing down on the wound with his hands. Doctor said he saved your life."

"Where's Achilles?"

"In KAT, the trauma hospital in Athens. Tembelos summoned a helicopter which came and took him away. He'll be all right, the doctor said. No lasting injuries."

Patronas looked around the room. Judging by the placement of the windows, it was the same one he'd been in the night of the fire, only instead of a gurney, there was a proper hospital bed and he was on it. A monitor with an eerie blue screen was tracking his heartbeats, the graph adjusting and readjusting itself, rising and falling with every breath he took, and he was hooked up to at least two intravenous drips, one a purplish bag of blood. He surreptitiously moved his hands down under the sheet, felt a length of tubing. *Shit!* They'd inserted a catheter, too.

Uncomfortable, he squirmed around on the mattress. He felt like he'd been tied in a knot, his insides fiercely constrained. He fingered the patchwork of bandages on his gut. "What's all this?"

"Doctor said he stapled you," said Evangelos.

Patronas nodded. That's about what it felt like.

"I shouldn't have shot him. I know that. But he was killing you, Yiannis. He was fucking killing you."

Patronas felt himself drifting off again. "Never mind," he said.

But Evangelos wanted to tell his side of the story. "After we got you settled, Nikolaidis called Stathis and told him what happened. After that, all hell broke loose. The newspapers got wind of it and people are saying I did it on purpose because Achilles Kourelas was *Chrisi Avgi.* But I didn't do it for that reason, Yiannis, I swear. I did it to save you."

"Stathis say anything about me?"

Unwilling to meet his eye, Evangelos nodded unhappily. "He wanted to know where Kourelas got the knife and how come you didn't search him before taking him away. He also quizzed me about the gun—why I still had it after what happened in Chios." Looking down, he hesitated. "You know, with the goats."

Patronas wished he could adjust the morphine drip, up the dose until he lost consciousness, drown Evangelos out somehow. It wasn't enough that he'd almost died. Evidently, Stathis planned to fire him, too. At the very least, hold a public hearing and feast on his entrails.

He had once seen a painting of Napoleon retreating from Russia. The emperor had been riding a horse—the landscape bleak and white with snow—and he had been surrounded by bloody soldiers. But it was Napoleon's expression Patronas remembered best, the look of abject despair. Lying there in the hospital bed, he understood how the man had felt.

Like the emperor, he'd bungled everything from start to finish. He'd assumed because Kourelas was Greek, he wasn't truly dangerous, and look where that had gotten him? Skewered like a *souvlaki* and his quarry nearly killed.

"I didn't know what else to do," Evangelos said.

Closing his eyes, Patronas lay there, thinking. *Even if I get fired, I can go back to working security at the archeological dig on Chios. Alcott's my friend. He'll take care of me.*

He sighed. Survival, not success. It seemed to be his destiny.

With a wife and son, it would be much harder for Evangelos. He couldn't afford to lose his job. The son, Nikos, needed special care; he'd perish without it.

"I'll do what I can to defend you, Evangelos," Patronas said. "If there's an inquest, I'll say you behaved heroically, took down an armed madman single-handedly and saved my life."

Drifting off to sleep, Patronas smiled to himself. *A hero, Evangelos? The opiates must be getting to me.*

Patronas thought he was hallucinating when Stathis showed up in the hospital room the next morning. As cocky as ever, his boss had brought a group of reporters with him, one from each of the major papers in Greece, and had a local photographer in tow. Worse was the way he was beaming at Patronas. Out of practice at smiling, he appeared to be baring his teeth, which made Patronas distinctly uneasy. He didn't know why Stathis had come or what he wanted—a worrisome place to be with his boss.

"There he is," Stathis said, rushing over to his bedside.

Posing next to the hospital bed, he put his arm around Patronas' shoulders and suggested the photographer take a picture, saying Patronas and his team had cornered a dangerous serial killer, a man who targeted even children because of their race. "Chief Officer Patronas fought to protect the people of Greece—native born and migrant alike—and almost lost his life in the ensuing firefight."

Patronas started to correct him, to say that as far as he recalled, there'd been no firefight, only a single, poorly thought-out gunshot, but seeing the expression on his boss' face, he decided to remain silent. Justice would be served, but not here, not now, and certainly not by Stathis.

Looking in the mirror over the dresser, Stathis wetted the tip of his pinky finger and smoothed down his eyebrows and moustache. He then posed for more pictures, angling his head first to the left and then to the right, speaking affably to the reporters the whole time. Cashing in on Patronas' injury.

"You'll be back in Chios before you know it," he told Patronas. "I've already authorized the airfare."

"But the case—" Patronas protested.

"The case is closed!" Stathis said.

His boss left fifteen minutes later, waltzing out as casually as he'd come, the reporters trailing after him. "I'm heading to Paros on vacation," he called out over his shoulder. "Let me know if you need anything."

Patronas didn't know whether to laugh or cry. At least he still had a job.

After Stathis left, Patronas slept for a few hours.

The doctor appeared at his side later that day and gave him a shot. "To prevent sepsis," he said. He then changed the dressing on Patronas' wound and adjusted his IV, removing the bag of blood and replacing it with another.

After that, there was a steady stream of people: Petros Nikolaidis and his wife, the latter bearing a plastic container of *avgolemono* soup, and Papa Michalis and Giorgos Tembelos, who had split the cost of a fancy tart made of almonds and ice cream. They brought in chairs and sat there talking. The room got hotter and hotter, the ice cream eventually melting and pooling on the nightstand.

"You okay, boss?" Tembelos asked.

Patronas raised a cautionary hand. "Not 'okay', Giorgos, *entaxei*."

He'd been on a campaign to rid his speech of foreign words such as 'okay' and had insisted his associates do the same. It hadn't gone well; Tembelos especially had mocked him, speaking German on occasion just to torment him. '*Guten Morgen, mein Herr,*' and the like. It was an insufferable situation, but Patronas was unwilling to concede defeat. Greek it was, and Greek was the language he'd use until the day he died.

Tembelos gave him a long look. "For God's sake, Yiannis, don't start that Greek-only crap today, not after what happened."

"We should preserve our heritage."

"Our heritage is in shreds … or haven't you noticed? One 'okay' more or less won't make any difference. You need to watch yourself with this Greek thing. First, it's the language, and then it's the homeland, and before you know it, you're joining *Chrisi Avgi*. It's not that big a leap from purity of the tongue to purity of the race."

"Oh, for God's sake, I'm not a fascist. Leave me alone."

Tucking an extra pillow under his head, Petros Nikolaidis' wife helped Patronas' eat the soup, holding the spoon up to his mouth so he could sip it. Her name was Thalia, and she had curly black hair and a broad, open face. She seemed a kindly person and was very patient with him, wiping his face gently with a napkin between mouthfuls.

"Given the fact that Achilles used a knife on you, Stathis believes he must have killed the boy, too," Tembelos told Patronas. "As for the firebombing, we found a container of gasoline in the house. Now, Stathis is pressuring us to arrest Costas."

"So what if there was gasoline?" Patronas said. "What does that prove? They were car mechanics. Of course they'd have gasoline."

"He wants to nail them for it."

"I know. He paid me a visit earlier today with a bunch of reporters. Seems to think our shooting of Achilles Kourelas is his ticket to stardom."

Tembelos snorted. "*As tous fane ta korakia.*" Let the crows eat him.

Patronas' pain had returned, and he could feel himself beginning to fade. "What else is going on?"

"Father, here, has been working at the school, doing what he can for the migrants," Tembelos said, gesturing to the priest. "The rest of us have been dealing with the fallout from the shooting. Appears that there'll be a hearing in Athens and we'll all have to go before a panel and defend ourselves—convince the powers-that-be it was the correct course of action."

"It wasn't," Patronas said. "The only thing we knew at that point was that Achilles Kourelas was an asshole. We had nothing linking him to either crime."

"He would have killed you, Yiannis. The man is crazy."

"I just wish it had gone differently."

"Wisdom behind me, had I but had thee before," Tembelos said. It was a famous Geek saying, one Patronas' mother had often recited.

"Wisdom in front of me would have been better."

The priest volunteered to stay with Patronas after Tembelos and the others departed. "I'll help you until you're back on your feet again, Yiannis. Be your eyes and ears."

"Do whatever you like, Father."

"A few prayers?"

Patronas yawned. "If you must."

CHAPTER TWENTY-ONE

———— ◆ ————

Honor good men.
—The Delphic Oracle

LYDIA PAPPAS LINGERED outside Patronas' hospital room, peering in as if afraid to enter. "I can come back later if you want," she said.

"No, now is perfect," Patronas said, beckoning her forward with his hand. "I had a bath and the doctor just left."

The bath had been an embarrassing affair. A stout Polish woman—a veritable giantess—had scrubbed him down with a washcloth, chiding him all the while, pushing him roughly this way and that. After shampooing his hair, she'd scrubbed the soles of his feet, his underarms and groin, even the inside of his ears, and rinsed him off with a hose. So thorough was the cleaning, Patronas felt as if he'd been through a carwash.

He was feeling much better this morning, far less weak and confused. The doctor attributed his improvement to the multiple blood transfusions.

"You lost a great deal of blood," the doctor said, "but we managed to stabilize the situation. Your wound is starting to heal, and there is no sign of sepsis. Starting today, I want you to start exercising. You can hold on to Kyria Wanda." He nodded to the Polish giantess standing next to him. " Walk up and down the hall."

"Maybe later," Patronas said, in no hurry to go anywhere with Wanda. "I'm a little tired."

Lydia Pappas had brought a bouquet of freesias that she set about arranging, filling the vase with water and setting it down on the nightstand next to him. "I came as soon as I heard."

She was wearing a voile dress with little flowers embroidered on it, the material so thin Patronas could see her bra, the line of her underpants. Her arm was still in a sling and her head was covered by the same kerchief she'd worn that night at Leandros—the one that made him think of Kazantzakis.

Patronas felt a little tremor of excitement. Hardly the time for it, given the catheter and the little nightshirt he was wearing. The heart monitor started beeping faster and faster the nearer she came, the machines he was hooked up to giving him away.

She nodded to the IVs. "What did the doctor say?"

"According to him, I'm full of other people's blood and doing just fine," said Patronas.

Self-conscious about his situation—the tubes and all the rest—he pulled the sheet up to his chin and ducked his head down like a turtle. "I'm supposed to go for a walk," he said. "Would you care to join me?"

After securing a robe from the nurse, they made their way slowly down the hallway, Patronas walking beside Pappas, clutching the pole with the IVs on it for support on one side, her arm on the other. After they returned, they sat together for a long time. Outside, the birds were lively and the scent of the flowers she'd brought hung heavily in the air.

Patronas described how an old woman he'd met on Patmos put seeds out on her windowsill for the birds, taming them over time. "I never saw anything like it. They'd hear her voice and come. She said it was a small price to pay for their company."

"I'll bring some seeds with me tomorrow," Pappas said. "Maybe we can get them to visit you, too."

"Don't let the doctor catch you or that Amazon he has working for him."

"Wanda? I met her."

Co-conspirators, they laughed together.

"I've been meaning to ask you," she said. "How did you get interested in astronomy? It seems a strange pastime for a cop. Did you study it in school?"

"No, nothing like that. I'm not a well-educated man. I never went to university. I taught myself."

He described his nights working security on an archeological dig on Chios, how there wasn't much on the hill where he was, only an immense blanket of stars. "I guess that's where it started. I ended up buying a telescope, a strong one, and scanning the sky. You can see the rings of Saturn through it, all kinds of stuff. I bought a book, too. I wanted to learn more about what I was seeing, everything I could—"

She leaned over and kissed him gently on the mouth, taking care not to disturb his IVs. Hearing the heart monitor, Wanda came rushing in to see what was going on and sent Lydia on her way.

Patronas watched her leave. "Well, what do you know?" he said to himself.

While Patronas was in the clinic, Lydia Pappas came every single day to see him, each time bearing a different gift: more flowers, an MP3 player so that he could listen to music, a bag of *amygdalota,* the almond cookies Sifnos was famous for, and even a pot one of her students had made with a sheriff's star etched on the side.

Usually she arrived late in the afternoon, after her classes had finished. Often they didn't speak, just sat and held hands. Sometimes Patronas would doze off while she was there. Other times, the reverse would happen; she'd be the one to sleep. He liked to watch her then, her face gradually relaxing, her breathing becoming deep and steady. Thought what he felt at those moments might well be the beginning of love.

The birds gradually found their way to his windowsill, and one afternoon, into the room itself, a group of sparrows flying around and around until they found their way out, with Lydia Pappas' help. She herded them in the right direction with her scarf, holding it to one side like a toreador and waving them over to the window.

"They'll be nesting in your IV if you're not careful," she said with a smile.

He and Pappas watched the birds pecking outside for a moment or two. "Give them more seeds," he said.

Smiling, she reached over and took his hand before sprinkling the seeds on the sill. "You're a good man, Yiannis Patronas."

Patronas spent a lot of time walking up and down the corridor as the doctor prescribed, nodding to the migrants who were still there. He'd visited Sami Alnasseri's aunt two or three times, sitting by her bedside and doing his best to communicate with her, using the translation application on his phone.

Although still in a great deal of pain, she seemed to welcome the company, and they worked out a kind of language between them, half-English and half-Arabic. *Congolezika,* he told himself—Greek slang for a babel of tongues.

She eventually admitted that Sami's friends might have been Greek. They had been foreign men, she was sure, information Patronas took with a grain of salt. Most probably all she meant was they were from some place other than Syria. "Sami, he say, they are rich."

This revelation worried him, for it contradicted everything he knew of Costas and Achilles Kourelas. But, remembering the boy's poverty, he decided it wouldn't have taken much to impress him. As a refugee, he had needs that were all-encompassing. Reluctantly, Patronas began to think Stathis might have been right after all: the killer was Achilles Kourelas.

Still, he had his doubts. Something about the case still bothered him. The solution seemed too tidy for one thing: both the arson and the boy's murder laid at the doorstep of one person, a man who lacked the means and the intelligence to defend himself. In his experience, things didn't happen that way. One question answered only gave rise to another and another, and so it was now.

When he questioned Sami's aunt about the fire, she said she hadn't seen the person who threw the Molotov cocktail and had no reason to believe anyone would want to harm her. "It is us, they were after," she said. "All of us, I am very sure. Not just me."

The doctor confided to Patronas that she needed skin grafts, that he was seeking to send her on to Athens, to a hospital with a team of doctors he trusted.

"Let me know if there's anything I can do," Patronas told him.

"Just do what you're doing. Keep talking to her. She is a lost soul, profoundly depressed."

CHAPTER TWENTY-TWO

---•---

Pray for happiness.
—The Delphic Oracle

PATRONAS WAS DISCHARGED seven days later, and he and Lydia Pappas went swimming that night. He'd taped a plastic bag over his bandage to prevent it from getting wet. Not very appealing, but somehow with Lydia, it didn't seem to matter.

They walked up the beach to the Platys Gialos Hotel and waded into the cove there, then swam along the rocky coast and out into the open sea. Lulled by the waves, they lay on their backs and held hands for a few seconds, then continued to swim. Soon they were surrounded by a vast darkness, the division between the sea and sky lost, the night seemingly endless and overtaking the earth. Overhead, the stars were radiant, so brilliant Patronas imagined he could see their reflection on the surface of the water. Lydia laughed as she swam, her hair undulating around her when they paused to rest, the long length of it moving back and forth on the current.

When they grew tired, they climbed up on the rocks that formed the far end of the cove and lay down on their backs. The night was warm and they stayed like that a long time. Someone had put up a metal pole and was flying a Greek flag. A gull was standing on top, watching them with frank curiosity.

Later Patronas couldn't remember who had reached for the other first, whether it had been him or Lydia. All he remembered was kissing her over and over, and his boundless joy when she drew him closer, and then closer still, shivering and crying out in pleasure.

He buried himself in her hair and licked the salt off her skin, called her name out loud until he could call no more.

His *neraida*.

* * *

Two days later Patronas moved out of Morpheus and into Lydia Pappas' studio apartment at Leandros. The summer study would be drawing to a close soon, so they didn't have much time, and they wanted to make the most of it. He was still on sick leave, so they took it easy, swimming in the afternoon and cooking the evening meal together. Patronas had never been with any woman but his former wife, and he found the experience exhilarating. Lydia didn't sulk, for one thing. Didn't argue, didn't rage. She actually seemed to like him, which was a revelation in and of itself.

His wife, Dimitra, had been less than forthcoming with her favors, so in his weakened state he found keeping up with Lydia more than a little challenging. Also, the incident with Achilles Kourelas had affected him more than he realized. Lydia woke him one night, saying he'd been whimpering in his sleep, crying out in anguish. The light of the full moon had been everywhere, and they'd lain in each other's arms, her face luminous in the moonlight, her reddish hair tangled up around him. Breathing in her scent, Patronas would gladly have died then and there.

It is enough, this. I need nothing more.

Kazantzakis said in *Zorba the Greek* that it is a sin to deny a woman when she summons you to her bed and you do not go. Patronas did his best, but he often needed a nap in the afternoon.

While Tembelos applauded Patronas' good fortune, he worried about the eventual outcome of his romance. "Only you would give your heart to a woman who lives in the United States, one you cannot afford to visit."

"Giorgos, I'm crazy about her. I'm going to ask her to marry me."

"For God's sake, Yiannis. You can't move to Boston, and she'd be a fool to stay here. Pull yourself together."

Papa Michalis had similar reservations. "You're at a crossroads, Yiannis," he told him one morning over coffee. "You've been alone for far too long. Even when you were married, you were alone. And now this brash young redhead comes along and sweeps you off your feet."

"She makes me happy, Father."

"Drunks say the same thing about whiskey. You must not let lust be the guiding principal in your life. You should see yourself. You're all … giddy." The priest made a kind of sweeping motion. "It's most unsettling, even a little unseemly in my view, given that you're an officer of the law."

"I'm happy," Patronas repeated.

"Happiness is an American state of mind, something those people feel they are entitled to and are always going on about. You and I, we are a mature people. We are Greeks."

Patronas continued to visit Sami Alnasseri's aunt in the clinic. After the doctor inspected his wound, he'd stop by her room and sit with her. They had formed a kind of a hesitant friendship. Thinking she'd be more comfortable if there was another woman present, Patronas invited Lydia Pappas along late one afternoon. It was quiet now in the clinic, the Syrian woman the only patient remaining.

Lydia took her hand and sat with her for the next hour. When Patronas returned to the clinic the following day, she insisted on accompanying him. The two women would always smile at each other and chuckle whenever he said something. 'A man,' they seemed to be saying in that universal female language they both shared. 'What do you expect?'

Lydia often brought the Syrian woman flowers or a box of sweets. Noor was elated and cried once at the sight of the roses, said something in Arabic neither Patronas or Lydia understood. The two of them spent many hours with her over the next ten days. Easing her suffering became almost a joint project between them. Once Lydia demonstrated what she did for a living with her hands—the pot making—and Noor nodded in approval.

They accompanied her to the ferry when she left for the hospital in Athens, pushing her up the ramp in a wheelchair, and promised to visit her there after her surgery. Lydia had arranged to have a vase of roses placed in her room in preparation for her arrival, and Patronas had asked Stathis to speak to the medical staff on the floor and tell them to treat her as a foreign dignitary.

Before she left, the woman grabbed Patronas' hand and held it. "Sami? What of him?"

"I will find the person who killed him," Patronas said. "I give you my word."

"Justice, you said before," she whispered. "Justice for Sami."

Patronas nodded. "Yes, yes. I promise."

AND THEN IT all came crashing down. It started with a phone call from Richard Svenson one morning, saying he needed to see him.

"I'll meet you at Narli's," Patronas said. "It's less than a block from Leandros."

"I'd prefer not to do it in Platys Gialos. I'm in Apollonia now. Let's meet in the lobby of the municipality building."

Reluctantly, Patronas agreed. He was on foot today and would have to take the bus. Nikolaidis was already in Apollonia, and Tembelos and the other two had taken off in the Rav to visit the village of Heronissos, far to the north. The priest had heard the best fish were there and had commandeered the vehicle at breakfast that morning. The old man had recently taken up driving, but he hadn't really gotten the hang of it, so Tembelos had gone along to supervise, to reach over and put his foot on the brake if Father got confused. Having nothing better to do, Evangelos Demos went along for the ride. Since traffic was rare on the road to Heronissos, Patronas had consented to the outing, thinking that at the speed Papa Michalis usually drove, they would get there faster if they walked.

He had no idea why the priest wanted to take up driving at his advanced age, but he seemed determined. "I thought the automobile was a fad when it first appeared in Greece," he told Patronas. "A misjudgment on my part."

Petros Nikolaidis was in the municipality building, documenting what had transpired preceding the wounding of Achilles Kourelas. "A mere formality," Stathis had assured Patronas. Still, it had to be done and Nikolaidis had volunteered.

"Wait for me inside the municipality building," Patronas told Svenson on the phone. "I don't have a car and I'll have to take the bus. It might take me some time."

It actually took him close to ninety minutes. Buses were few and far between in Platys Gialos and he'd just missed the last one. When it finally did arrive, it made multiple stops, one every block or so, discharging islanders all along the road. Tourists were also onboard. The locals ignored them with well-practiced neutrality—outsiders, they were simply invisible to them—content to chat with one another in Greek. Causing a further delay, the tourists would stand in the doorway of the bus, guidebooks in hand, and ask the driver directions in bewildered voices. Parallel universes.

Petros Nikolaidis was still laboring away when Patronas finally got to the municipality building; he said Richard Svenson had never appeared. The only people in the lobby were locals seeking tax stamps, and it had been like that the entire day.

Exiting the building, Patronas walked through Apollonia and then on up the hill to Artemonas, searching the restaurants and coffee houses. Svenson might have gone for lunch prior to their appointment and been delayed. However,. he saw no trace of him.

An alarm was beginning to sound in his head, and he called the summer study, only to learn that Svenson had departed more than three hours before, saying he was heading back to Platys Gialos.

Patronas quickly called the owner of Leandros and asked him to check and see if Svenson was in his room. Within minutes, the man phoned back and said no one had answered the door at the apartment.

"What about the kids? Are they there? If so, put them on."

"They're always in class at this hour. They usually turn up here around four. You can always tell … the music."

"Did you see Svenson come in? The people at the summer study said he was on his way there."

"No, and he usually stops by the office to say hello. Real friendly, the professor. Typical American. Wants people to like him." The owner hesitated. "I have a master key. If you want, I can unlock the door and check inside for you."

"Do that and get back to me." Patronas gave him his cellphone number and hung up.

The owner called back within minutes. "His computer is on, but he's not there."

Growing anxious, Patronas called Tembelos on his cellphone and summoned him and the others back to Apollonia. "Richard Svenson has gone missing."

They spread out and searched the island, dividing it into quadrants. Concentrating on Platys Gialos, Patronas and Evangelos Demos worked their way through the village, interviewing the staff at Flora's, the taverna Svenson had said he frequented. While the people they spoke to said that they knew Svenson on sight, as far as they knew, he hadn't been around today.

Tembelos was exploring Apollonia with Nikolaidis and Papa Michalis. There were no ferry boats off the island until four p.m., so they held off expanding the search to Kamares. Turning up nothing, they continued on to Castro and Faros.

While in Kamares, Patronas had stopped at the headquarters of the Coast Guard and alerted the staff to Svenson's disappearance. Not wanting to cause a panic, he'd told them not to search the boat before it departed, but to stand by in case he needed them. He would call if he and his men didn't find him.

By the time he reached Castro, the sun was going down. Tourists were sitting outside the bars, drinking beer and watching the light fade from the sky. Patronas studied the medieval citadel at the top of a mountain, its eastern flanks plunging nearly straight down into the sea. A maze of narrow alleyways, the area had been occupied for centuries, each subsequent civilization building on the remnants of the one before. Patronas kept losing his way, taking a side street that led nowhere or back to where he'd started, which only added to his growing anxiety.

Although he searched every square inch of the village, stopping to question each person he met as before, he came up empty-handed.

A tiny chapel occupied an islet some distance away, a stone bridge leading out to it. Tourists were making their way there, stick figures in the distance. For a moment he stopped to watch them, but could see no one who resembled Svenson.

The village of Faros fronted a shallow bay. Seaweed darkened much of the water, undulating slowly in the current. The beach was more dirt than sand, muddy. Little more than a collection of rooming houses, cafés, and hostels, Faros appeared far less prosperous than Platys Gialos, its inhabitants surviving on a much poorer class of tourism. He spoke to each of the residents in turn, but again, no one had seen the American.

Before returning to Platys Gialos, he called the Coast Guard and told them they needed to start searching the boats—public or private, it didn't matter. Svenson had vanished and they had to find him.

Patronas went back to Flora's in Platys Gialos after leaving Faros, thinking Svenson might have turned up there for dinner. The taverna was crowded, its tables full. The waiter he spoke to—the dark-haired son of the owner—told him Svenson and his students usually came in around eight o'clock, but he hadn't seen them tonight.

Patronas and his men ate a quick meal, the inevitable *tyropitas* and a platter of *soutzoukakia,* meatballs flavored with cumin, before continuing the search. Patronas was desperate now. It was getting late. Soon they'd have to call off the manhunt—no one to talk to, everyone in bed.

The kids had returned from the summer study and they aided in the search, as did Lydia Pappas after Patronas called her to say Svenson was missing.

Charlie Bowdoin was distraught. "Jesus, where did he go? What could have happened to him?"

"I don't know," Patronas said grimly.

Gilbert and Nielsen were equally glum. Silently following Patronas' instructions, they combed the grounds of Leandros and the uninhabited area between the beach and the migrant camp, shining their flashlights into the dry riverbed. Lydia Pappas had taken it upon herself to tackle the Greeks in the neighborhood, going from house to house, seeking some clue as to the professor's whereabouts.

Close to midnight, Patronas returned to Leandros and ordered the owner to let him into the professor's apartment. Unsure of what he'd find, whether it was a crime scene or not, he donned his protective gear beforehand. Inside, he found the rooms to be in good order. Svenson's clothes were all put away—either hanging in the bedroom closet or folded neatly in the drawers of the dresser. The dishes had all been washed and were stacked up in the drainer, a clean dishtowel laid over them. There were no toiletries in evidence in the bathroom; they'd all been stowed away in a small leather case.

Opening the door to the balcony, Patronas stepped outside and lit a cigarette. The moon was high overhead and it was a beautiful evening, a thin line of clouds along the horizon catching the light. It felt strange to be here, looking down on Lydia Pappas' terrace. He wondered if Svenson had seen them together, been aware of their deepening relationship.

The apartment itself was a mirror image of hers. It appeared the professor had been working at the table in the kitchen. As the owner had told Patronas earlier, the American's computer was still on and a cup of coffee, now filmy and cold, sat on a coaster next to it.

Pulling up a chair, Patronas quickly scrolled down the computer screen, seeking information as to what Svenson had been working on, what might have led him to contact him. Although it was hard to type with gloves on, from what he could tell, the American had been writing a paper on the shrine in Cappadocia, probably in preparation for his upcoming visit there.

Patronas' men had followed him into the apartment, and he ordered them to turn the place inside out. "Suit up and go through everything. Take it room by room."

Dressed in a hazmat suit, Evangelos Demos dutifully began opening and closing drawers. "I don't understand it," he told Patronas. "A place the size of Sifnos …. Surely someone must have seen him."

"Apparently not," Patronas said impatiently.

Patronas was still working on the computer when Tembelos appeared at the door to the kitchen. "Coast Guard's here," he said. "They found him."

CHAPTER TWENTY-THREE

———— ✦ ————

He who becomes a sheep is eaten by wolves.
—Greek Proverb

Leaving Svenson's apartment, Patronas walked to the marina in Platys Gialos with Tembelos and the Coast Guard officer who'd reported the find. The wind had picked up, and it tore at their clothes as they made their way out onto the quay, waves slamming into the distant sea wall. Disturbed by their presence, a gull left its perch on the mast of a sailboat and took flight, wheeling high overhead, cawing raucously.

Another Coast Guard officer was waiting for them, standing on a small floating dock that ran perpendicular to the quay. Seeing Patronas, he pointed to a black Zodiac.

The yellow light of the mercury lamps was garish against the darkness, and it heightened the eerie, science fiction atmosphere of the scene. Svenson's Zodiac was anchored about midway down, located between a small wooden fishing boat and a midsized yacht flying a German flag. Again, Patronas thought of parallel universes.

And now a third universe had been added to the mix, that of the migrants.

The wind was brisk and the Zodiac was bobbing up and down, a length of rope hanging off the port side. Something about the rope didn't look right to Patronas. It appeared too taut, like a fishing line that had gotten snagged. Far beneath it he caught a glimpse of a white shape.

Pulling on his protective gear, Patronas jumped down into the boat and began tugging on the rope, trying to pull it up. Something was holding it back and he searched the dark water again for the source. About two meters down, he spotted Svenson's body. Arms outstretched, the American was caught in the rope.

* * *

"An accident?" Tembelos asked.

With the help of the two Coast Guard men, he and Patronas were in the process of laying Svenson's body out on the quay. Borne by the waves, the Zodiac kept shifting, drifting farther and farther away, only to return again when the wind changed direction. It was proving to be an arduous task.

After Patronas had called, the dispatcher at the Coast Guard station had checked the registration of Svenson's boat, found out where he'd anchored it, and dispatched the two men there. It had been a sensible move, saved them countless hours.

The men had inspected the Zodiac and seen the same white shape in the water Patronas had. Not wanting to disturb it, they left it in place, pending his arrival. They would take Svenson's remains to Athens on the cruiser after Patronas finished processing the scene. All four were wearing protective gear—probably an unnecessary precaution, given how long Svenson had been in the water—but Patronas had insisted on it anyway.

Garbed in his hazmat suit, Tembelos was a strange vision in the night, his voice deeply muffled by a mask. "What's the term?" he asked Patronas, "death by misadventure?"

"Not a chance," Patronas said. "Svenson was murdered. Same killer, different means."

Undoing the front of his suit, Tembelos reached into the pocket of his shirt with a gloved hand and pulled out an envelope. "I found this in his apartment. There were several of them. I bagged the rest, but I wanted you to see it."

A woven red anklet, it was nearly identical to the one found on Sami Alnasseri.

Behind his goggles, Patronas sensed his friend was watching him.

"This mean Svenson did it?" Tembelos asked.

"I don't know, Giorgos. I just don't know."

"It would fit. Someone, maybe a migrant, knew he was responsible, that he'd murdered the kid, and took care of it. Revenge is big in that part of that world."

It was nearly two a.m. when the doctor at the clinic arrived to sign off on Svenson's death. Patronas had summoned him to the marina, telling him to get there as fast as he could, that there had been another death.

The doctor knelt down next to Svenson. "Looks like he drowned," he said after a long moment.

"Are you sure?" Patronas asked. "Check him carefully."

Pulling on gloves, the doctor methodically inspected Svenson's body, starting at the top of his skull and working his way down. "It looks like he has a contusion on his head, but there's no telling where it came from. It might well have come from hitting the dock when he fell overboard." He offered this in a hopeful voice.

"So … not necessarily murder?"

"This is beyond my level of expertise," the doctor responded. "You need a coroner to look at him."

Together, Patronas and Tembelos raised Svenson up and placed him in a black body bag.

Before zipping the bag closed, Patronas took a final look at the American's lifeless form. Svenson was dressed in shorts and a t-shirt from a Grateful Dead concert, a skull split by a bolt of lightning. *Ironic*, Patronas thought grimly, *given the way the American died.*

Svenson's clothes were soaking wet and clinging to him, a tendril of seaweed caught in his hair. Patronas ran his gloved hands over Svenson's head, seeking to establish the size and shape of the contusion the doctor had mentioned. And then, with a heavy heart, he closed the bag.

"I'll fill out the paperwork and get him ready to go to Athens," Patronas told Tembelos. "After that, let's call it a night. We can start again in the morning."

He was convinced the American had been knocked out, trussed up in the rope, and thrown into the water to drown. No one frequented this place. There would have been no witnesses. As with Thanatos, whoever had done this had chosen his killing ground well.

Lydia Pappas was waiting for Patronas when he got back to the apartment, sitting outside on the terrace in a cotton nightgown. The spotlights around Leandros had been turned off, and the candle in the lantern on the table flickered unsteadily. On the second floor, all was quiet.

So tired he could barely think, Patronas wondered how much to tell her. "Svenson's dead," he said, fumbling for the words. "Judging by his appearance, he fell off the boat and drowned. It probably happened not long after he called me, at least fifteen hours ago. He didn't say anything to you, did he? Why he wanted to speak to me?"

Lydia Pappas shook her head. "I didn't see him today."

She got up and began walking back and forth. "I can't believe it. Richard was always so careful on that boat. The way he wound the ropes …. He wouldn't quit until he got it exactly right, one concentric circle after another. The kids and I used to tease him about it. I can't believe he drowned … not someone like him. It's impossible." Her voice rose. "First the Syrian boy and now Richard. Who's next? Me?"

"Hush, Lydia," Patronas said. "I won't let anything happen to you." Taking a deep breath, he said it again in a louder voice. "I love you."

It seemed wrong to be telling her this tonight, but Patronas wanted to get it said, to have her hear it from him. The stabbing had scared him. Who knew what lay ahead? Whether or not he'd get a second chance.

"Oh, Yiannis, what's going to happen?"

A simple answer seemed beyond him. Age, fatigue? Patronas wasn't sure. "I don't know," he said

"You'll catch him. I know you will." Lydia Pappas sounded like she was trying to convince herself. "You're like Diogenes with his lantern, searching the world for an honest man." She smiled then. "Only it's not honesty you're seeking. It's the reverse."

A poor joke, but Patronas laughed anyway. "That's me as a cop. What about me as a man?"

"I love you, Yiannis. Surely, you know that. You're the only man in my entire life who has valued me the way I want to be valued, who recognizes my true worth."

They spent the night lying next to each other on the bed, their fingers touching. Framed by the window, the moon illuminated a square patch on the floor. Although faint, the light made Patronas uneasy. He felt exposed, the dark corners of the room full of some unseen threat.

Lydia Pappas eventually slept, but he lay awake until morning. Something kept bothering him, something he should have done, but hadn't.

THE NEXT DAY was even worse. The coroner in Athens—a dour man everyone joked was as lifeless as the corpses he worked on, called Patronas and reported that the DNA on the knife from Thanatos did not match that of either Achilles or Costas Kourelas, nor was there any trace evidence suggesting the two had been anywhere near the vicinity when the boy was killed.

"They've done jail time and seem pretty familiar with police procedure," Patronas said. "Is it possible they wiped everything down?"

"Highly unlikely. There was a lot of territory to cover—the pole and chain, the platform, not to mention all that paraphernalia scattered around. It would have been virtually impossible to clean it all. Neither man is the killer you seek, Yiannis. It's as simple as that."

"And the fragments of glass from the fire?"

"Ditto," the coroner said. "There was nothing on the glass that would have linked them to the bombing."

So Achilles Kourelas had suffered in vain.

Patronas felt like vomiting. "Did you tell Stathis what you found?"

"What I *didn't* find," the coroner said, as ever, quick to correct him. "No. I decided to let you do the honors. I don't envy you, telling him that your people made a mistake and shot an innocent man." The coroner gave a dry laugh. "Your boss is not known for his compassion." Still chuckling, he went on, "One thing of note: those bones you sent me were indeed very old—at least two thousand years or more. I've taken the liberty of sending them on to the archeological department at the University of Athens. Let's see what they come up with. However, they have no relevance to the child's death. Also, the lock that held the chain …. I looked it up, and it, too, is ancient, dates from the time of the Dorian invasion, roughly 1100 B.C. According to the sites I checked on the Internet, similar locks are still in use in Karpathos today. But I don't believe yours came from there. No, given the pitting and erosion of the metal, I'd say it's at least three thousand years old."

"Where would a person find a lock like that?"

"Most probably in a museum. Or perhaps a private collection. Such artifacts are exceedingly rare. Oh, by the way, your drowning victim arrived here in the lab at dawn this morning and is prepped and ready to go. He's at the top of my to-do list."

Patronas winced at the man's choice of words. The coroner always appalled him, his cavalier attitude as he spoke about the most repellant aspects of his job, the cheerful way he went about his work, whistling as he removed someone's heart and tossed it on the scale. On occasion, he'd even given the dead nicknames, usually after the shadow puppets much beloved by children in Greece: 'Karagiozis,' if the corpse in the mortuary had a big nose, 'Kollitiri,' if it were of diminutive stature, and 'Veligekas,' if it resembled a Turk.

Distraught already, Patronas didn't want to get into the specifics of what the coroner planned to do to Svenson, the sawing open of the American's head and the cutting of the y-shaped incision, the stitching back together afterwards, usually with black thread so thick it resembled twine.

"As we'd anticipated," the coroner went on, "the child died of catastrophic blood loss. It was over in a matter of seconds. As soon as the killer nicked the boy's jugular, he was gone. The results of the toxicology screens should be available later this week. I wish I could get it to you sooner, but unfortunately, such tests simply cannot be hurried. Once I have them in hand, I should be able to tell you if the boy was drugged beforehand. Let's hope and pray that he was."

Patronas and his men were sitting in a vast room in back of the municipality building, dealing with the fallout from the American's death. Needing more space, they'd moved out of the murder room and taken up residence here. Judging by the layout—the cafeteria-like counter and groupings of tables and chairs—it had once served as the hotel dining room.

They had been on the phone all morning, alerting the American Embassy as well as his employers in Greece and the United States to Svenson's death. Patronas had personally given the professor's family the news, a long, involved process as Svenson had an ex-wife, three children in various parts of the world, and last, a live-in girlfriend in Boston—Brazilian, from the sound of her. He'd also contacted the dead man's colleagues at the university, his department head, and the dean. It had been a lengthy ordeal, a series of heart-wrenching calls, the people he spoke to shrieking and crying when he told them what had happened. One man hadn't bothered to hang up, just put the phone down and disappeared. Given that it was an overseas call and it took over an hour to get the situation rectified, this caused Patronas a great deal of distress. "Anybody there?" he kept shouting. "Please, please, hang up the phone!"

As these conversations had to be conducted entirely in English, he had consulted the Divry's Greek-English dictionary beforehand and written out phonetically what he wanted each of his men to say, coaching them on the proper way to pronounce 'condolences' and 'sympathy.'

Evangelos Demos, as to be expected, couldn't get his mouth around the words and ended up saying, 'Sorry, sorry, Svenson dead,' which didn't ingratiate him or the Greek police department with the Americans.

The officials at the summer study wanted to know where they could locate a grief counselor to console Svenson's students, saying it would be a great loss for them; the professor had been well-liked. Patronas had done his best, but psychiatrists who dealt with post-traumatic stress were few and far between in Greece, so no luck. Not knowing what else to do, he'd sent Papa Michalis to minister to them.

Papa Michalis called in later to report that Svenson had been one of the most popular faculty members, and by and large, his students were inconsolable. "It's hard. I don't know what to tell them."

"You hear anything suspicious? Any clue as to who might have done it?"

"No, nothing. Mostly, they just cry."

So far, Patronas had been able to keep the news of the murder away from the press, but given Svenson's reputation and foreign nationality, it was only a matter of time before reporters got wind of it. He could just see the headline: 'A Serial Murderer on Sifnos.' It would destroy the island.

He couldn't stop thinking about Achilles Kourelas, shot in that ill-conceived bust, one he himself was responsible for. If what the coroner said was true, Kourelas was innocent of all wrongdoing. So what if he'd been a thug and assaulted him? He shouldn't have been injured the way he had—shot like a rabid dog in front of his father.

Deeply depressed, Patronas again recalled Napoleon. Not the Napoleon who'd returned in defeat from Russia, but the one on Elba.

Thinking he might as well get it over with, Patronas took a deep breath and called Stathis. "Sir, we might have a problem."

CHAPTER TWENTY-FOUR

—— ◆ ——

Also the dragon, earth-borne in craftiness,
is coming behind thee.
—The Delphic Oracle

"WHAT DO YOU really know about Lydia Pappas?" Tembelos asked Patronas. And I don't mean in the biblical sense, which you no doubt are eager to share. I'm talking about her character. Could she possibly be involved in this?"

"In Svenson's murder?"

Tembelos nodded. "Stranger things have happened. Look at that Michael Douglas movie, the one with Sharon Stone. He was a cop investigating a murder and fell in love with the chief suspect, a woman who got her kicks from sticking ice picks in people."

"Lydia Pappas is innocent. I'd stake my life on it."

His friend snorted. "Let's hope you don't have to."

They were eating lunch in a taverna in Apollonia. The first call from a reporter had come in before they left to eat, and within minutes, it had been followed by a deluge—phones throughout the municipality building ringing off the hook. Patronas had left Evangelos Demos behind to deal with them, thinking that it took his associate so long to gather his thoughts, let alone articulate them, the reporters would eventually hang up in frustration.

"What thoughts?" Tembelos said cheerfully when Patronas told him this.

Tembelos continued to joke around, trying to cheer him up, but Patronas held up a hand, signaling him to stop.

"I can't get the image of Achilles Kourelas out of my mind," he said, "the way he clawed the earth with his fingers and lay there, bleeding. I knew we had no proof, but I proceeded anyway. It's on me this time, Giorgos. That shooting is on me."

Affected by the coroner's report, they were both drinking ouzo, throwing it down, shot after shot. Getting drunk wouldn't help matters, but at this point, Patronas didn't care.

"He'll be all right," Tembelos said. "As my mother used to say, 'The bad dog dies hard.' And Kourelas is a very bad dog."

"Still ...."

Fronting the street, the view from their table didn't amount to much, but the *bifteki* they'd ordered had proven surprisingly tasty, flavored delicately with mint and nicely charred. Hungry as he was, Patronas could barely swallow and he pushed his plate away.

A group of women were inspecting a rack of clothing on display across the street, and he watched them for a moment, trying to guess their nationality. A fanciful establishment, the store featured shorts made of peek-a-boo lace and hats with huge, floppy brims, as well as other items that gave tourists a bad name. *English or German, had to be.*

"So back to Lydia Pappas ..." Tembelos started to say.

"I told you, she's innocent."

"Yiannis, we're running out of suspects."

"For God's sake, Giorgos. First of all, she's a small woman and as such, lacks the physical strength, the musculature needed to hoist a ten-year-old boy over her shoulder and carry him up to Thanatos, let alone string him up and hang him over the pit. The murder of Svenson would have been even more difficult. Neither crime was easy to execute. It would have taken someone with," his voice trailed off, "*panagia mou.*"

Tembelos stopped chewing. "What?"

"Did we fingerprint those kids or swab them for DNA?"

"Nope. I'm pretty sure we only did Svenson that day."

They sat for a moment in silence, looking at each other.

"Shit," Tembelos said. "It was them, wasn't it?"

Patronas nodded. It had been in front of him the whole time. He just hadn't seen it.

The means, the opportunity .... All he needed now was the motive.

WHEN PATRONAS RETURNED to the municipality building, he found an isolated spot and called Charlie Bowdoin on his cell phone. What he was planning was highly unorthodox and bordered on entrapment. He didn't want to be overheard.

"Hey, Charlie," he said, working to keep his voice level. "It's Chief Officer Patronas. I know you must have heard the news about Professor Svenson by now, and I just wanted to tell you how very sorry I am. It must have been a terrible shock, and I was wondering how you're doing."

In a hollow voice, Bowdoin said he was all right. Then he asked for specifics as to how Richard Svenson had died.

"We believe it was an accident," Patronas said, "that he somehow got tangled up the ropes, tripped and fell overboard."

"Awful," Bowdoin whispered. "I can't believe it. To die like that ... Professor Svenson. You didn't know him. He loved the sea."

He and the other two boys had just returned from class. They'd been reassigned to another adviser, he told Patronas, and planned to finish out the term. "We figured we got this far, we might as well complete the course. It won't be the same, though, without him."

Patronas took a deep breath. "You three were a great help to us during the search and I wanted to thank you."

To show his gratitude, he offered to take them out to dinner that night, and Bowdoin readily assented. They arranged to meet at Flora's at eight thirty; then Patronas hung up the phone.

Sitting back in his chair, he closed his eyes. *"Epityhia!"* Success!.

The three students were already sitting at the table when Patronas arrived. Clearly arguing about something, they'd stopped when they saw him. They had all dressed with care and were far more subdued than he'd ever seen them, their hair slicked down and wet from recent showers. They stood up to greet him, Bowdoin insisting he take the chair at the head of the table.

They spoke respectively about Richard Svenson, reminiscing about their time together in a mournful way.

"A tragic loss," Patronas said.

Gilbert nodded. "I told him I wanted to learn how to dive and he taught me. I never would have learned if it hadn't been for him."

"You could feel his passion when he was teaching," Bowdoin said. "He really wanted you to learn. He was a man obsessed."

It went on like this for some time, a kind of impromptu memorial service.

Eventually Patronas asked them what they wanted to eat and they ordered. Between mouthfuls, the three continued to extol the virtues of Richard Svenson and express their sorrow over his death.

They're good, Patronas concluded as he listened. *If I didn't know better, I would have thought they cared.*

"What was he doing on the boat, anyway?" Bowdoin gave Patronas a searching glance.

"I don't know," Patronas said. "Something drew him there, but we'll probably never know what it was. As far as we're concerned, it was a tragic accident."

"Are you going to check his cellphone records?" Nielsen asked.

"We don't have that capability," Patronas said, "nor do we have the manpower. Government can barely pay our salaries."

He was watching Nielsen carefully and thought he saw something. It wasn't much—nothing he could take to Stathis or a jury. Only a release of tension in the boy's shoulders, a subtle exhalation as if he had been holding his breath. Also, the other two seemed to visibly relax.

Patronas studied them for a few more minutes. The why, the reason they'd killed Sami Alnasseri, continued to elude him, but the rest he was pretty sure he'd figured out. Svenson must have gotten there before him and that was why they'd killed him.

They spent quite some time together, and by the end, the boys were completely at ease, teasing each other and joking around.

It turned out Bowdoin had started out his life in Texas and still subscribed to that state's cultural values. "As soon as I finish college, I'm moving back there. Get a ranch on the plains and raise some cattle."

"You have a cowboy hat?" Patronas asked with a smile.

"Yup. And a gun." He mimed firing off a revolver with his hand.

The other two exchanged glances. "Charlie just talks big," Gilbert said. "He's actually pretty harmless."

"How about you?" Patronas turned to Nielsen. "Do you have a gun?"

"No. Guns are Charlie's thing, not mine."

Patronas was trying to determine the identity of the ringleader, the so-called criminal mastermind, but as with the motive for the crime, he couldn't quite get there. One minute, it appeared to be Bowdoin who was in charge, the next it shifted to Gilbert or Nielsen. It was almost as if they were running a relay and passing the baton.

According to case studies Patronas had read, often a psychopath will partner with a weaker person. A symbiotic relationship, each would then feed off the other, challenging their co-conspirator to commit ever more heinous crimes, to escalate to a higher level of violence, the relationship reinforcing the darkest aspects of both personalities. It had happened in Columbine, Colorado, and elsewhere, and Patronas found himself wondering if the same pattern was in play here.

If it was, the dominant personality was definitely Charlie Bowdoin. But he didn't present as a psychopath, nor did Benjamin Gilbert, which left only Michael Nielsen. Patronas tried to remember the physique of the person who'd thrown the firebomb, the man he and Tembelos had chased across the fields that night. Whoever he was, he'd been fast—that much was certain—and Nielsen, if he remembered correctly, was a runner. Another piece of the puzzle slipped into place.

At one point, Patronas flicked his fingers through Nielsen's hair, saying he'd seen a mosquito and wanted to kill it. Pretending it was an accident, he yanked out two or three strands, saying they'd caught on his ring, after which he carefully folded them up in a napkin, taking care not to touch them more than necessary. The chain of evidence wasn't as pristine as he would have liked, but he didn't know what else to do. He was after Nielsen's DNA, but he didn't want to tip his hand, to put the students on notice. He used a similar trick later during dinner, asking the waitress to bring everybody a beer.

"Never mind bringing glasses. We'll drink it out of the bottle."

Unsophisticated, the boys had initially wanted to order the Greek equivalent of steak, but Patronas demurred, saying they had to try *paidakia,* lamb chops—they were far better. He also requested a *xoriatiki* salad with extra olives.

When the meat came, he demonstrated how to eat the chops, picking them up with his fingers and gnawing on the bones. As intended, the Americans followed suit, gobbling them down and leaving behind a pile of bones. They also ate the olives in the salad and spat out the pits. Patronas looked over their leavings, praying the coroner would have enough.

"When are you leaving Greece?" he asked.

"In ten days," Bowdoin said. "We're going to Turkey after we leave Sifnos. Professor Svenson arranged everything and we thought it was the least we could do, to honor his wishes. You know, see the things he was so excited about." He shrugged. "Kind of a tribute to him."

"And after that you'll go home?"

Bowdoin nodded. "That's the plan."

After he paid the bill, Patronas sent them on their way. "It's late and you've got class tomorrow. Why don't you head back to Leandros and get some rest?"

They thanked him politely and departed, walking along the beach toward Leandros, wading in and out of the water. They weren't talking as they splashed along the shore, each keeping his distance from the other two, isolated and alone.

Patronas watched them go; then, pulling on a pair of latex gloves, he collected the bones from each of their plates, dropped them in separate bags and labeled them with the appropriate name. He did the same with the olive pits and the beer bottles, the napkins and forks—all of it. Repelled, the customers at the other tables watched him with disgust.

"For my dog," he said.

When he got back to the municipality building, he called the coroner and left a message, saying he was shipping some key evidence to him early the next morning that he needed processed as fast as humanly possible. "Fingerprints, saliva, anything you can match up. The suspects are leaving the country soon. We have to hurry. We're running out of time."

CHAPTER TWENTY-FIVE

———◆———

The tailor is at fault and they beat the cook.
—Greek Proverb

Aт BREAKFAST THE next day, Patronas ordered his men to monitor the kids throughout the day, dispatching Evangelos Demos to the summer study to work as a janitor, Tembelos to do the same later at Leandros. Equipment in hand, they were to go from room to room and pretend to clean. Petros Nikolaidis would drive to Kamares and arrange with the harbor patrol to keep watch on the ferries in case the suspects tried to board one and flee.

"A bucket and a mop?" Tembelos said. "Really, Yiannis. After all these years, this is what you and I have come to?"

"Only you. As of this morning, I'm still a cop."

Patronas still had a job as far as he knew, although Stathis had been noncommittal on the phone after Patronas had disclosed the coroner's findings.

"A mistake, huh?"

There'd been a long silence as Stathis digested this fact, after which he stated that as of this moment Evangelos was on administrative leave, pending a formal investigation, and could no longer serve as a policeman in any capacity. Hence, his assignment as a janitor. The fate of Patronas, on the other hand, was anybody's guess.

"You were the officer-in-charge," Stathis said. "That makes you responsible for the shooting of Achilles Kourelas."

"You had a hand in this, sir. You ordered me to question him."

"I did *not* tell you to let Evangelos Demos keep his gun after that debacle on Chios. Just the opposite. 'Remove that man's weapon,' I told you at the time. 'He's an imbecile. He cannot be trusted.' But did you? No, you *forgot*. Nor did I tell you to try and put Achilles Kourelas into the backseat of a car without searching him for weapons, a flagrant violation of procedure. And I most certainly did not tell you to have one of your subordinates shoot him."

"It was an accident. Achilles stabbed me and everything went to hell."

"Patronas, I talked to his doctor. Achilles Kourelas was shot less than five centimeters from his *heart*."

Patronas continued to argue, claiming Evangelos Demos lacked the necessary skill to shoot anyone, *anywhere* on purpose. "It was a lucky shot. He's no sharpshooter."

"*Lucky*? Do you even realize the pile of shit you've landed me in? *Chrisi Avgi* is clamoring for my head, thanks to you. They're claiming we shot Kourelas on purpose, to terrify their membership and shut down the party."

"You know that's not true."

"All I know is you're in trouble, Patronas. If you were here, I'd fucking skin you alive." And with that, Stathis slammed down the receiver.

But he hadn't fired him. At least not yet.

Waiting to hear back from the coroner, Patronas took the Rav and drove to Kamares to meet Petros Nikolaidis. It was a bright, sunlit morning and he was struck anew by the island's beauty—the villages scattered along the brows of the hills and thickets of olive trees, their leaves like flecks of silver in the early morning light, and beyond it all, the dark blue waters of the Aegean. He could see the island of Antiparos rising in the distance like a sea serpent, its bulk dusky against the sky, Paros and Serifos and countless others. The sea was threaded with whitecaps, a lone sailboat off the coast nearly horizontal in the wind.

He fooled around with the radio, seeking old-style Greek music, cantatas maybe, or ballads from the war. All he could find was modern stuff that sounded like a mix of static and thunder. That morning, he and Lydia Pappas had talked about taking a vacation together after the case was over, swimming in secluded coves, eating *gavros*—fish the size of french fries—and sleeping out under the stars.

Like Orpheus, the god of music she'd spoken of, he'd wake her at dawn with a song. Propose marriage when the time was right.

He'd found her presence a great comfort after the case unraveled. Today might be shit, but if he was lucky, the two of them might have tomorrow.

The ringing of his cellphone jarred him out of his reverie, and he pulled over to the side of the road to answer it.

It was Stathis, calling back. "I forgot to ask you the status of the case. Have you solved it yet? Do you have a viable suspect or was Achilles Kourelas your only lead?"

"I solved it, sir. I'm sure of it."

"You're sure of it?" Stathis' laugh was ugly. "A little late for that, isn't it, Patronas? Won't do Achilles Kourelas, our shooting victim, much good now, will it? Won't keep the press off our backs." His boss went on for some time, raking him over the coals. "One of your suspects is dead, the other's in the hospital, so by process of elimination, who does that leave us with?"

"Three of Svenson's students: Michael Nielsen, Benjamin Gilbert, and Charlie Bowdoin. Americans college kids, they're enrolled in a summer study here. I have reason to believe they killed Sami Alnasseri and Richard Svenson. They might even have firebombed the camp."

"You better watch your step. You can't afford to mess up if Americans are involved. *Tha se stavrosoun.*" They'll crucify you.

"I sent samples of the kids' DNA to the lab and I won't make a move until I have the results in hand. I don't want to be accused of framing them and have everything blow up in my face."

"No, no, we don't want an incident like that one in Italy where the police arrested an American girl and charged her with murder, only to have the judge throw the case out after she'd spent four years in jail."

"Amanda Knox."

"That's the one. Everybody involved in that case ended up looking like jerks. We don't want that, do we, Patronas?"

"No, sir."

Noting the 'we,' Patronas relaxed. Stathis was back onboard. His job was safe.

Stathis said he would speak with the coroner, see if he could speed things up. "Let me see what I can do. Keep me informed."

After hanging up, Patronas mentally reviewed the case for the hundredth time, seeking to determine which of the three students had been the instigator. But no matter how many times he went over it in his head, he couldn't come up with a definitive answer. All of them seemed to be what they claimed—college students on a lark in Greece. Foolish, yes, but hardly lethal.

If he only knew which one was the leader, he might be able break the other two. Turn Papa Michalis loose on them and garner a confession.

He considered contacting the administrators at their universities—Hobart College in the case of Charlie Bowdoin, the University of Virginia in the case of Benjamin Gilbert and Michael Nielsen—to see if any of the students had been in trouble, suspended for assault, for example, but decided against it. College administrators might be required to notify a student's parents if there was an inquiry from the police, in which case, the kids would undoubtedly learn of it and he'd lose whatever advantage he had.

Patronas sat there for a moment, going over his options. Maybe he should call the police in their hometowns. Colleagues, they might be more likely to help. These kids weren't minors. If they had criminal records, perhaps they could be shared. If there was indeed a psychopath among them, it was unlikely the murder of Sami Alnasseri was his first foray into violence. Whoever it was had probably been at it since childhood.

He did a quick calculation. Seven hours' time difference—six in the morning, American time. He'd have to wait. No good would come of calling a police station at the start of the workday.

Petros Nikolaidis was waiting for him in Kamares, standing in front of the headquarters of the harbor patrol. Together, they went inside and briefed the officer in charge, a handsome young man with a Cretan accent. Patronas had made copies of the students' passports, and he handed the man the photos.

"This is what the suspects look like. Under no circumstances can they be allowed to board a boat and leave Sifnos. We must do everything in our power to keep them here."

"We'll do our best," the officer said, "but there must be at least a hundred people leaving Sifnos on any given boat. It's a mob scene when one of those ferries departs."

PATRONAS ATE A hasty lunch in Kamares, a tired gyro wrapped in pita bread. After he finished, he drove back to the municipality building and set about calling America. He had his Divry's open to the word 'arrest' on the table and the language application up and ready on his phone.

The first police officer he spoke to—a stiff, by-the-book sergeant named Wilson in McLean, Virginia—made it clear from the beginning he wasn't going to help. "You have to go through the proper channels," he told Patronas, "fill out the requisite paperwork. I cannot release potentially damaging information over the phone."

"Are you saying there is damaging material on Benjamin Gilbert?"

"No, I'm saying that you have to go through channels. But I can tell you right now juvenile records are sealed here. They're sacrosanct and nobody can touch them."

"Sacrosanct, what is this … 'sacrosanct'?" Feverishly thumbing through his dictionary, Patronas continued to plead with him, "Was Gilbert ever arrested?"

They went back and forth for a few more minutes, Wilson growing more and more impatient with Patronas' halting English.

"I repeat: juvenile records are sealed," the American said. And with that, he hung up.

The officer in San Diego was equally unhelpful, echoing the sentiments of his colleague in Virginia. "What you're asking is impossible. The file of a juvenile? You'd need a court order to open it. "

"We believe he murdered a ten-year-old boy."

"I'm sorry, Mr. Patronas, but we are responsible for the well-being and safety of more than a million people here and we have their hands full. We don't have time to do your job for you."

Patronas could hear phones ringing and people yelling in the background. There was truth in what the American said.

The last person Patronas spoke to, a police officer in Wellesley Hills, Massachusetts, was even more short with him. "Can't do it," he told Patronas. "How do I know you are who you say you are? That you're not someone wanting to blackmail that boy's family?"

An odd response, Patronas thought. One that indicated the man was familiar with Bowdoin.

But no matter how hard Patronas pushed, the policeman refused to clarify his statement.

After he hung up, Patronas sat there, wondering what he should do. Maybe Stathis could get something out of the Americans. Contact the attorney general or the FBI. He didn't know how it worked. But reaching out to them from here was hopeless.

Chapter Twenty-Six

A cassock does not make someone a priest.
—Greek Proverb

Patronas met with his men that evening in Kamares. A harbor patrolman named Stelios Mavros had volunteered to take over the stakeout at Leandros so that they could go to dinner. After they finished eating, Patronas planned to send them on their way—Nikolaidis to his home on Sifnos and Evangelos Demos, Giorgos Tembelos, and the priest back to the Morpheus Hotel to get some sleep. He himself would relieve the harbor patrolman at the apartment building and work surveillance there throughout the night.

He spoke to Lydia Pappas before he left for Kamares—a hurried, whispered conversation in the bedroom after she returned from work. He outlined his theory about the murder and warned her to be on guard. "No telling what those three are capable of. Lock your door and keep it locked."

Shocked, she dropped down on the bed. "I can't believe they did it."

"All evidence points in that direction."

"I know a child psychiatrist in Boston who has violent kids in her practice. 'They're pretty scary,' she told me. 'There's something dead in their eyes and they give off a kind of chill.'"

"Is she afraid of them?"

"Not for herself, she said. For the other people in their lives."

She looked over at him. "I never felt that way about them, not once the whole summer. They were obnoxious, sure, but that was it."

They talked for a few more minutes. "Did you ever see the Syrian child around here?" Patronas asked. "The boy must have crossed paths with them at some point before they killed him."

"No, never." She hesitated for a moment. "There are migrant children out in the street here sometimes, running around. They get in the way of the cars and people yell at them. I'm not sure, but he might have been one of them."

"Did Bowdoin and the others yell at them?"

"No, but Richard Svenson did. He had a pretty short fuse and he didn't like it when they got in the way."

"Did he ever threaten them?"

"Not that I remember. I think for the most part they were invisible to him. Greece wasn't his country and he knew he'd be leaving soon. The migrants weren't his problem."

Pushing her hair back from her face, she sat for a few minutes, lost in thought. "I just can't believe what you told me—that those three boys are murderers. I assumed they were just spoiled brats. Immature, maybe, but certainly not dangerous."

"You said they spied on you."

She laughed. "I'm a middle-aged woman. In a way, their attention was a compliment."

They continued to argue about the character of the students. Lydia Pappas defended them, claiming Patronas was wrong, and the three were innocent. As a cop, he only saw the worst in people. "Kids make mistakes. That's all that spying thing was. Youthful high jinks. They would never hurt anybody."

Patronas finally stood up to go. "Be careful," he said. "You might not believe it, but those boys are dangerous. They have already killed two people."

He'd been expecting her to kiss him goodbye, but she stayed where she was. "It must be a heavy burden," she said coolly. "All that cynicism. It must be a very heavy burden."

PATRONAS FOUND HIS men waiting for him outside Stella's Taverna. They were all starving and ended up ordering half the things on the menu. To start with, *papoutsakia*, little shoes, an eggplant and meat dish crowned with béchamel; *domates gemistes*, tomatoes stuffed with rice, onions, and currants; *keftedakia*, meatballs, and for the grand finale, *stavlisia*, immense porterhouse steaks weighing in at close to a kilo each, one per person. This was in addition to fried potatoes, three different kinds of pitas, and various other tidbits.

Although the food was delicious, the meal got off to a rocky start. Papa Michalis was morose, full of tales about the woeful afternoon he'd spent with Svenson's students, who had cried all over him, and Tembelos was surly, still angry about the housekeeping assignment.

But it was Evangelos who was the biggest problem. Having just learned from Stathis he'd been suspended, he'd set about consoling himself with food, emptying entire platters onto his plate. After he consumed three quarters of the potatoes, the others revolted; there'd been a lot of angry back and forth about portion control and Evangelos' walrus-like size. Eating no more than one's share and the like, lessons the others said he should have learned as a child.

Feeling like a grade school teacher, Patronas intervened. "Look, it's been a bad couple of days. Go easy on each other, okay?"

"Okay?" Tembelos raised his eyebrows. "What's that you speak? Could it be the dreaded English?"

"What can I say? I took your advice. I became bilingual."

"It wasn't me," Tembelos said, his mood brightening. "It was that redheaded vixen, the Greek-American woman. What's her name? Pappas. She's the one. She's the reason you abandoned your mother tongue."

"It's true," Patronas said. "Thanks to Lydia, my skills in many things are improving."

Tembelos smiled. "I'll just bet they are. You two going to continue to cohabitate?"

The priest raised his head. He'd been squirreling away food on his plate, fearing another onslaught by Evangelos, stockpiling what was left of the french fries. He was making little piles and appeared to be counting them.

"Cohabitate?" he asked with a frown. "What is this? I am unfamiliar with the term."

Patronas poured more wine into his glass. "It means I'm living in sin," he said.

Papa Michalis pondered this news for a few minutes, his expression thoughtful. "Marriage, of course, would be the answer to such a situation, this moral quandary you've gotten yourself into, although I'm not sure I would recommend it. I'd need to meet the lady first. All those years in America …. She's bound to be full of erroneous modern ideas."

Familiar with the priest's beliefs, Patronas laughed to himself. Papa Michalis' idea of erroneous modern ideas was giving women the vote. The old man despised Hillary Clinton, not because of her political beliefs, but because she wore pants.

"Why don't you come back with me tonight and meet her?" he told him. "Once we're done here, I'm going to ask her to marry me. You've known me a long time, Father, and I would like your blessing."

Tembelos interrupted. "So my cousin, Calliope, is out of the picture?"

"I'm afraid so, Giorgos. No hard feelings."

"Actually, I'm surprised the two of you lasted as long as you did. I was sure one date with her would do it. Way too close to your previous model—the fearsome and all-knowing Dimitra."

"Calliope did seem to have a lot of opinions."

Enjoying themselves, the group began to itemize the peculiar opinions of their womenfolk, their wives' ill-conceived ideas.

"Nothing tasty," Evangelos said. "No salt, not fat, no sugar. And no matter what she does to lentils, at the end of the day, they remain what God made them, lentils. I've never eaten mouse droppings, but I'm willing to wager they taste the same. As for zucchini, another favorite of hers, it's mostly water. Water and mouse droppings—that's what she feeds me."

"No casual look-see at female sunbathers at the beach," Tembelos said when his turn came. "No girly magazines, no nudity on television or in the movies."

"No extended visits from my mother," Nikolaidis said.

After two liters of *retsina*, a potent local wine, they were all very jolly.

"Here, here!" Tembelos tapped his glass with a spoon. "In conclusion, marriage is an evil most men welcome. Our ancestor, the ancient philosopher, Menander, got it right."

"*Sosta*," Nikolaidis said. You speak correctly. "When you get right down to it, women are a pain in the ass."

Scandalized, Papa Michalis spoke of the Holy Mother and the female saints of the church, women who were 'chaste and pure.' When Tembelos and the others ignored him, he began quoting St. Paul's Letter to the Corinthians, deepening his voice and doing his best to sound like God.

"'BRETHREN, love is patient and kind…. It is not arrogant or rude… irritable or resentful; it does not rejoice at wrong, but rejoices in the right. Love bears all things, hopes all things, endures all things.'"

Tembelos waved him off. "We're talking about marriage, Father, not love. One sets your heart racing while the other …" he made a hopeless gesture with his hands. "*Varka vouliagmeni*." It's a shipwreck.

Evangelos smiled for the first time that night. "Amen," he said and popped the last meatball into his mouth.

Patronas didn't join in. Unlike these poor idiots, he and Lydia Pappas would live happily ever after. He was sure of it. She was a good woman. Like a geisha, she would make his life a pleasure.

He was paying the bill when his cellphone rang. Pulling it out of his pocket, he looked down at the number on the screen. It was a 228 exchange, Sifnos.

"You'd better come," the harbor patrolman, Stelios Mavros, said. "The kids have disappeared. I can't find them anywhere."

THE DOOR TO the students' second-floor apartment was open, but it was obvious they had cleared out, packing in haste, if at all. Clothes were strewn across the floor and their razors and toothbrushes were still in the bathroom. Patronas picked up a tube lying next to the sink and read the label. Medicinal, it had been prescribed by a doctor to treat Michael Nielsen's acne.

Patronas and his men searched the apartment thoroughly, but found nothing to indicate where the students had gone. They had taken their laptops and phones with them, so there was no way to check the sites they'd visited on the Internet, the recent calls they'd made.

"Athens?" Patronas said out loud.

It was the logical choice. And from there, back to the United States. That's what he would have done in their place. Their parents would hire lawyers to defend them and fight their extradition to Greece. Chances are they would never spend a day in jail.

Remembering the Syrian boy, he slammed his fist down on a table.

"They had everything, those kids," he told Tembelos. "And Sami Alnasseri, what did he have? Nothing. Who spoke out for him when he was alive? Who sought to make his lot better? He was nothing in life and he'll be forgotten in death. Just a statistic, one more lost child from the Middle East."

"Ach, Yiannis, it's the way of the world."

"As long as I live, I will never understand it. Those three were blessed in every sense of the word, and yet they ended up without conscience or heart."

"I repeat. It's the way of the world. An easy life does not guarantee goodness."

Pawing through the fugitives' possessions, they noticed that despite the disorder, the kids had been careful—no scraps of paper in the wastebasket, no ticket stubs or scribbled notes. Aside from the acne prescription in the bathroom, there was no trace of their respective identities in the room. Whether from watching crime shows on television or thanks to their own innate intelligence, their leave-taking had been sophisticated. It was a wonder they hadn't snipped the labels out of their clothes.

"What tipped them off?" Patronas asked Tembelos.

"Young Stelios, your harbor patrolman. They were used to seeing you hanging around, given your relationship with the fair Lydia, but when he showed up tonight in a uniform, they must have realized you were on to them."

Patronas turned to Stelios Mavros. "When did you first notice they were missing?" he asked.

"Around ten thirty. I was sitting outside the apartment when I smelled smoke. I was afraid it was another firebomb and I ran to check. Some idiot had poured gasoline into a trashcan on the street and set it on fire."

"It was the kids," Patronas said. "They set the fire to distract you."

Stelios Mavros considered this and nodded. "Figures. They had their music turned up real loud, and when I got back, I could still hear it. Only the CD had changed—the same song over and over, 'Before You Accuse Me.' That's when I got suspicious and went upstairs to check."

"Trying to get in your face. The song was a message."

Lydia Pappas had come out of her apartment and was standing there listening to the conversation. She was barefoot and dressed in thin, lavender pajamas, her hair tied back with a ribbon.

Preoccupied, Patronas continued to speak with Mavros and Tembelos. Eventually she went back inside and closed the door.

He followed her with his eyes, wondering if he should talk to her, ask her if she'd spoken to the kids while he was at dinner, alerted them somehow. Not deliberately, just let something slip. But in the end, he decided not to.

If she was innocent, a conversation like that would destroy their relationship, and if she was involved …. He closed his eyes, remembering what Tembelos had said about the woman with the ice pick. All he knew about Lydia was what she'd told him. What if, like the cop in the movie, he was wrong about her?

He continued to question Stelios Mavros. "How much time were you actually away from the building?"

"Forty-five minutes, maybe a little longer. I phoned you right after."

So the kids had an hour's lead.

Grabbing his phone, Patronas called the Coast Guard in Kamares and told the dispatcher the suspects were headed their way, most probably in a white Jeep. Then he rounded up his men and they sped to the harbor to head them off.

When they got there, Patronas spied a group of uniformed officers working their way through a surging crowd of people, photos in hand. They were pulling individuals out and questioning them, and the family members of the people they'd seized were shaking their fists and shouting at them. A boat was due to arrive and it was a chaotic scene. Long lines of tourists were shoving their way forward, and cars and trucks were gunning their engines, blowing their horns.

"When's the next ferry?" Patronas asked.

"In fifteen minutes," one of the Coast Guard officers said. "We checked everybody after you called, but those boys of yours never turned up."

"There's no airport on Sifnos," Patronas said "Only a heliport, and that would pose too great a risk. If you were a fugitive, how would you get away?"

The man thought for a moment. "Their best bet would still be by boat. As we've seen from the migrants, there's really no way to monitor the people passing through Greece. There's a multitude of islands and boats of every description, some registered, some not. Even if we wanted to, we couldn't seal it off. You want to come, you come. You want to leave, you go. And there's nothing any of us can do about it."

A Hellenic Seaways ferry arrived not long after. An immense red catamaran, it dwarfed the other vessels in the harbor, its prow like a vast pair of scissors cutting into the sea. The traffic out of Sifnos was going in the opposite direction tonight, the people boarding the ferry far outnumbering those coming ashore.

Spreading out, Patronas and his men joined the throng of tourists, pushing them aside and running up into the hold of the boat. Far below, the propellers were spinning in preparation for the ferry's departure, creating massive whirlpools, white and frothy in the darkness, the churning water slamming against the pier. It was late and Patronas saw people bedded down on the floor, others with their heads on the tables in the lounges, fast asleep. The journey to Piraeus took less than three hours, so few people bothered to rent cabins.

Patronas checked all the public areas, the snack bar and the dining room, the first and economy class. When he was sure the students weren't there, he ordered crew members to unlock the doors of the cabins.

When he explained what he was after, the crew willingly joined the search. Together they scoured the boat, going from cabin to cabin, even inspecting the engine room and the storage cabinets where they kept the fire hoses—any place a person might hide out.

But Gilbert, Nielsen, and Bowdoin were nowhere to be found.

Patronas eventually released the ferry, telling the captain he could leave. He watched it go with a sinking heart.

CHAPTER TWENTY-SEVEN

———— ◆ ————

Why are you going barefoot on thorns?
—Greek Proverb

I T TOOK PATRONAS and his men until early the next morning to discover the escape route the students had followed. After untying Svenson's Zodiac, still anchored at the marina in Platys Gialos, they had taken off on it, bypassing Sifnos altogether and heading for the island of Antiparos, a distance of roughly thirty kilometers. It must have been a harrowing journey at night.

The captain of a rented sailboat had seen them. Afraid the Zodiac might capsize in the heavy seas, he had notified the office of the Coast Guard, which in turn had informed Patronas. "Three people were on board," the man said. "Young foreigners, from the look of them, not Greeks."

Boarding a Coast Guard cruiser, Patronas and his men raced to Antiparos in pursuit. Patronas feared the trip would be too much for Papa Michalis and ordered the old man to stay behind, suggesting he continue his ministry at the summer study.

"Keep your ear to the ground, Father. See what you can learn about our fugitives."

"What is it you're hoping to learn?" the priest asked.

"Their history, if they bragged about doing something like this before, any previous acts of violence, and where they might be going. That's the main thing."

The rest were already on board the cruiser, even Evangelos Demos. Patronas had asked Stathis to lift his associate's suspension, saying he needed the extra manpower. His boss had reluctantly agreed.

Patronas had visited Lydia Pappas at Leandros before he left. Still a little suspicious of her, he'd been vague about where he was going. She'd been very unhappy.

"When are you coming back?" she asked.

"I don't know."

"I'll be going back to the States soon, Yiannis. We're running out of time."

"In case you've forgotten, I'm investigating a murder and my time isn't my own. I don't get to choose the days I work. I'm a cop, for Christ's sake."

Her face softened and she reached out to touch his sleeve. "I know, I know. I'm sorry. Just come back alive."

Standing on the terrace, she watched him until he was out of sight, something no one had done since his mother died.

"Stop being a cop," Tembelos told Patronas when he voiced his doubts about Lydia Pappas.

"Come on, Giorgos. Don't you think the timing was suspect? I tell her and," he snapped his fingers, "ten minutes later, they're gone."

"If she was guilty, she would have taken off, too."

"She defended them."

His friend groaned. "You yourself said she lacked the musculature to carry the boy up to Thanatos. *You* convinced *me*."

"Maybe they're in it together. Maybe she's working with them."

"Something's wrong with you, Yiannis. You can't let anything go. You just keep poking at it like a snake until it rears up and bites you. You're allergic to happiness."

Furious, Patronas stayed outside on the deck of the police cruiser while Tembelos and the others went below. He resented the way his friend had dismissed his fears about Lydia Pappas, mocked him for his suspicions. Women were tricky; surely Giorgos, a married man, knew that. Vigilance was everything when it came to women.

When the boat got underway, he gripped the railing and scanned the sea for the Zodiac. The wind was up, hitting him so hard in the face that he had to take a step backward. Water came spilling across the deck; and he had to fight to keep his balance on the slippery metal. He was soaked by the time the cruiser reached Antiparos.

As the boat drew close to shore, he was dismayed to see Antiparos wasn't one island, but many. A few had names, the captain informed him: Despotiko, Strogili, Tourlos, and Preza. A wealthy ship owner, Goulandris, owned one, but for the most part, they were uninhabited.

Patronas debated searching them, but decided no one could survive on those rocks for long, not without food and water, and subsequently directed the captain to head into port instead. The village was similar to those on Sifnos, the majority of the whitewashed buildings occupying a low-rising hill above the harbor.

Vast swaths of the Antiparos remained undeveloped, he noticed, a landscape of empty beaches and secluded, blue-green lagoons, reminiscent of the Chios of his childhood. The water sparkled in the sunlight, so clear he could see all the way to the bottom.

Following a lengthy search, they found the Zodiac, a hole torn in its side, abandoned on the beach of Livadia on the western side of the island.

Patronas waded ashore and made his way over to it. The beach was deserted and the Zodiac was listing to one side, half-submerged in the shallows. Seeing the gaping hole in the rubber, he was sure the kids had sunk it deliberately, seeking to obliterate every trace of their presence here.

"What do we do with it?" he called to Tembelos.

"Leave it," his friend yelled back. "We'll come back for it after we catch them."

Patronas had been keeping Stathis informed, so he called him now. "We found the Zodiac with a hole punched in its side. Afterward, we searched the island, but we didn't find them. My guess is they used Antiparos as a stepping stone on their way to Paros. I don't know how they're getting there, but that's how I would have played it if I were them. It's the closest destination, less than a mile away. They're athletes. If they had to, they could swim there."

"If they decide to hide out on Paros, it won't be easy to find them," Stathis said. "Five thousand people live in the port alone and that's not counting the tourists. Cruise ships stop there on a regular basis, three, sometimes four a day, so there are those people, too. It's a pretty loose place. Nobody knows or cares who you are or what you do. It's a lot like Mykonos in that respect. Those kids want to disappear, they found a good place."

"We're on our way there now in the cruiser. My guess is they'll try and get to Athens at some point and from there on to the United States."

"I'll call Venizelos Airport," Stathis said, "tell the security people to keep an eye out. Check the passenger manifests for all outgoing flights to America."

PAROS WAS AS Stathis had said, a throbbing tourist mecca. A ten-story cruise ship had just docked in the port of Parikia, and the streets were packed with foreigners of every age and description. Turkey must have been on the boat's itinerary, for Patronas saw a group of men in fezzes. Germans, from the look of them. A large quay jutted out over the water, and the cruiser drew alongside, anchoring there, the crew throwing out a length of rope and securing the vessel.

In contrast to Sifnos, the buildings in the port were a hodgepodge of historic styles and elements—neoclassical mansions interspersed with the boxy, whitewashed houses of the Cyclades—the two traditions forming a nearly seamless tableau. One of the most famous sites in the Orthodox world,

Panagia Ekatontapiliani, Our Lady of One Hundred Gates, was in Parikia, Nikolaidis told him. Built by Justinian the Great, it dated from the sixth century AD.

Walking to the police station to meet Stathis, Patronas scanned the faces of the people. He stared hard at the English speakers, seeking to spot the Americans, but saw no one resembling the three students. By his calculation, nearly eighteen hours had elapsed since the suspects left Sifnos. They now had a significant head start.

Stathis was waiting for them at the police station. He started in on Patronas as soon as he entered, cursing and insulting him, as angry as Patronas had ever seen him. Calling him names—*tis manas sou o kolos,* your mother's ass—and other idiomatic expressions of a less than affectionate nature.

"How the hell could you let them get away? Sifnos is not that big. Surely you could have prevented this." On and on, it went. As the proverb said, Stathis passed him through fourteen generations.

But beneath Stathis' usual self-serving bluster, Patronas sensed fear. His boss was afraid that the kids weren't done and would cut a swath through Greece the way those boys in Columbine had their high school.

Cut from the same cloth, Bowdoin, Nielsen, and Gilbert were equally dangerous. The killing of Sami Alnasseri was testament to that. His boss was right to be frightened.

The coroner called in the middle of Stathis' tirade to report he'd successfully matched the DNA Patronas had sent him—the saliva on the beer bottles and Nielsen's hair follicles—to the DNA on the metal pole and lock from Thanatos.

"All three of your suspects handled it. There is no question in my mind."

"What about the knife?"

"I haven't processed it yet or the glass from the fire. I just wanted to let you know that in my opinion, you've got it right this time. Bowdoin, Gilbert, and Nielsen killed that little boy. I don't know why. That's up to you to establish. But they were definitely present when the crime was committed and undoubtedly were the ones who strung him up and slit his throat."

Stathis had overheard the conversation and was already on his cellphone, speaking to his colleagues in Athens, instructing them to put out an all-points bulletin for the three. "Contact Interpol and flag every flight heading to the United States from Europe."

His boss did a little victory dance after he hung up, hopping around like Zorba on the beach in the movie. "We've got those bastards. We've got them."

Patronas wasn't so sure. So far the kids had outsmarted them every step of the way. Like a fool, he'd been taken in by their boyish antics. Whoever their leader was, he was a brilliant strategist. The Zodiac had been a masterstroke, a nearly foolproof method of escape.

'Professor Moriarty,' the priest had taken to calling the ringleader, after Sherlock Holmes' legendary adversary, and Patronas concurred.

Let Stathis talk all he wanted. It wasn't over yet.

JONATHAN ALCOTT CALLED later in the day to report he had heard back from his colleagues in Boston. "Although Richard Svenson was a brilliant scholar, he was considered to be a bit of a rogue," he told Patronas. "Well known in the academic circles for his unorthodox teaching methods. Supposedly, he often took things too far, dwelling on the more grisly aspects of ancient religions in his classroom, of which, if my source is to be believed, there were many. Once he even had his students stage an ancient religious rite—Phoenician, my source said it was—so that they might experience firsthand 'the mindset of the pagans.' Svenson's words, not mine."

Another piece of the puzzle dropped into place. "What did this reenactment entail?" Patronas asked.

"The last time we spoke, you mentioned human sacrifice. Evidently, that was the key element. He instructed one of his students to act as a priest and pretend to slit another student's throat, to mime collecting the victim's blood in a basin. Pretty unsavory, if you ask me. It got him into terrible trouble, and as far as I know, he never did it again." Alcott hesitated for a moment. "The administrators at the university called him out, saying there'd been numerous complaints from parents, but he insisted it was his prerogative as a professor, a matter of academic freedom. By the way, he was on extended leave when he got killed, but whether this was imposed on him by the university or entirely voluntary, I don't know. My guess is they were trying to force him out."

Patronas was writing furiously. "Anything else?"

"Two more things. He got into trouble for diving off Cyprus in a restricted area. Also some artifacts he was responsible for disappeared." Alcott paused and Patronas heard him shuffling papers. "Phoenician relics, a lock of some kind. The person I spoke to said it was priceless, there being only two or three like it in the entire world. Its loss caused a big uproar at the time."

There we have it, Patronas said to himself.

Besides thievery, he wondered what else Svenson had taught his students, if ritual murder had once again been part of the curriculum.

From what Patronas had seen on the Internet, people around the world continued to practice human sacrifice. One man on the Indian subcontinent confessed to killing his neighbor, certain the Hindu goddess, Kali, would welcome the sacrifice and reward him with the necessary funds to buy a car. Another had wanted to win the lottery. And then there was that awful group in London who'd killed and dismembered a boy and thrown his remains in the Thames River because a witch doctor from their native land claimed the child was possessed by demons.

If God, the one his mother had believed in—not Kali and her friends—decided in His infinite wisdom to put an end to the human race, Patronas, for one, would vote for it. Sifnos had convinced him. Leave the grasshoppers and the zebras, the meadowlarks and the snakes, but get rid of man.

Seeking the three fugitives, Patronas and his associates worked their way across Paros over the next forty-eight hours. Tembelos, responsible for the airport, checked every flight that left the island while Patronas, Evangelos Demos, and Petros Nikolaidis spoke to the charter boat captains and ticket agents, the staffs of the hotels and the restaurants.

During the day, they inspected the sunbathers at the beach and at night haunted the clubs the port was famous for and the bars young foreigners were known to frequent. They ate on the run, *souvlakia* and *tyropitas* mostly, a slice of pizza on occasion. They labored around the clock and hadn't showered or shaved since arriving on the island.

The fevered pace was taking its toll. Patronas, for one, was so weary he could barely put one foot in front of the other.

After they completed the search in Parikia, they moved on to Naoussa, another large tourist center, and from there to villages up and down the coast. It being late summer, there was an enormous number of ferries. Working with the Coast Guard, they inspected every one of them prior to departure. They even spoke to the crews of the cruise ships, ordering them to be on the lookout for stowaways.

The coroner continued to call with updates, additional evidence of the Americans' complicity in the crime. The toxicology screen had come back, and there was evidence the child had ingested Rohypnol.

"What's Rohypnol?" Patronas asked.

"It's potent date rape drug. Give it to someone and you can do just about anything you want with them; they won't remember it. It's easily available on college campuses throughout the United States, but in Greece it would be nearly impossible to obtain, as the drug is virtually nonexistent here. The students must have brought it with them."

"So, the Rohypnol alone would indicate American involvement," Patronas said.

"Indeed. As far as I know, its use is only prevalent in the United States, and even there only among the young people, those roughly the same age as your suspects."

The coroner went on to say that according to the trace evidence on the fragments of glass, Michael Nielsen, as Patronas suspected, was the one who'd thrown the Molotov cocktail into the migrant camp. However, there was little to link the students to the murder of Richard Svenson. His body had been in the water too long and all trace evidence had been washed away.

The coroner had also heard back from the archeologists at the university. The baby's skeleton dated from the time of the Phoenicians, perhaps even a little before. After Patronas hung up, he called Jonathan Alcott and told him to organize his dig; the bones were old.

"I'll get on it today," Alcott said. "I know some experts in the area and I'll call them. They'll be ecstatic."

Proof of the kids' guilt in the death of Sami Alnasseri continued to accumulate. The priest called and said a staff member at the summer study told him Michael Nielsen had been in trouble in high school.

"It raised questions about his suitability for the program, but in the end they decided to take him. Allegedly he stalked a girl in his class, following her home from school and peering in the windows of her house. A couple of times he wore a mask of some malevolent movie character named, of all things, 'Freddie,' which terrified her. What jumped out at me was that her dog disappeared around the same time."

The priest was excited. Patronas could hear it in his voice.

"I don't know if you are aware of this, Yiannis, but if he did indeed kill her dog, that indicates he was already a very dangerous individual. Such activity at an early age is considered one of the three identifying characteristics of serial killers. As children, they wet the bed, torture animals, and set fires. It appears that with Michael Nielsen, we have two out of three."

"So he's a psychopath?"

"I prefer 'evil.' I loathe psychiatric terms."

A TECHNICIAN IN THE coroner's office called to report that the lab was finished with Svenson's body and that Patronas needed to inform the American's family.

It was a very sad conversation, Svenson's son sobbing and wanting to know how much coffins cost in Greece, whether or not his father's body was fit to travel. He and Patronas spoke in code; neither uttered the words 'embalmed' or 'decayed.'

As far as Patronas knew, no one had come forward to claim Sami Alnasseri's body. The child's remains still rested in a drawer at the morgue. He intended to fly to Athens after the case was over and arrange a proper burial for the boy. He'd even looked up Muslim funeral rites in preparation—how Syrians laid their dead to rest. He and Sami's aunt would go to the cemetery and do whatever was necessary. He'd pay for everything out of his own pocket and place the child's treasures next to him in the coffin.

He'd had so little, Sami—not just worldly goods, but so little time.

Patronas had called the victim's aunt at her hospital room in Athens a couple of times to check in. She'd had her surgery and was doing about as well as could be expected, she said. "A woman comes every morning and makes me walk. It is very hard and hurts much."

"Did the graft take?"

"Yes. The doctor, he is pleased. He brought people to see and everybody, they are smiling."

Thinking he might need to make further arrangements for her, Patronas asked where she planned to go after she was discharged from the hospital.

"I don't know. Maybe to Germany to be with my brother," she said. "I am a leaf in the wind."

"We're closing in on Sami's killers." Patronas struggled to pronounce the words correctly in Arabic. "Soon we will arrest them and it will be over."

Her voice caught. "It will never be over, not for me. It will hurt my heart always."

As it will mine, Patronas thought, but didn't say.

PATRONAS HAD TRIED repeatedly to get in touch with Lydia Pappas. Not for a lengthy talk—there was no time for that—just to check in. He'd called from Antiparos and from Paros multiple times. After ringing for a few minutes, her phone always went straight to voicemail.

He tried again now from the hotel room. As before, the phone rang and rang, but she didn't pick up. Worried, he called the owner of Leandros and asked him to check her apartment.

A few minutes later, the man called back. "She's sitting out on the terrace by herself. I told her you were trying to reach her and to call you."

Lydia was as friendly as ever when they finally connected. "Oh, Yiannis, I'm so glad you called. How's it going?"

"Case is still in limbo." Still suspicious of her, he was unwilling to say more.

Her phone had been giving her trouble, she said. It didn't always ring when it should and she didn't know what was wrong with it. "Probably need a new one." Her classes were winding down and she'd been writing up the final evaluations of her students.

Slowly, they moved on to more serious topics.

"I've been thinking about you," Lydia said. "The way you screamed in your sleep after that man knifed you. I don't know how things work here, but in the States when a cop gets injured on the job, they have to talk to somebody. You might want to consider it. According to psychiatrists, physical or emotional trauma can affect a person for a long, long time. They call it 'post-traumatic stress disorder.' "

Swell, Patronas thought, *she wants me to see a shrink.*

"Sometimes I can't sleep at night either," she confessed. "I start thinking about the fire in the camp and it's like I'm reliving it—the smell of the smoke, the sound the branch made when it fell on me. I just can't get away from it. It's even worse with the child. What was his name, Sami? I'll be doing something and suddenly I remember him and find myself in tears."

"You can't just walk away from these things, Lydia. They affect you. All your life long, they affect you. Call it what you will, post-traumatic stress or battle fatigue, but you're not the same person you were before and you never will be. Maybe talking to a shrink can help you deal with it, but it never really goes away."

"You were so upset about that child. It was almost as if he were your son."

Patronas closed his eyes. *How could I have ever doubted her?*

Seeking to change the topic, he described Antiparos and how beautiful it was. "I'll take you there when the case over. You'll love it. It'll cure what ails you."

"I'm just a little depressed tonight. I always hate the end of summer."

Patronas pictured her sitting outside on the terrace, her hair like burnished copper in the light of the candle. Her loneliness was almost palpable.

Seeking to cheer her up, he started singing "Autumn Leaves," an old American standard from his youth, crooning about 'those summer kisses, those sunburned hands' he used to hold.

Unfortunately, his serenade had the opposite effect. It made her cry. "I wish you were here," she said.

"Ah, Lydia, what am I going to do with you?"

"Love me. That would be a good start."

"No need to start. I already do, you know that. You're my lady, my *neraida*."

PATRONAS AND HIS men were bunking in a single room in an industrial area. A dismal, claustrophobic space, it was so small the four could barely turn around, and the bathroom door would always mysteriously open whenever someone was in there, going about their business. However, it was cheap, and Stathis was in town.

Sitting on the bed in his underwear, Evangelos Demos complained bitterly about the accommodations, saying the beds were lumpy, the air-conditioning nonexistent, and toxic fumes were emanating from the bathroom. "Every time I go in there, I can't breathe."

"Neither can we," Tembelos told him. "You stink up the whole place."

Evangelos continued to list the defects of the room: the likelihood of bedbugs in the mattresses and lack of water pressure in the shower, the way the toilet leaked and spewed yellowish water into the hall.

"*Re, touvlo,*" you brick, "you're not here on vacation," Tembelos said.

"That's right," Patronas bellowed angrily. "In case you've forgotten, you're here to get justice for Sami Alnasseri and the migrants burned in the fire, to catch the individuals who committed those crimes and put them in jail, to get justice for all those who suffered at their hand. You understand, Evangelos? You're a policeman and that's what you're here to do. Not take goddamned showers."

"Justice for Sami," he repeated again. "Do you hear me, Evangelos? Do I make myself clear?"

"Yes," said Evangelos. "Justice for Sami."

The three of them chanted this over and over again the next twenty-four hours. Half mantra, half prayer, it seemed to spur them on when their energy flagged and they grew too exhausted to continue.

Stathis was coordinating the search for the killers from a desk at the police station, manning the phones and speaking to his counterparts in Athens and Europe. Interpol had stepped in, as had the American FBI. The net his boss had cast now covered two continents, but as of now, it remained empty.

Deeply discouraged, Patronas lay down and stared at the stained ceiling. Tonight justice for Sami seemed far away.

CHAPTER TWENTY-EIGHT

———◆———

Be benevolent to your friends.
—The Delphic Oracle

PATRONAS WAS FAST asleep when his phone started to ring. Stathis, he assumed, hearing the distinctive ringtone, the one that sounded like a declaration of war.

Ignoring it, he rolled over and tried to go back to sleep. His men were equally comatose—all snoring, not quite in sync, each inhaling and whistling in a different key. They'd gotten in very late the previous night and dropped their uniforms where they fell. The stench of sweaty clothes and unwashed men lay heavy in the room.

A half hour later, Stathis turned up at the hotel and banged on the door. "Patronas, you in there? Open up!"

Patronas looked toward the window. The sun was barely up. Something major must have happened to have brought his boss out at this hour.

"What is it?" he asked sleepily.

"Three people matching the suspects' description were seen in the parking lot of the Athens airport late last night. A security camera picked them up. I reviewed the footage and I'm sure it's them."

"So they're on their way home."

"Ticket counters aren't open yet, but yes, sooner or later, they're going to try to board a plane for America."

Patronas was wide awake now. "And we're going to stop them?"

"Of course, I'm going to stop them. What do you think? I'm not going to let them get away!"

Interesting the way his boss had switched pronouns. Now that victory was in sight, he was intent on making it his.

"I've ordered plainclothesmen to stand guard at all the departure gates for flights to the United States," Stathis said. "They've been briefed as to what the kids look like. It's just a matter of time."

Patronas, self-conscious about standing in the doorway in a state of undress, tried to cover himself up with his hands. Rather like Botticelli's Venus, the one standing on the half-shell, only she'd been young and beautiful and had a lot more hair.

By this time, the others were up, Tembelos hastily pulling on his trousers. "How did they manage to get to Athens?" he asked.

"I'm still in the process of piecing it together, but as near as I can tell they left for the island of Serifos almost immediately after they got here, long before any of us arrived on the scene. The boat that took them was owned by a local fisherman. He said the kids approached him at the harbor, asked him to take them and he agreed, hoping to make some extra money. He didn't think anything of it at the time, just assumed they were island hopping. After they reached Serifos, they boarded a Blue Star ferry to Piraeus and hid out there until last night when they made their way to Athens and the airport. Those Blue Star ferries make the rounds in the summer: Serifos, Sifnos, Paros, Naxos, Mykonos, and back again. They're huge and hold over two thousand people. We weren't expecting them to board on Serifos, so no one was checking. They just waltzed up the ramp and there they were. It was a clever move."

Stathis said he was taking the 8:40 a.m. flight to Athens. Since he had the case well in hand, he saw no need for Patronas and the others to fly out with him. They could journey to Athens just as the suspects had. By boat.

"Third class," he said.

AFTER HIS BOSS left, Patronas called Papa Michalis on Sifnos and told him to get himself to Piraeus as quickly as he could. "We're heading there now. I'll call you when we arrive and tell you where to meet us."

"What's the rush, Yiannis? Why the early wake-up call?"

"The kids turned up on a security camera at the airport."

It wasn't necessary to bring the old man along, but Patronas wanted him there when he questioned the three students, remembering the ease with which the priest broke suspects down and got them to talk. Patronas planned to interview Nielsen at length, seeking to understand the boy's character, the forces that had shaped him and led him to do what he did. Hopefully, Papa Michalis would aid in that understanding.

The need to confess was universal. With any luck, it would come into play with Nielsen.

Even though Patronas had been a cop his entire adult life, this being Greece, he'd never met a genuine psychopath before, a person utterly devoid of human emotion. The prospect of meeting one now scared him a little.

He tried to remember what the priest had said that first morning in Sifnos. Something about how they were about to enter the kingdom of evil. And so he was … so they all were.

As a child, he'd studied the faces of criminals in the newspapers, trying to see if there was a difference between them and the other adults in his life, if their sins had branded them. For the most part, they hadn't, as far as he could tell. The men facing the camera looked just like everyone else. When Adolf Eichmann had gone on trial in Jerusalem, reporters wrote that the ex-Gestapo agent seemed more like an accountant than a murderer, 'appearing to be normal in every respect.' A man who had done his best to destroy of an entire race of people.

Patronas' experience bore this out. Although he'd encountered his share of killers, they'd rarely embodied the base evil depicted in the movies. For the most part, they'd been ordinary men. Like Eichmann, maybe even a little drab.

Michael Nielsen might well fall into that category. Unlike the two killers at Columbine, Nielsen wasn't a loner, nor had he been the victim of bullying in high school or a toxic home environment. He was obviously disciplined—Patronas recalled the boy's runner's physique—and the priest reported Nielsen had the best academic record of the three. So what was it that made him different from millions of other kids? What anomaly had set him apart and led him down this path?

PATRONAS AND HIS men bought tickets on a Blue Star ferry, the fastest boat they could find. It departed at 10:45 a.m., arriving in Piraeus at close to five. A long trip, but Patronas welcomed it. Just to sit and watch the sea, knowing the suspects were in hand, would be heaven.

Each man had taken his turn in the shower prior to departure, one after the other, and the air in the hotel room was so hot and damp, it felt like a jungle. Wiping the mirror with his sleeve, Patronas did what he could to make himself presentable, parting his hair and carefully smoothing it down. He'd steamed his uniform along with himself in the shower and he slipped it on now. If there was a press conference, no doubt Stathis would occupy center stage, but he still wanted to look his best.

He and his men were in a state of high excitement, happy to close the case and finally return home—Nikolaidis to Sifnos, the other two to Chios.

Patronas called Lydia Pappas before he left for Piraeus and impetuously invited her to join him in Chios in a week's time. "I'd like to introduce you to the people I know on the island and meet my relatives."

"How long should I plan on staying?" she asked.

A little sly, the question. Patronas smiled to himself. "Let's start with ten days and see how it goes."

He was thinking of asking her to marry him in the same place his father had proposed to his mother, on the beach of Emborio on the west coast of the island. Surrounded by umbrella pines, it was a quiet place—the only sound, the black pebbles rolling back and forth in the surf. As there was no sand, tourists rarely ventured there. With any luck, he and Lydia would have it to themselves.

He'd do it casually. No mush, no flowers or champagne. They were both adults. He'd simply say, 'Marry me,' and that would be that.

PATRONAS AND TEMBELOS took adjoining seats in the economy section of the ferry. The television in the salon was broadcasting the news and they watched it. Grim-faced, the commentator reported that the countries in the European Union, seeking to stop the influx of migrants, were closing their borders with Greece, stranding more than fifty thousand in the country.

Patronas turned away, not wanting to hear what the prime minister in Athens had to say about the crisis, or worse, the German politicians who'd orchestrated the tragedy—Merkel first inviting the refugees and then withdrawing the invitation. People would die as a result, most probably of starvation or disease, exactly as they had in 1941.

"Will you look at that?" Tembelos nodded to the television. Reporters were interviewing a migrant in the pouring rain. He was standing in a sea of Red Cross tents, thousands of displaced people as far as the eye could see. Each tent was filled with people hoping to cross the border and make their way on into Germany—people who were now hopelessly. stranded. Ten, twenty thousand … it was difficult to say.

Wanting a cigarette, Patronas left the salon and pushed open the door to the deck. Like the tents on television, it too was packed with migrants: Syrians in family groups and gangs of men from Afghanistan and Bangladesh, others whose origins he couldn't identify. So many he couldn't make his way forward and was forced to retreat. Whatever they were, they were all traveling light, most with only a backpack, and he had no idea where they were bound or what their fates would be once they got there.

Looking at them, he wouldn't have known he was in Greece.

He ended up standing at the prow of the boat, leaning over the railing and cupping his hands to light a cigarette, match after match blowing out in the wind. A teenager—Syrian from the look of him, although Patronas couldn't say for sure—was standing nearby, a cheap wooden cross on a cord around his neck. Patronas had been told they did that sometimes, the migrants, tried to pass themselves off as Christians, thinking they'd get better treatment, but somehow he didn't think that was the case with the boy. Hollow-eyed, he was staring at the sea, his face filled with such abject despair, Patronas wondered if he might be contemplating suicide—as if each kilometer the boat traveled was carrying him farther away from something or someone he couldn't bear to part with. Patronas offered him a cigarette and the boy took it, nodding his thanks and giving him a tentative smile.

Cigarette in hand, Patronas pointed out the islands in the distance and said their names, indicating the boy should repeat them after him. They continued in this vein for a couple of minutes, Patronas endeavoring to teach him a few words in Greek—man, boat, sea—the boy growing more and more animated. He embraced Patronas when he turned to go. *"Efxaristo,"* he said in Greek. Thank you.

Tembelos was still engrossed in the newscast when Patronas returned. "Reporters say we're witnessing one of the greatest migrations in human history."

"I can well believe it," Patronas said. "There's more than a thousand passengers on the boat today. You've never seen anything like it. Talk about a sea of humanity."

The image on the television changed, this time to a scene in Macedonia along the northern border of Greece, men in police uniforms shouting and pulling migrants down from a barbed-wire fence.

"Maybe I should retire." Tembelos said. "I don't want to spend the rest of my days locking these people up until we can deport them to Turkey."

"Greece will survive. All this, it's just a momentary setback."

"A 'momentary setback'? Jesus, Yiannis, what's wrong with you? Don't you see what's happening?"

"So far we haven't lost anything of value, Giorgos. Unlike the rest of Europe, we're feeding these people, feeding them when we don't have food ourselves. The soul of Greece is intact. We are what we have always been."

"But for how long? That's what I want to know. How fucking long?"

Papa Michalis was waiting for them in Piraeus, standing at the bottom of the ramp when they got off the ferry. Flagging down a cab, they piled into it and headed to the airport.

Patronas hadn't been in Piraeus in over a year and was repelled by what he saw. Most of the stores were gone and the streets were teeming with migrants, men mostly, gangs of them. Groups were sleeping out in the open on the pavement while others worked their way through the traffic, begging for handouts. A crowd of people came pouring out of the subway. He watched them for a moment, seeing not a single person, not one, who was recognizably Greek.

Far worse was the evidence of economic decline, the eroding fortunes of Greece. Buildings on either side of the road, one of the major thoroughfares in Athens, now stood empty, and there were signs everywhere advertising space for rent. Many of the abandoned stores had broken windows and nearly all were covered with graffiti, spray-painted in lurid colors. Not even the local church had been spared, its entranceway desecrated by a skull with dollar signs in the eye sockets, a phrase written in Arabic.

Tembelos nudged Patronas. "Behold, your nation's capital."

"A momentary setback," Patronas repeated. "Soon we'll be back on our feet again."

"No, we won't. Not in our lifetimes."

Seeking to save money, Patronas had opted to take a single cab to the airport, a choice he had come to regret. Early evening, it was still very hot in Athens and he and three of his men were wedged tightly in the backseat—close to a ton of perspiring, suffering human flesh. When Patronas' cellphone rang, there wasn't enough space to reach his hand into his pants pocket to retrieve it, not without groping one of the others. It continued to ring for the next thirty minutes.

Stathis was calling. "The Ride of the Valkyries," over and over.

CHAPTER TWENTY-NINE

———— ♦ ————

With silver spears, you may conquer the world.
—The Delphic Oracle

As soon as Patronas arrived at the airport, he paid off the driver and hurried to the office on the second floor where his boss was waiting. Tembelos and the others were close on his heels. The airport was busy, but not unduly so, orderly lines of foreign tourists waiting to check in at the various counters with their luggage.

Stathis was standing in the midst of a group of men—policemen, judging from the uniforms—and they were all shouting, obviously upset. The room itself was large and full of television monitors, the screens displaying various areas of the terminal in rapid succession. The men and women who'd been scanning the screens had stopped what they were doing to watch the fight.

The three Americans were nowhere to be seen. Perhaps his boss had locked them up someplace else in the airport, Patronas thought, willing himself not to panic, or already transported them to the Koridallos prison complex in Piraeus.

Catching sight of Patronas, Stathis walked over. "Unfortunately, there has been an unforeseen complication."

"What do you mean?" Patronas fought to keep his voice down. "Where are they?"

"They slipped through the net and got away. I had plainclothesmen stationed at all the departure gates, checking the passengers boarding the planes. The problem is, they only screened the ones leaving for the United States. They neglected those heading elsewhere."

"Where's Nielsen?!" Patronas cried.

"On his way to Turkey. I don't know how the three of them got past security, but somehow they did. Maybe nobody paid attention to them because they changed their appearance, dyed their hair, even put lifts in their shoes, and no longer matched the description on the flyers we distributed. They're clever boys. Anything is possible. Or the person checking the passports got distracted and didn't inspect them as carefully as he should have. Given what I've seen of the assholes here, that would be my guess. All I know is they managed to escape. When I found out they were missing, I went from counter to counter and spoke to the ticket agents. An employee of Turkish Airlines said he'd just booked three American kids onto a flight to Istanbul. I checked the passenger roster and there they were."

Stathis casually admitted he'd been delayed getting to the airport. Because of the traffic in Athens, the trip had taken him twice as long as it should have. By the time he got there and realized what had happened, the kids were already in Turkish airspace.

"I just assumed they'd be going home. It was a mistake," he admitted reluctantly.

Patronas reached for his cigarettes. Lydia had asked him to quit smoking and he'd tried, but the situation demanded nicotine, whiskey … something. "What are you going to do?"

"The Turkish government will never return them to us; that much is certain," Stathis said. "They'll check with the American Embassy and do whatever the ambassador says—probably put them on a plane to New York."

"They're going to go free? After what they did?"

Stathis raised a hand to silence him. "Calm down, Patronas. Justice will be served. Maybe not in the form you anticipated, but trust me, it will be served."

His boss had something up his sleeve, something furtive and illegal. Patronas could almost smell it on him.

"You might say, the Turks and I have an informal reciprocity agreement," Stathis explained. "I do for them and they do for me—not officially, of course, under the table—and the job gets done. I just called and told them the situation and they agreed to grab those kids as soon as they get off the plane and hold them for us."

"On what grounds?"

Stathis chuckled. "It's Turkey, Patronas. The police there have a free hand. They do what they want." He sounded more than a little envious.

"You can't just stuff them in a plane and bring them back to Greece. They're Americans. What if they refuse to go?"

"I have no intention of bringing them back to Greece." The way Stathis said it made Patronas' blood run cold. "I have something else in mind for them."

"Surely you want them to stand trial for what they did?"

"I don't care if they stand trial or not. I just want them punished."

* * *

Stathis had already bought a ticket for himself, and he instructed Patronas to do the same for himself, Tembelos, and the priest. Evangelos Demos was to go back to Chios, Nikolaidis to Sifnos. "Flight's short, less than an hour."

Patronas wondered why his boss wanted them to come along. *As protection, probably. If everything went to hell, he would have someone to blame.* It had happened before. Stathis had fired him two years ago after a murder case on Chios collapsed, waited until the publicity died down and then reinstated him. "Nothing personal," he'd said at the time.

Sitting in the terminal waiting to board, Patronas got out his notebook and flipped through the pages, reviewing what Svenson had said during his interview about his upcoming trip to Turkey. Patronas thought the suspects might be planning to follow the same itinerary.

They'd as much as told him what their intentions were the night they'd eaten dinner together at Flora's after Svenson died, saying they wanted to go to Ephesus as the professor had planned and from there on to Cappadocia as a way of 'paying tribute to him.' They'd virtually given him a roadmap and he'd ignored it.

Much as he hated to admit it, Stathis wasn't the only one who'd fucked up. He had, too.

A Chiot to his core, Papa Michalis was pathologically distrustful of the Turks and kept dragging his heels on the way to the gate, saying he needed to stop and catch his breath.

"Come on, Father," Patronas urged. "Our plane leaves in thirty minutes. We have to hurry."

"I hope you are aware of our shared history with the Turks, Yiannis. How they murdered sixty thousand of your ancestors on Easter Sunday in 1821. Threw the Greek residents of Smyrna into the sea."

"A long time ago, Father. Come on. Let's get a move on."

The flight to Istanbul was surprisingly short, barely long enough for Patronas to buckle his seatbelt and drink the free soda the flight attendant gave him before the plane landed. Stathis was waiting for him at the gate. "The Turks have them in custody."

"No problem then?" Patronas said.

"Not for us," his boss said. "Their problems, on the other hand, are just beginning."

The airport itself was far bigger and more congested than the one in Athens, the vast lobby crowded with people in native dress, garments Patronas had only seen in geography books or on television newscasts. A group of Sunni women waited by the elevator, clothed entirely in black. Their hair and faces, everything but their eyes, was veiled. A few were wearing sunglasses as well, making them appear like apparitions from another world. In marked contrast were the people dressed in Ihram clothing in preparation for their Hajj pilgrimage to Mecca; both men and women wore pure white cotton garments. Others were clad in the tunics, vests, and loose pants of Pakistan. Pashtun hats from Afghanistan were also in evidence on some of the men as was a kind of flattened turban. Patronas saw few women in Western dress, tourists mainly. The vast majority wore traditional garb, the long robe-like dresses and headscarves of Turkey. In spite of the heat, a few had on handsome knee-length jackets as well.

Walking among them, Patronas felt farther away from home than he'd ever been in his life. The language, the features and physiognomy of the people, everything was unfamiliar. He felt unsteady, as if he'd lost his balance, the culture of the Middle East closing in on him from all sides. A pair of young women in floor-length robes and scarves hurried past, their eyes downcast, accompanied by a much older man in a caftan. *Father? Husband?* Patronas couldn't help but wonder. He paused for a moment, looking up at the list of departing flights: Sana, Islambad, Yerevan, Tbilisi. He doubted he could locate half on a map.

"My mother was from Asia Minor," the priest said, "and she said that at Turkish weddings, they hoist the mother of the groom up in a chair; the bride has to crawl under her. They do it to show her, right from the beginning, what her place is."

"On the floor," Patronas said and everybody laughed.

"My wife and I visited Istanbul a couple of years ago," Tembelos said, "but we didn't see anything like that. Turks were real friendly. When we said we were from Greece, they called us *sympetheroi.*" The in-laws. "But even then, you could tell the country was in a state of flux, and that it was growing more and more conservative. Outside some of the mosques there were soldiers with machine guns—Sunni, Shiite, I never could figure it out. What impressed me was the way everybody stopped talking when the muezzins called them to prayer." He laughed. "Imagine trying that in Athens."

"Hard to believe religion can make such a difference," Patronas said.

"Of course it does." Papa Michalis motioned to the masses of people moving around them. "You yourself might have no need of faith, Yiannis, but what most people believe and worship defines them."

Feeling uneasy, Patronas studied the list of flights again, curious about the passengers on those planes. Was there really no connection between those people and him? No common bond? He was an atheist. Did that really define him?

* * *

STATHIS LED THEM down to the lowest level of the airport and along a dimly lit corridor. At the very end was a small, windo wless room. Dank and cell-like, it had dingy walls and a cement floor. A fluorescent light flickered overhead, and there were three chairs in a row, a card table set up in front of them. The three suspects were standing just inside the door, their hands cuffed behind them. They'd been roughed up. Gilbert had the beginnings of a black eye, and all were subdued. Bowdoin was whimpering quietly while Nielsen stared defiantly ahead.

A heavyset man in a uniform appeared to be in charge. He greeted Stathis warmly and whispered something in his ear.

"Good, good," Stathis said.

Two other officers were with him, and he gestured for them to bring the students' luggage forward. "Are these yours?" he asked each of the Americans in turn, gesturing at the suitcases.

When the kids nodded, he removed their handcuffs and ordered them to initial a piece of paper. When Gilbert balked, saying he couldn't read Turkish and didn't know what he was signing, the officer grabbed him by the hair and slammed his head hard against the table. Handing Gilbert a pen, he pointed once again to where he was to sign. Crying, Gilbert quickly wrote his name where the man had indicated.

The officer then put the handcuffs back on and had his men seat the students in the chairs.

After that, things proceeded quickly. Pulling on latex gloves, the Turks began opening up the suitcases. Inside, hidden away in the interior pockets of each of the bags, was a sealed plastic pouch of white powder. The pouches weren't large—no more than five centimeters square—but, realizing instantly what it was, Patronas knew it would be more than enough.

Removing the pouches from the suitcases, the Turks handed them to the officer-in-charge, who deftly slit them open with a knife and tasted the contents of each in turn. "Heroin," he said in English.

The kids went crazy. "It's not ours! Somebody planted it on us!"

They continued to yell, swearing they'd never seen the pouches before and didn't know where they'd come from. The Turkish policemen nudged each another with their elbows and laughed at their distress.

Stathis, too, was enjoying the show. "Heroin?" he sang out. "My, my, you're in a world of trouble, my friends. Well and truly fucked."

"Aren't they allowed to call their parents?" Patronas asked.

"All in good time," the Turk said, unperturbed.

When Patronas stepped forward to read the name tags on the suitcases, his boss pulled him back. "Stay out of it," he said fiercely.

Gathering up the bags of heroin and putting them in a briefcase, the officer ordered his men to take the students away and stalked out of the room.

By this time, all three of the kids were in tears.

Stathis watched them go. "You see, Patronas. I told you I'd take care of it."

"It was you?"

His boss nodded smugly.

Patronas just stared at him. If the rule of law was indispensable to civilized society—the *only* thing that separated it from the time of the Neanderthals—then his boss had just returned them to the cave. Stathis' actions were a travesty, a violation of the Greek constitution, every law he was sworn to uphold.

The frame-up had been deftly done. Either Stathis had brought the heroin with him from Paros—it was commonly used there and would have been easy to obtain—and planted it in the suitcases when he got to Istanbul, or he'd arranged to have the Turks do it for him. It didn't really matter. As his boss had said, the Americans were well and truly fucked.

Years ago, there'd been a poster in the airport with the picture of a young man behind bars in what looked like Devil's Island. The caption had read: 'If you get caught with drugs in Turkey, you're in for the hassle of your life.' There'd been a movie, too, about an American drug smuggler in a Turkish prison, *The Midnight Express.* Tourism in Turkey had plummeted ninety-five percent upon its release. It was as close to a vision of hell as Patronas had ever seen.

Knowing what lay ahead, Patronas felt a little sorry for the students—not much, just a little. He wished it had gone differently, that they'd been charged and gone to trial, been sentenced in a Greek court. Given the conditions in the Turkish prisons, he doubted the kids would last a month. What Stathis had done to them amounted to a death sentence.

"They'll never see the light of day again," Stathis said, as if reading Patronas' mind. "The penalty for trafficking here is twenty years, which is doubled if heroin is involved, making it an even forty. And if the perpetrator is part of a criminal conspiracy—defined by Turkish law as more than two people as was the case here—they add another twenty to the sentence for a grand total of sixty years. Sixty years of what in their criminal code is defined as 'heavy imprisonment.' "

Devil's Island, in other words.

CHAPTER THIRTY

———— ◆ ————

A serpent, unless he devours another serpent,
does not become a dragon.
—Greek Proverb

Patronas got his chance to talk to Michael Nielsen the following day. Overseen by a burly Turkish policeman, he and Papa Michalis sat with the three Americans in their cell in Maltepe Prison where they'd been transported in a police van after leaving the airport the previous night.

A collection of red-roofed buildings on the outskirts of Istanbul, the prison was so large, it was like entering a small city. The cell the students were in was part of a unit, seven rooms housing four inmates each, opening into a larger space. A single shower and a hole in the floor, an old-fashioned Turkish 'squat,' served the twenty-eight prisoners who were housed there. The primitive toilet smelled so bad it was like breathing in raw sewage. Drawn by the stench, clouds of flies were buzzing around the cell; a sheen of filth coated every surface.

Taking it all in, Patronas again doubted the kids would survive their incarceration. Terrorists were housed in the same prison, and they would know via the prison grapevine the crime the three were accused of—the murder of a Muslim child. They might well take matters into their own hands. He wondered why the Turkish officials had chosen to house the three kids with the general population, if it had been deliberate. As Americans, they would have been far better off in solitary.

He had asked to speak to them, telling Stathis he still had questions about the murder he wanted resolved before returning to Greece. "I promised the boy's aunt I'd find out what happened to him. I gave her my word."

Stathis had arranged the interview with the appropriate Turkish authorities, making it clear that even if the three confessed, it would make no difference. "They're staying in Turkey, Patronas. Nothing you do can change that. There will be no extradition to Greece."

As soon as Patronas entered the cell, the students started begging and pleading with him to get them out of prison.

"Did the guards let you call your parents?" Patronas asked, thinking he would do it himself if they hadn't. It was their right as prisoners, whether here or in Greece. He'd notify the American Embassy, too, if he had to.

Bowdoin nodded. "One phone call apiece, just like in the movies. My parents were real upset and said they'd get here as soon as they could, but it would take time—what with getting tickets and waiting for connecting flights and all this other crap. In the meantime, I'm stuck here in this hellhole." He slammed his fist against the wall. "Fuck!"

He, too, had been beaten since the last time Patronas had seen him. There were black and blue marks on his face, wrists, and neck, and his shirt was torn in places. All three stank, their pants stained and foul-smelling. The Turks must have kept them in that room at the airport for a long time before moving them here, denied them access to a bathroom.

"What about the American Embassy in Ankara?" asked Patronas.

"My parents said they were going to call them," Gilbert volunteered. "Demand that they send somebody to help us out. But so far it's been nothing doing. You're the first person we've seen since we got here."

The parents of Nielsen and Gilbert were also en route to Istanbul. The latter's father was a lawyer, and Gilbert said his father was less than optimistic about their prospects.

"I swore up and down that we weren't dealing drugs," the boy said, "that someone had planted them on us. But he said, given the evidence, it would be hard to convince the Turkish authorities of our innocence. Also, the fact that we're Americans would probably count against us. He told me he and my mother would do what they could, but that I might be looking at sixty years in prison." Gilbert started to weep. "I don't want to stay here! I want to go home."

Bowdoin couldn't sit still. "I still can't believe it," he said, pacing back and forth, "Heroin? What … are we crazy? Everyone knows what happens if you traffic drugs in Turkey."

"We're not here about the drugs," Patronas said, cutting them off. "We're here about the killing of Sami Alnasseri, the ten-year-old boy you strung up in Thanatos."

The students exchanged uneasy glances. "I don't know what you're talking about," Bowdoin stammered, not meeting his eyes.

"We found the knife," Patronas said. "Your fingerprints are all over it."

"Damn it, Charlie," Nielsen said, glaring at him.

Again, the three looked at each other.

Bowdoin hesitated. "Will it go better for us if we confess?"

"Of course it will," Patronas said expansively, knowing it was a lie. "We'll keep it informal, just a couple of questions. As this is Turkey, I have no authority here, which means nothing you say can be used in court. Afterward, I'll tell the Turkish authorities that you cooperated. I'll say you're just kids and they should give you a second chance—show you some leniency. We have a reciprocity agreement with them and they'll listen to me." More lies.

That seemed to reassure them, and one by one, they began to talk. Unlike Patronas' earlier conversation with them, it was Michael Nielsen, not Charlie Bowdoin, who took the lead this time.

"Svenson wasn't involved," he admitted. "It was just us."

Patronas opened up his notebook and wrote the date and the time. "Why Sami Alnasseri?"

"He stole Charlie's iPad."

"An iPad!"

Michael Nielsen nodded. "That's right."

Patronas kept his head down and concentrated on entering this information in his notebook, afraid if he looked up, his horror and repulsion would show in his face.

"It was brand new," Nielsen insisted as if that explained everything. "When we caught him with it, he just laughed."

Sensing Bowdoin was the weakest link, Patronas turned to him. "You can speak freely, Charlie. Go on, I won't hurt you. Confession is good for the soul."

"The three of us discussed it and decided he needed to be punished," Bowdoin said.

Although they continued to talk for the next ninety minutes, the motive for the crime remained murky and confused in Patronas' mind. An unholy combination of adolescent bravura—evidently Nielsen had dared the other two—and television-spawned violence. Once they'd gotten started, drugging and kidnapping the boy, it had been too late to turn back and they'd gone ahead and killed him, goading each other on. There had been no true leader, no Charlie Manson or demonic puppet master. They'd taken turns, according to Bowdoin; the group had acted in tandem.

As Patronas had anticipated, Michael Nielsen was the worst. "I wanted to feel what it was like to kill," he said. "To cut a person's throat and feel their life ebbing away. To hold the power of life and death in my hand … to play God."

Although he was doing his best, the boy was far from convincing in the role he's assigned himself, that of a bloodthirsty maniac. He sounded arrogant and more than a little silly, an actor reading the script of a bad movie.

Bowdoin was different, an avowed racist. When Tembelos pressed him about the Syrian, he brushed him off, complaining that 'those fucking people are ruining the world.' Growing up in Texas, he fancied himself an expert on the problem and said Europe needed to send the migrants a message. "Machine guns," he said, "that's the answer. Blast every last one of those sons of bitches to hell and back."

Again, Patronas questioned what he was hearing. As with Nielsen, there was a false element in Bowdoin's little speech, a staged quality. Patronas was sure Bowdoin had heard the words elsewhere and was just repeating them. Maybe his father had said them one night over dinner, or a local politician in Bowdoin's hometown. Such people existed in America. George Wallace wasn't that long ago.

"What about the fire?" Patronas asked.

"That was us, too," Bowdoin said. "We figured you'd think a Greek did it and that he killed the kid, too, and we'd be off the hook. A group of Greeks beat a Pakistani to death in Athens, and we assumed you'd think the death of the kid was the same kind of thing."

"We almost did," Patronas said under his breath, remembering Achilles Kourelas.

Gilbert was far less forthcoming, shrugging when Patronas asked him why he'd participated in the killing. "Temporary insanity?" he offered.

He tried to sound as callous as the others, but he couldn't quite pull it off. Alone among the three, he seemed to realize the gravity of what they'd done.

Sensing they'd reached an impasse, Papa Michalis stepped in and took over the interview a few minutes later. "How did you convince the boy to come with you?" he asked Nielsen.

"We promised him a bicycle," Nielsen said. "We even asked him what color he wanted. 'Red,' the little fucker said. 'I want a red bicycle.' "

"None of you speak Arabic. How did you communicate with him?"

"We looked the words up on the computer. There are sites that tell you how to sound things out and that's what we did. He was always around, playing in the street with the other kids, so it was easy to find him. Before we spoke to him, Charlie, here, bought a soda and we laced it with drugs and gave it to him. After that, we told him about the bike and the rest was easy."

He smirked. "He actually thanked us."

"Those people love handouts," Bowdoin said. "They just take and take." He drawled these last few words, and again, Patronas had the sense he was repeating something he'd heard.

Translated, the kid didn't matter. He was nothing.

Patronas shook his head. The part about the bike made him want to cry.

He remembered what Lydia Pappas had said about someone watching her at Thanatos. "Were you there when Lydia Pappas found the body? Were you spying on her?"

"Yeah," Bowdoin said. "We were deep into the ritual when we heard her coming, pretending to be Phoenicians and all that shit. Michael was the high priest, and we were all calling to Moloch. We didn't want her to see us, so we stopped what we were doing and hid in the bushes. It was about an hour after we killed him. The blood was already pretty dry."

"I was all for killing her, too," Nielsen said, a swagger in his voice, "but these guys wouldn't let me."

"After she left, we wiped everything down and ran for it," Bowdoin said. "I threw the knife off the rock, thinking no one would find it. She had her phone out and we knew she was calling the cops."

"How'd you get away?" Lydia had specifically said she'd seen no cars in the parking lot.

"We stayed well behind her and skirted around the museum, then hiked back down the hill. We knew the way. We'd mapped it out before we killed him. There's a little path not far from the migrant camp. Using the Jeep would have been too risky. Svenson would have known."

"Is that how you got Sami up there?"

"Yup. We'd already drugged him, so we had to carry him part of the way. We'd rehearsed going back and forth one night, so we knew what we were doing."

Very gently, the priest continued to probe. "There was very little blood at the scene. What did you do with it?"

"We drank it." Nielsen widened his eyes, obviously seeking to shock the old man.

Thinks he's the star in a feature film. Patronas could hear it in the young man's voice, how entertained he was to have been involved in a murder. Soulless and foolish and a killer of children.

"Svenson had us reenacting religious rites all summer," Bowdoin explained. "He told us people had practiced human sacrifice in the old days and that it had brought them power and prosperity, so we wanted to try it out."

"The red ocher and the beads?" Papa Michalis asked.

"They were Svenson's," Nielsen said. "I bought the metal pole at a hardware store in Kamares and the chain there, too, but everything else came from him. He had all this crap, tons of it, and I figured he wouldn't miss it."

"The anklets we found in his apartment?"

"I put them there. I wanted to confuse things, make you think he was culpable."

A big word, *culpable.* Unfamiliar, Patronas could only guess at its meaning. The kid might be a psychopath, but he had a fine vocabulary.

Looking off into space, Nielsen seemed to lose his train of thought for a moment. "Using the lock was a mistake. Svenson had it in his room and I took it. He'd showed it to us once and I remembered where he kept it. I wanted to make everything authentic, you know? As close to the original as we could get. He got suspicious and confronted me. We were in deep by that point and we couldn't have that."

"So you killed him, too?" Papa Michalis stated this quietly.

Nielsen nodded. "I called him and told him I'd left something on the boat the last time we went out and I needed to get it—a watch my father had given me for my birthday. He said he had an appointment with you, but if I hurried, he could meet me before."

"And the three of you were waiting for him?"

"Yes."

"How'd you get away from school? Didn't you have classes that day?"

"Svenson had already left, so we didn't have to stay. He was our adviser, and that's how it worked. After he died, they gave us another adviser, but he was it for us then."

"Who hit him?"

Looking down at his hands, Nielsen inspected his fingernails. "I don't remember."

"It was you, Michael," Bowdoin said, his voice rising. "You hit him and hit him and then you threw him into the water. You did all of it, every last fucking bit."

Gilbert was in tears. "And we just stood there and watched."

In spite of himself, Patronas was troubled by the fate of the students, and he spoke to the Turkish authorities at the prison before he left, flashing his badge and asking if there wasn't some way to release the three boys into his custody.

The official he spoke with was extremely polite. "We know what they did," he said in English. "Your commanding officer explained it to us when he called and asked us to hold them at the airport. They are very bad people, your supervisor said. They killed a ten-year-old Muslim boy, a refugee from Syria."

"It happened in Greece. We have jurisdiction."

The man gazed at him thoughtfully for a few minutes. "Don't you wonder what made them do such a terrible thing?" he asked. "What manner of people they are? Was it because the boy was a Muslim and America is at war with Muslims? Or maybe it was sadism that motivated them, the desire to hurt. Either way they should not walk the earth with the rest of us. They should be in prison. Here or Greece, it doesn't really matter. While I believe you are sincere, Mr. Patronas, your concern is misplaced. You should be mourning the victim, not seeking freedom for his killers."

"The drugs were planted," Patronas said. "I'm sure of it."

"I'm sorry, Mr. Patronas, but I am afraid I must refuse your request. They are our prisoners now and they will stay here with us. They will not leave Turkey."

Standing up, the Turk escorted Patronas and the priest to the door. "Good day, sir. Give my regards to your commanding officer, Mr. Stathis."

PATRONAS HAD THE cellphone number of Benjamin Gilbert's father and he called him. When the man answered, he introduced himself and told them he'd just visited his son in his cell in Istanbul.

"Benji, oh my God … is he all right?" the man asked in an agitated voice.

"As well as can be expected," Patronas answered. "The prison where he's staying is a pretty rough place."

"My wife and I are in Munich, waiting to catch the plane to Istanbul with our lawyer. If everything goes according to plan, we should be there later today. I spoke to the parents of the other two and we're planning to get some funds together, hopefully, pay a fine and get them out. How's the system work over there? How soon can we post bail?"

Poor, trusting Americans. Thinking money would solve everything,

"I don't know what the custom is," Patronas said. "I'm not sure they even have bail in Istanbul, and I doubt you can buy the Turks off."

"There must be *something* we can we do," the man howled.

"You need to get Benji and others out of the cell they're in and into solitary. They're in a compound with the general prison population; and it will go badly for them if they stay there. There are Jihadists in that place. Muslim fanatics who hate Americans.

"I'll see to it. Thank you."

Hopefully, the man would never learn the full extent of his son's crimes, would go on believing until the day he died that smuggling heroin was the worst thing his boy ever did. Patronas wished that for him. The alternative was too painful to contemplate.

He tried unsuccessfully to reach the other two sets of parents, but eventually gave up. They must be in transit, and Gilbert's father would tell them what he'd said. They had money and influence, contacts within the State Department and the American Embassy in Ankara. Perhaps they'd succeed in building a wall around their children, protecting them from the local inmates.

MALTEPE, WHERE THE prison was located, had once been a summer resort for rich Ottomans, Papa Michalis informed Patronas as they made their way to the waiting taxi. "My mother was from Istanbul and she often spoke of it."

Still in shock over what they'd learned, neither wanted to discuss the students.

Getting carried away, Nielsen had even gone so far as to reenact the child's terror, demonstrating how the little boy had writhed and screamed when they chained him to the pole then brought out the knife.

"You should have seen him."

Raising his hands in the air, Nielsen cried, "Allah, Allah!'" mimicking the child's Syrian accent. Bowing and playing the fool.

It was quite a show. Unable to control himself, he'd laughed hysterically. Bowdoin had also been amused.

"Show them what he did, Michael!" he shouted, egging his friend on. "Come on, show them!"

Knowing the drugs had worn off before the boy was killed made Patronas want to vomit.

Maybe the Turkish official was right, after all, he thought. The world would be a better place without them.

CHAPTER THIRTY-ONE

---·◆·---

Do not wrong the dead.
—The Delphic Oracle

MALPTEPE WAS OVERRUN with sprawling apartment buildings. All that
was left of its former grandeur was the view. Patronas could see the Sea
of Marmara and the archipelago of the five Princes Islands in the distance,
small outcroppings of land in the seemingly endless water. A large mosque
dominated a nearby hillside. Built in the traditional style, it was a magnificent
structure, blue-gray with a large dome and four delicate minarets.

The prison was far from the center of Istanbul, and the drive to the hotel
where they'd arranged to meet Stathis took over two hours. The road they
were on traversed almost the entire Asian side of the city. The suburbs were
densely settled, and there was a tremendous amount of traffic. Patronas saw
a family picnicking by the water, smoke rising from their grill, and beyond
them, a group of boys playing soccer on the grass. *Not so different from us*, he
concluded, studying them from the window of the cab.

They sped down a street full of stores selling women's evening dresses.
Heavily beaded and obviously expensive, the gowns were elaborate affairs in
every color of the rainbow, at least a third of them strapless.

"Where do they wear them?" Patronas asked the priest. "From what I've
seen, women keep themselves pretty covered here."

"What do I know of women's fashion," the priest said, "here or elsewhere?
I am a man of God, a priest."

Aside from the historic district, many areas of Istanbul appeared to be
under construction: work crews pouring cement, giant cranes erected over
vast holes in the ground. They crossed the Bosphorus and headed toward
the Golden Horn. The park fronting the water was beautifully cared for, its
lush gardens planted with rose bushes. Every two or three kilometers, there

was a shiny new playground for the children, exercise equipment for their parents, and metal grills for cooking. Immense apartment buildings covered the low-lying hills on both sides of the water, their balconies overlooking the luminous channel that separated the two continents.

"A boomtown, Istanbul," Patronas told Tembelos and Papa Michalis. The feeling of prosperity was almost palpable. It didn't seem fair to him, Turkey ascending while his homeland, a far nobler and more ancient country, was in economic freefall.

"The seventh largest city in the world. The population of Istanbul is over fourteen million," the priest told them, "almost five times that of Athens."

As they neared the historic center of Sultanahmet, the priest pointed to the high stone wall, saying, "It was built by the Roman Emperor Theodosius in the fifth century AD. It's only been breached twice since then, once in the thirteenth century by the men of the Fourth Crusade, the other in 1453 when the Ottoman Turks overran the city."

While waiting at a red light, Patronas noticed a group of men washing their feet in a low marble fountain outside a mosque. They all seemed to know one another and were chatting amiably.

"*Wudu,*" the priest said. "It's a Moslem ritual. Worshippers must be clean and wear good clothing before presenting themselves to God. The devout face Mecca and pray five times a day, reciting prayers that are over fourteen hundred years old. There are many rules, and they abide by each one. For example, no one is allowed to wear shoes in a mosque. It's well organized; they have attendants at the entrance who take the shoes and store them while people worship. The religion is a living force here and throughout the Middle East. It influences absolutely every aspect of life."

And therein, yet again, Patronas thought, *lies the difference between us.*

STATHIS WAS WAITING in the lobby of the small hotel in Sultanahmet. It was very hot outside, and in contrast, the high-ceilinged room felt like an oasis. Overhead, huge fans whirled slowly, and the Turks eating in the adjoining dining room were chatting with one another and chuckling —what the priest called, *kefi,* Turkish for 'good spirits.' On the walls were many paintings— scenes from the age of Ottomans—and on the shelves, knickknacks of every variety—china dogs and cats, porcelain shepherdesses, even a clock, its dial held in place by a pair of half-naked blackamoors. Patronas felt strangely at home, the décor eerily reminiscent of the furnishings in his mother's house.

His boss was sitting in an upholstered chair, drinking a demitasse of Turkish coffee. "How'd it go?" he asked when he saw Patronas. He remained where he was, hadn't bothered to get up.

"They admitted they murdered Sami Alnasseri. Reason didn't amount to much. The boy stole an iPad from one of them. Ritual killing also came into play, or so they wanted me to believe. According to them, Richard Svenson had reenacted a ritual murder one day in class, a rite of human sacrifice from Phoenicia. They'd been intrigued and wanted to try it out themselves. Nielsen gave me a lot of crap about it. Pretty creepy, the things he said. But I don't think that was the real reason they killed him. Thrill-seeking would be my guess. Racism played a part, too. It was pretty clear they despised Sami Alnasseri because of what he was." Not wishing to forget anything, Patronas scanned his notes. "They also admitted they threw the firebomb."

"Why?"

"To mislead us into thinking *Chrisi Avgi* was responsible for the killing. They didn't mention the group by name. All they said was there were plenty of Greeks who hate the migrants and they wanted us to think one of them did it."

"And Svenson?"

"Him, too, sir. Everything."

"So the case is closed." Stathis folded his hands over his chest, an evil Buddha. "Well done, Patronas."

Patronas took a deep breath. Might as well get it said. "Before I left, I asked the officials at the prison to release them into my custody so I could take them back to Greece for trial, but they refused."

"You did what?" Stathis choked on his coffee.

Leaping to his feet, he approached Patronas. "I told you there would be no extradition, none, even if those boys confessed," he said, jabbing him in the chest with a finger. "The order I gave you was very clear: talk to them, but leave things as they are."

Patronas addressed him in a controlled manner. "With all due respect, sir, I didn't think it was right what happened at the airport. I wanted to get justice for Sami Alnasseri, not to avenge him. I am a cop. That's *not* my job."

Nor yours, he wanted to add, but didn't, convinced his boss would fire him on the spot.

Stathis eyed him coldly. "After what happened with Achilles Kourelas, you have the nerve to criticize me? What right do you have to tell me how to do my job?"

"Planting the heroin, sir. It was wrong."

"Not as wrong as shooting an innocent man."

They argued for a few more minutes, Patronas refusing to back down. It wasn't the fate of the students—they could rot in hell as far as he was concerned—it was the cavalier way Stathis had set them up. First, you do something like that to them, and then you do it to someone else—maybe someone innocent this time. Before you know it, you're finished, not just as a cop, but as a human being. It was a bad road to start down.

"The Embassy has been notified and their parents are coming tonight," he said. "All hell's going to break loose."

"Let it. The Turks will never release them. They know those kids killed a ten-year-old Muslim boy. And they'll prosecute them for that if they have to. There's no longer a death penalty in Turkey, but at the very least they are looking at life imprisonment."

Patronas continued to berate his boss. Worried, Tembelos signaled him with his eyes to stop. Even the priest, the arbitrator of all things moral, was shaking his head.

Eventually Stathis returned to his coffee, taking a prissy little sip. Frowning, he set his cup down on the table in front of him. "You are a stubborn man, Patronas, insubordinate and full of yourself. I'll let it pass this time, but see that you don't do it again."

Tembelos pulled Patronas away before he could respond. "Don't ruin your career over this," he whispered. "Those kids got what they deserved."

"They'll die in that prison."

"Let it go, Yiannis. For God's sake, just let it go."

Eager to return home, Stathis and Tembelos were planning to return to Greece the next morning. Papa Michalis wanted to stay on in Istanbul for a few more days and visit the Patriarchate, the seat of the Greek Orthodox Church, and search for his mother's childhood home.

Worried, Patronas insisted on accompanying him. They'd spend twenty-four hours sightseeing and then head back to Chios. Patronas was very clear on that point—twenty-four hours, not a single minute more. The old man couldn't be permitted to roam the streets of Istanbul by himself, not dressed as a priest and most likely seeking to convert the natives. *Athyrostomos*—a mouth without a door—Father was. No good would come of it.

They gathered for a farewell dinner that night at Asitane, a restaurant famous for serving traditional Ottoman fare. Pleased with the tidy outcome of the case, Stathis had offered to treat.

The restaurant was located off a cobbled square not far from the Church of the Holy Savior, which had been deconsecrated by the Turks some time ago and renamed the Kariye Museum. "It is renowned for its frescoes and mosaics," Papa Michalis said, "some of the most beautiful in the world." He insisted they visit it before the meal.

The mosaics were indeed spectacular, virtually indistinguishable from oil paintings, the one of the Christ and the Virgin Mary especially compelling. Sadly, the people who had once worshipped there were all gone, the majority expelled by the Turks in 1922, the remainder in 1956. There *were* Greeks in the church, but they, too, were tourists.

Like the priest, Tembelos was a reluctant visitor to Turkey, and kept referring to Istanbul by its Greek name, *Constantinopolis,* the City of Constantine the Great, and making poisonous remarks about Kemal Ataturk, the founder of the modern Turkish state who had engineered the destruction of the Greek community.

"Why the hell is his photo everywhere?" He pointed to a picture of Ataturk at the entrance to the restaurant.

Such displays were on walls throughout the city. Patronas had seen them on billboards and in every store they'd visited since their arrival. Sometimes Ataturk was pictured in a fez, other times, staring somberly ahead. Given that he'd engineered the destruction of the Armenians and the burning of Smyrna as well as the expulsion of over a million of their Greek countrymen, the photos made him nervous.

"It's like he's looking over my shoulder," Tembelos said, equally spooked, "waiting with a scimitar in his hand to cut off my head."

"Keep your voice down," Stathis hissed. "They love him here. He's like a father to them."

"I love my father, too, but I don't have a picture of him in every fucking room of my house."

The food offered in the restaurant was unlike anything Patronas had ever tasted—the combinations of fruit and meat, the intricate seasonings. He ordered something called *kavun dolmasi*—melon stuffed with ground lamb, nuts, and currants—a recipe the menu said dated from the fifteenth century. He found it surprisingly delicious, one of the best things he'd ever eaten. The priest was working his way through *mutanjene*—an elaborate concoction of lamb, apricots, raisins, figs, prunes, and almonds—and Stathis was enjoying sea bass roasted with rose water. Unwilling to experiment, Tembelos and Evangelos Demos had ordered kebabs, the closest thing to Greek food they could find on the menu.

Between mouthfuls, the priest explained there were many similarities between the cuisines of the two countries. "Take *mamoulia*, for example, a cookie stuffed with nuts that we make on Chios. The Turkish version is identical. Even the name is close, *mamul.* And then there's *barbounia*—in Turkish, *barboun.*"

"Who got there first?" Tembelos asked. "Us or them?"

"With respect to food, I believe it was the Turks. As for everything else— science, philosophy, theater, democracy—it was us."

"It appears democracy is still giving them some trouble," Tembelos said.

This time Stathis lost his temper. "*Scase!*" he bellowed. Shut up. "You want to get us arrested?"

After they finished eating, they sat around the table for a long time, drinking *raki* and reviewing the facts of the case, deeply troubled by the three kids and what they'd done to Sami Alnasseri. The crime made no sense to them. Unable to let it go, they kept going over the details, trying to process it.

"Ritual murder in this day and age?" Stathis said. "They must be mad."

"A little," Patronas said. "Mostly just young and jaded, seeking excitement anywhere they could find it." He said he intended to hold a funeral, a proper Muslim one, and bury Sami Alnasseri in Athens. "Focus on the victim," he told the others, "not the killers."

That is what a judge had told Patronas when he first joined the force. Over the years, he had found it to be good advice, a way of keeping himself grounded. "No one should enter into the mind of a murderer," the judge had said. "Such darkness is contagious and it will eat into your soul."

"Since there's no mosque in Athens," Patronas said, "I'll have to organize everything myself. I've been reading up on Muslim ritual, funeral rites in Syria specifically. Instructions on the Internet were pretty clear and I am sure I can do it."

"Won't you need a cleric to preside?" the priest asked.

"No. Sami's aunt can say the necessary prayers: 'In the name of Allah and in the faith of the Messenger of Allah,' and I'll join in, if she wants. I've been working on that, too, so I can pronounce the words properly. Soil cannot touch the body, so I'll have to buy a piece of wood and place it over him before we start to fill in the grave. After that, we throw in three handfuls of soil apiece."

Papa Michalis nodded. "Three of everything, a trinity of sorts."

"We already violated Muslim tradition by performing an autopsy on him. I'd like to get at least this much right."

Rosy-faced, Tembelos tossed down another shot of raki. "Who else is going to be there?" he asked.

"No one. Just his aunt and me."

"I'll come," he said.

"As will I," Papa Michalis said. "If you think it will make her too uncomfortable to have a Christian priest present, I will stand off to the side, but I want to be there when you lay him to rest."

Stathis had been listening intently to the conversation. "We'll bury him in the First Cemetery of Athens," he announced. "I'll have to pull some strings, but I believe it can be done. Given the extent of her injuries, the boy's aunt will probably still be in a wheelchair, so I'll arrange transport for her as well—get a nurse to accompany her. As a Muslim woman, she'd prefer that, I think, rather than having one of us help her."

A compassionate remark, sympathetic. Patronas stared at Stathis for a long moment.

A man of many parts, his boss. He wasn't just a pompous fool. There was kindness in him as well. Pity even.

Tembelos volunteered to ready the grave while Patronas was in Istanbul, and all four agreed to chip in to pay for a gravestone.

"Has to be modest," Patronas said. "Muslim law is strict on that point."

AFTER BREAKFAST THE next morning, Patronas and Papa Michalis set off to explore Istanbul, buying tickets for a hop on/hop off tourist bus, thinking it would be the best way to get an overview of the city. Stathis and Tembelos had already left, flying out on Turkish Airlines. They'd arranged to meet in two days' time and finalize the arrangements for the funeral of Sami Alnasseri in Athens. After he buried the boy, Patronas planned to return to Chios immediately. He'd spoken to Lydia Pappas the previous day. She had already bought her plane ticket and would be arriving there in five days. He needed to figure out where to put her. Sharing a cot in the police station wouldn't do. At the very least, she'd expect a bed.

Patronas and the priest boarded the bus in Tacsim Square and climbed up the circular stairs to the top. They took a seat at the front and put on their headsets. It was a glorious day. The bus started out, circling the Golden Horn and then moving along the Bosphorus. They crossed the Galata Bridge a few minutes later. Long lines of men were casting off the bridge, pulling up slippery little fish and dropping them in plastic buckets. A couple of women in headscarves were standing with them, also with poles in hand, doing the same.

The view took Patronas' breath away. Bordered by the Bosphorus and the strait of the Golden Horn, the Sea of Marmara to the south and the Black Sea to the north, the seven hills of Istanbul were surrounded on all sides by shining water.

The priest said there was even a word for it in Turkish, a special term to describe the way the light played across the surface of the Bosphorus, the historic border between Asia and Europe. Boats of every description were sailing back and forth between the two, leaving scythe-like wakes on the golden surface of the water. In addition to the fishing boats and tourist crafts, oil tankers were lumbering ponderously ahead, moving slowly in the direction of the Black Sea and Russia.

The bus ride took over two hours, and by the end of it, Patronas understood why the Greeks still grieved over the loss of the city more than six hundred years before. His mother had always referred to it as *i polis*, the city. There was only one city in the world, she often said, and it was here.

Sitting out in the open air, he had the same sense he'd had at the airport, that he was as far from home as he had ever been. He stared at the people in the crowded streets, the women pushing strollers. Familiar, yet somehow not. He felt like he was at the edge of the known world. Not that there was an abyss on the other side, only the unknown. The world of Allah, not of Christ.

They spent a long time at Hagia Sophia, the crowning glory of the Byzantium Empire, and if the priest was to be believed, one of the greatest achievements in human history. Few of its precious mosaics had survived the Ottoman occupation—nothing like the walls of gold Patronas had read about in school. The priest was quiet as they walked through the church. In the process of being restored, the main room was barely visible beneath the scaffolding. There were quotations in Arabic from the Quran throughout, huge round signs in every corner. "It's not a living church anymore," the old man said. "It's a relic. Do you know what Justinian, the emperor who built it, said upon entering?" He looked over at Patronas to make sure he was listening. "He said, 'Glory to God that I have been judged worthy of such a work! Oh, Solomon, I have outdone you!' " He shook his head sadly. "What we lost as a people …."

"What we continue to lose," Patronas said.

After leaving Hagia Sophia, they toured the Basilica Cistern, a vast subterranean water source, and the Blue Mosque.

Built by the Romans, the cistern was a dank, cavernous place with water dripping from the ceiling. At the back was a giant sculpted head of Medusa, lying on its side. In contrast, the Blue Mosque was full of muted light, filtering down through the stained windows in the dome. The walls were made up of ceramic tiles, countless designs in every shade of blue.

Seeing people kneeling in worship, Patronas felt like he was trespassing, and taking the priest by the arm, he led him back outside.

Curious, they also visited the harem, part of the enormous palace complex of Topkapi, the historic home of the sultans.

"The Ottomans were a most peculiar group of people in my opinion," Papa Michalis said after they concluded the tour. "Did you hear what the guide said about African eunuchs guarding the entrance to the harem? And how the Sultan's mother picked the concubine her son would sleep with, like a madam in a brothel?" The priest sniffed. "Even their entertainment was off—dwarfs in little ships sailing around the pool in the courtyard and doing acrobatic tricks."

"Three *hundred* women under one roof. Think of that, Father." Patronas shook his head in disbelief. "And I could barely manage one."

"Don't fault yourself." The priest laid a consoling hand on his arm. "Your wife, Dimitra, was an exceedingly difficult woman. Hercules himself would not have been able to subdue her."

Their final stop before heading to the patriarchate was the Grand Bazaar, to be followed by a side trip to its cousin, the Spice Bazaar, a short distance away.

The sales people were aggressive, and they talked the priest into buying a black leather satchel. Large and unwieldy, it resembled a mailman's bag and hung almost to his knees. To prove the bag was leather, not plastic, the salesman set it on fire with his cigarette lighter, clinching the deal for the old man.

"You're always saying, 'Lay not up for yourselves treasures upon this earth, which moth and dust doth corrupt,' " Patronas said. "And now look at you: you're laying up purses."

"This is different," the priest said primly. "As the salesman demonstrated, it is genuine leather and in case you are unaware, moths do not eat leather."

They both loved the Spice Bazaar, with its burlap sacks full of every imaginable spice. The smell alone was worth the trip. Patronas ended up buying a kilo of lokum, a glossy, gelatinous Turkish candy, and an herbal love potion/aphrodisiac in case he suffered a failure to launch with Lydia Pappas. He also bought a fez for Nikos, Evangelos Demos' handicapped son, and an ornate Turkish sword, its scabbard encrusted with fake jewels.

Intrigued by the idea of cherry-flavored tobacco, Patronas toyed with the idea of buying a hookah as well, but in the end decided against it. Cherry-flavored or not, it would still be tobacco. And as a policeman, he would be unwise to take up hashish.

Lydia Pappas called him as he was leading the priest out of the bazaar. A cruise ship had just arrived and busloads of European tourists were pouring in, the smell of spices gradually being replaced by that of sunscreen.

Seeing fresh game, the clerks in the stores perked up and began setting out fresh trays of lokum, calling for the tourists to sample some. "Very tasty, my friends. Old family recipe."

Taking a handful, Patronas ate the sweets one by one while he talked on the phone. He described his day in Istanbul and told her how he and his men were planning to bury Sami Alnasseri in Athens as soon as he returned to Greece.

"I would like to be there, too," she said. "To bear witness, if nothing else."

The priest was watching him. "Was that her?" he asked when Patronas hung up. "The woman you profess to love?"

"Yes, that was Lydia Pappas, the woman I love and intend to marry."

"In a church?"

"Probably not. In a civil ceremony."

"So … not in the eyes of God?"

"Father, I tried that—the crowns, the candles, the priest—and you saw how it went. Years of misery."

"And you think it will go better this time?"

"Look at it this way, Father. It couldn't be any worse."

After leaving the bazaar, they took a taxi to the Patriarchate, located in the Church of St. George, a surprisingly modest building in the Phanar district, after which they visited the *Panagia ton Vlachernon,* one of the most cherished churches in the Orthodox world. It was here that the Greek residents of Istanbul had taken shelter during foreign invasions. The famous *Akathistos Hymnos,* recited the first five Fridays of Lent, was first chanted here in 626 AD by the Greek residents in gratitude to the *Theotokos,* Mary, the Mother of God, who had miraculously repelled the Persian fleet, thus saving them.

Patronas had often attended those Lenten services and sung that hymn with his mother. Remembering her, he began to chant its most famous stanza. The priest joined in a moment later, and together they sang the words in the empty church, their voices echoing off the stone walls:

> Unto the Defender General the dues of victory,
> and for the deliverance from woes, the thanksgiving
> I, Thy city, ascribe Thee, O Virgin
> And having your might unassailable,
> deliver me from all danger
> so that I may cry unto Thee:
> Rejoice, O Bride unwedded.

A shiver ran down Patronas' spine. He imagined the people, cowering behind these walls in the fifteenth century, praying for salvation as the Ottomans laid siege to the city, praying to the Virgin to protect them.

Remembering Sami, he wondered who the boy had called out to in his final minutes, if there was the equivalent of the Holy Mother in his faith.

And if there was, why she hadn't answered.

The priest said his mother had lived in Balat, an old Greek and Jewish neighborhood not far from the Patriarchate. Built on a steep hill, the area, although shabby, was picturesque with cobbled streets and old buildings painted a myriad of bright colors. The upper floors of many jutted out over the pavement, a feature dating from the time of the Ottomans, when Muslim women, in virtual hiding, had watched the world go by from second-story windows.

They passed one house that was literally falling down, its wooden staircase eaten away and almost entirely gone. In spite of this, people were living inside. Patronas saw pots of well cared-for geraniums sitting on the windowsills and heard a radio playing from somewhere deep within.

Stathis had warned them to be careful, saying some of the people living in Phanar and Balat were hostile to Greeks and it might be unsafe for them there. Patronas' experience bore this out. Many of the windows and doors were heavily barred, and signs advertising security systems were in evidence on nearly every building. The people he passed all kept their heads down. A few, upon encountering the priest, even went so far as to cross the street in order to avoid him.

Although they searched for over two hours, address in hand, the two never found the house where Papa Michalis' mother had come of age. The street names had all changed. Istanbul was a different place than it had been in 1922, the year she and her family fled Turkey. The old quarter of Balat felt haunted now, melancholic and full of shadows, and Patronas was glad when Papa Michalis suggested they abandon the search and leave.

AFTER DINNER—A MACKEREL sandwich, one of the famed delicacies of Istanbul—they took a one-hour cruise on the Bosphorus. The boat was small and packed with Turkish twenty-year olds. Patronas and Papa Michalis were the only foreigners. To Patronas' surprise, the young people fell silent when the muezzin made his call at sunset and sat there respectfully without saying a word. The only sound was the water lapping against the wooden hull of the boat.

Youngsters on an outing, the girls had taken great care with their appearance. Their eyes were beautifully made up, and the fabric of their scarves matched that of the summer dresses they wore under their long jackets. The work of a female relative, he guessed, a mother or a grandmother. Although lovely, the garments were obviously homemade.

A co-ed group, they were all talking and laughing together in a way Patronas hadn't seen in years. There was a kind of purity in their conduct, male and female alike, an innocence he remembered from his own boyhood, when just saying hello to a girl in his class had been a major adventure.

Maybe there was something to Islam, after all.

When he proposed this to Papa Michalis, the old man nodded. "I know it is a blasphemy, but I was thinking the exact same thing."

Strung with lights, the suspension bridge connecting Europe to Asia came to life a few minutes later. The colors changed every few minutes on the network of cables that supported it—one minute purple, the next blue. Patronas watched it for a few minutes, thoroughly enjoying himself.

"Look, Father!"

The priest barely looked up. He had gone quiet since leaving Balat.

"What's the matter?" Patronas asked. "Are you upset because we didn't find your mother's house?"

Papa Michalis waved him off. "Not important," he said. "Just an old man's fancy." He paused for a moment. "The truth is, I can't get those boys out of my mind. The ones who killed him."

Patronas looked out at the night, seeking to hang on to the beauty of Istanbul. He would be meeting Lydia Pappas in less than twelve hours and he wanted to sit there, daydreaming about her. To write bad poems in his head about catching stars and weaving them in her hair. He didn't want to remember Sifnos. He wanted to put the case behind him and forget about it.

But there was no stopping the old man. When upset, Papa Michalis would talk and talk, and tonight, apparently, he was very upset.

"Look at the bridge, Father," Patronas said again. Red and green now, the lights might serve to distract him.

But Papa Michalis was intent on having his say. "I know everyone says the migrants will ruin everything, overturn Western culture like a canoe and bring about the end of the world as we know it. Jihadists on every corner and so forth and so on. But I think the problem is different. I think it's the growing amorality of the young. There was nobody like Michael Nielsen and those other two when I was growing up, not even in America. Nobody who slaughtered children. No one who killed for sport."

"Why do you think he did it?"

"Well, Richard Svenson certainly played a role. One shouldn't speak ill of the dead, but that man had no business being in a classroom. You have to take responsibility for what you teach, Yiannis. It's imperative. I don't know if you're aware of this, but the Nazi party gained its first adherents, not in the streets of Germany, but in its *universities*. They assumed because dogs could be bred successfully—I believe the Doberman Pinscher was cited—the same could be done with people."

"I don't follow. What do the Nazis have to do with Richard Svenson?"

"It's what he *taught* them, Yiannis. Don't you see? It can't be amoral what you instill in the young. It has to have value, be as close to the truth as possible."

"Christian truth?"

"*Moral* truth. Whether it's Christian or not doesn't matter. That's where Svenson went wrong. The reenactment of a blood rite—that's essentially what led to this. He might have intended it as theater, but Nielsen and the other two took it to the next level. All that nonsense Nielsen said about wanting to feel the child's life ebbing away. Playing the high priest …." The old man snorted. "It was Satanism, pure and simple. And Svenson taught it to them."

Sticking his hands in the sleeves of his robe, he wrapped his arms around himself. "His ideas were toxic, a celebration of brutality and violence. The world is a fearful place and religion, be it pagan or not, can provide a bulwark against the darkness. But evil is also there in this, the possibility that we can harness and contain it—ride it, in other words. A great thrill, I imagine, opening up that portal and staring down at hell."

He had more to say, but Patronas tuned him out, concentrating instead on the gentle murmuring of the Bosphorus, the soft slapping of the water beneath him. He'd be sorry to leave Istanbul. It was the most dazzling place he'd ever been. He wished his mother was still alive and he could tell her.

"*I polis,*" he whispered, looking across the strait toward Asia. The city.

Still profoundly unsettled, the priest continued to talk. "What we teach the young will determine our future, maybe even the future of the world. And what is it they learn from us? Promiscuity, alcoholism, and drug addiction. Don't look at me that way, Yiannis. I know what I'm talking about. I may be old, but I hear things. I get around." His voice had risen, becoming strident.

The Turkish kids had fallen silent and were watching him with growing alarm.

Time to put an end to this. "I don't know, Father. I wouldn't blame Svenson. I think it might have just been them."

"It's all of us, I tell you. Western civilization only had one mooring and that was religious faith, and in Greece at least, it has been well and truly decimated. No one listens to priests anymore. No one strives to follow the words of Christ. For centuries, the church tried to contain the kind of savagery we saw on Sifnos, tried to instill a belief in the sanctity of life. Yet somehow, it never really succeeded. Violence lives in the human heart, Yiannis, that's all there is to it. With the least provocation, men will pick up a sword and chop their neighbors to pieces. They do it in the name of Christ. They do it in the name of Allah. But in the end, they always do it. The need to annihilate those who are different is strong in us—the ones with darker skin or who worship a different god, the heathens and the infidels. And now, sadly, the strangers in our midst—the migrants."

Patronas had never seen Papa Michalis so worked up. The search for his mother's house must have upset the old man more than he realized, reminding him of the life she'd been forced to endure as a refugee, those years of poverty and alienation. Perhaps that was why Greece treated the migrants better than the rest of the Europe. There had even been talk of awarding the women on the island of Lesvos the Nobel Peace Prize, because its citizens *knew* how it felt to be uprooted. Their parents and grandparents had lived through a similar cataclysm, suffered as much or more than the Syrians had.

Still, he believed the priest was wrong about the case. It hadn't been bigotry that motivated those kids. It was something missing in their souls.

"Those three were the ones responsible, Father," Patronas said. "It wasn't society or mankind. It was just them."

"I'm afraid they are not alone. There's a whole army out there now, in every Western nation. Let's pray someone like Hitler doesn't come along and set them in motion."

"It was just them," Patronas repeated. "It wasn't Svenson. It wasn't the rest of us. It was just them, Father: Nielsen, Gilbert, and Bowdoin. They were evil people, from the devil's farm."

As they were exiting the boat, one of the Turkish girls approached Patronas. "Is he all right?" she whispered, nodding to Papa Michalis. Her friends were watching her, their faces full of concern.

"Yes, he's fine. Just a little tired."

When she reported back to her friends, they all smiled at Papa Michalis,, obviously relieved.

"If this is Islam, I'll take it," Patronas said to himself. As an antidote, it would be extreme, but if, as the priest said, the alternative to religious faith was Michael Nielsen, they'd all be better off.

But then there was ISIS and Al-Qaeda, young men as crazy and violent as any who'd ever walked the earth. They were far worse than Nielsen and they numbered in the tens of thousands.

Sitting there that night in Istanbul, Patronas recalled the Book of Revelation, St. John's fiery vision of the end of the world. Like Papa Michalis, he felt the world was far less safe than it had been when he was a boy, had grown dark and would grow darker still. He could almost hear the trumpets heralding the Apocalypse start to sound.

CHAPTER THIRTY-TWO

———◆———

On reaching the end, be without sorrow.
—The Delphic Oracle

THEY BURIED SAMI Alnasseri on a Wednesday morning, three days after Patronas returned from Istanbul. Stathis had succeeded in securing a plot in the First Cemetery. He even rented a hearse to transport the body from the morgue to hospital where the boy's aunt was staying, so that she and Patronas could prepare the child for burial, according to Muslim custom. The coroner had refused to wash the body, saying it was a religious rite and Patronas must see to it.

Patronas had read that the body must be placed on a high table. He followed the instructions, placing Sami Alnasseri on a gurney in an empty surgical suite. Then it must be washed carefully three times in a process called *ghusl*. The person doing the cleansing must start at the right shoulder, move to the left, and then work their way down. Although she was still in a wheelchair, Sami's aunt managed to raise herself up and lean against the gurney. As a woman, she was not permitted to wash the boy's body herself, so she instructed Patronas, overseeing what he did and correcting him when he made a mistake.

Lying there exposed, Sami Alnasseri looked small and defenseless, much younger than his actual age. Out of deference to the aunt, the coroner had bandaged the wound in the child's throat and the y-shaped incision from the autopsy that ran down the length of his body. Patronas tried to shield the area with a cloth so that she wouldn't see it, but she pushed his hand away.

"You must clean," she said. "Everywhere, clean."

After he'd cleansed the body, she demonstrated how he was to place the boy's hands on his chest, right hand on top of the left. Together, they enshrouded him in the three white cotton sheets Patronas had purchased.

"*Kafan*," she said, indicating they must start with the sheet on the right. After they finished the wrapping, she helped him secure the sheets at the child's head and feet with ropes and tied another length of cord around the middle of his body.

Watching her work, Patronas felt a wave of pity. She was obviously familiar with the ritual that attended death in her culture, deftly tying the ropes around the corpse and knotting them. Her hands flying, she could have done it blindfolded.

"I know how," she said, reading his mind. "I have many dead, many people."

Tembelos arrived not long after. He and Patronas carried Sami Alnasseri out to the parking lot where the hearse was waiting and laid him inside.

Lydia Pappas, who had come from Sifnos to help with the preparations, joined them there. She'd spent the previous day with Sami's aunt, seeking to learn what the Syrian woman wanted to wear to the service. After taking her measurements, she'd purchased the necessary garments. She'd also arranged for a hairdresser to come to the hospital that morning to wash and set the woman's hair.

Noor was now wearing what Lydia Pappas had bought her: a long, caftan-like dress made of a silky, expensive-looking fabric and a matching headscarf. Both were blue, so pale as to appear almost white. She also had on new shoes, white patent-leather ones, which, in spite of the heat, she wore with heavy white stockings.

Lydia wheeled her out to the handicapped van Stathis had found, then up the ramp to where the female attendant waited inside. The two of them would ride with the Syrian woman to the cemetery and keep her company on the hour-long journey across Athens.

Stathis had found a place for Noor to live after she was discharged from the hospital. For a small fee, a relative of his had expressed willingness to take her in and care for her. The woman had grown up in Alexandria, Egypt, and knew rudimentary Arabic. A widow, she was alone and welcomed the company.

Patronas had rejoiced when Stathis told him this and offered to contribute. "Let me handle it," his boss had said. "You'll be retiring one of these days. You need to hold on to your money."

Perhaps a new era was dawning in their relationship, a wary friendship. Patronas couldn't really see it. But then again, the world was full of surprises.

Located behind the Temple of the Olympian Zeus and the old Olympic stadium in central Athens, the First Cemetery contained three churches. Hundreds of the most illustrious people in recent Greek history were buried there—actors, poets, singers, politicians. And now, little Sami Alnasseri would join them.

They passed many crypts as they made their way toward the gravesite. Some dated from the last century and were surrounded with towering palm trees; others were far more recent. Patronas was carrying the remains of the child in his arms, Lydia Pappas and Giorgos Tembelos taking turns pushing the boy's aunt in the wheelchair. Stathis was behind them, walking with the two workmen who would fill in the plot once they'd finished. Papa Michalis was far behind, staying at a discreet distance.

A few of the family tombs were actual buildings, constructed out of white marble—small replicas of the Acropolis, with columns and fanciful porticoes. Some featured life-sized sculptures—grieving women, angels triumphant. Gripping the armrests of the wheelchair, Noor looked around in wonder.

Patronas had asked her if she wanted flowers to decorate the grave, but she shook her head. "No, no. It is not done."

The service itself didn't take long. Noor quietly led the ritual, facing Mecca and chanting the *Salat al-Janazah*, the Islamic funeral prayer:

> O God, forgive our living and our dead, those who are present among us and those who are absent, our young and our old, our males and our females. O God, whoever You keep alive, keep him alive in Islam, and whoever You cause to die, cause him to die with faith. O God, do not deprive us of the reward and do not cause us to go astray after this. O God, forgive him and have mercy on him, keep him safe and sound and forgive him, honor his rest and ease his entrance; wash him with water and snow and hail, and cleanse him of sin as a white garment is cleansed of dirt. O God, give him a home better than his home and a family better than his family. O God, admit him to Paradise and protect him from the torment of the grave and the torment of Hell-fire. Make his grave spacious and fill it with light.

Patronas had printed out the Arabic words phonetically, and he and the others did their best to join her. There weren't enough people in attendance to make the odd rows of mourners the Muslim rite required, but Patronas positioned his friends carefully, one a little closer to grave, another a little farther back, in an effort to honor the tradition. It was a hot day and the air was dusty, the sky nearly white with heat.

As Sami's aunt was not allowed to witness the actual internment, Lydia

Pappas wheeled her a small distance away, talking and gesturing in an effort to distract her.

Tembelos had prepared the grave the previous day, and he and Patronas carefully positioned the body at the bottom, making sure it was lying on its right side and facing Mecca as was the Islamic custom.

After they finished, they all recited, "In the name of Allah and in the faith of the Messenger of Allah." Patronas then covered the shroud with the wooden board he'd brought and laid some stones on top of it, after which each of them stepped forward and threw the requisite three fistfuls of earth into the grave.

The workmen immediately went to work with shovels to fill in the grave and finish the task. The headstone had been ordered, but it would take some time. Patronas planned to return from Chios when it was ready to supervise its installation. The boy was well positioned, not far from Andreas Papandreou, a former prime minister, and Odysseas Elytis, the Nobel Laureate in poetry. Patronas wondered what the famous Greeks would have made of the little Syrian. His mother had believed in all manner of spirits—ghosts, poltergeists, angels. Today, he hoped there were such things, and the spirits, such as they were, would be benevolent and welcome the child into their midst.

Weeping quietly, Lydia took his hand and led him out of the cemetery.

They all shared a meal afterward in a fish restaurant in Mikrolimano, a picturesque harbor with tavernas facing the water. Sami's aunt was very tired and fought to stay upright in her wheelchair. She appeared deeply touched by what Patronas had done and thanked him again and again.

"Sami, he is not forgotten," she said. "In Sifnos, you say these words to me, but I did not believe. You made it truth."

PATRONAS AND LYDIA Pappas spent the night at a hotel in Varkiza, a seaside resort forty kilometers from Athens. They'd accompanied Sami's aunt back to the hospital and helped the attendant resettle her in her room, then journeyed on from there in a police car Stathis had put at their disposal, the burgeoning relationship between Patronas and his boss in full flower. Tembelos and Papa Michalis were already in Chios, having flown out immediately after the funeral, and Stathis had returned to his office at the police station, saying he had work to do.

Patronas had bought a gold wedding ring in Athens the day he arrived from Istanbul. He'd had Lydia's name engraved inside, reserved a room at the Golden Sands on Chios, and ordered a local florist to fill it with roses. The priest had promised to get a church for them and Tembelos had offered to serve as best man. Eleni, Tembelos' wife, had volunteered to cook the wedding feast. Or they could go out, whatever Patronas preferred. Patronas wasn't planning on a lengthy engagement. Forty-eight hours at the most. If everything went according to plan, in less than three days he would be a married man.

Later, he and Lydia sat outside on the terrace of the hotel, watching the night. The lights from the hotel were reflected in the still water at their feet, stirring and breaking up when a gust of wind swept across the bay. The *gri gri* fishermen were hard at work, shining lanterns off the sterns of their boats in an effort to attract mackerel and *marida,* a tiny anchovy-like fish much loved as an appetizer in Greece. The technique was an ancient one, the light fooling the fish, who believed it was the sun and would swim to the surface, where fishermen lay in wait with their nets. Patronas could see a man with a net in his hand as well as the teeming fish flashing silver all around his boat, leaping and splashing in the dark water.

His cellphone rang. Startled, he looked down at the screen, wondering who it might be at this hour.

It was Tembelos, calling to tell him he'd just spoken to his wife and asked her to purchase the *stefania,* crowns, and *lambadas,* the decorated candles used in Orthodox wedding services. Also to speak to a priest and reserve a church.

"You're good to go," his friend said. "God help you."

"Someone getting married?" Lydia asked when Patronas closed the phone. He realized she must have overheard part of the conversation.

"I don't know. Maybe. You want to get married?"

Tears filled her eyes. "Sure," she said, making light of how moved she was. "Sure, Yiannis. Why not?"

IN THE END, they didn't use any of things Tembelos had purchased. They got married in a civil ceremony in Athens. Lydia wore a white lace beach cover-up she'd found on a rack on the sidewalk in Varkiza, and Patronas, a fresh shirt, pants, and a tie.

She had insisted on the latter, and when Patronas objected, told him, "There's a Greek proverb: 'A potter puts the handles where he wants.' I'm a potter and that's what I want."

"You're not going to put handles on me, are you?" Patronas asked. "Or a leash or a muzzle?"

"I won't, Yiannis, I promise. It'll be good, you'll see. I have some money and we'll buy a house in Chios, live out our days there. Watch the moon rise over the sea like we did last night in Varkiza. We're together now. All is well."

From Coffeetown Press
and Leta Serafim

———◆———

Thank you for reading *From the Devil's Farm*. We are so grateful for you, our readers. If you enjoyed this book, here are some steps you can take that could help contribute to its success and the success of this series.

- Post a review on Amazon.com, BN.com, and/or GoodReads.
- Check out Leta's website or blog and post a comment or ask to be put on her mailing list.
- Spread the word on social media, especially Facebook, Twitter, and Pinterest.
- Like Leta's Facebook author page and Coffeetown Press's Facebook page.
- Follow Leta (@SerafimLeta) and Coffeetown (@CoffeetownPress) on Twitter.

Good books and authors from small presses are often overlooked. Your comments and reviews can make an enormous difference.

L ETA SERAFIM IS the author of the Greek Islands Mysteries: *The Devil Takes Half* and *When the Devil's Idle*, as well as the work of historical fiction, *To Look on Death No More*. She has visited over twenty-seven islands in Greece and continues to divide her time between Boston and Greece.

You can find her online at www.letaserafim.com

The Greek Island Mysteries
Books 1 and 2

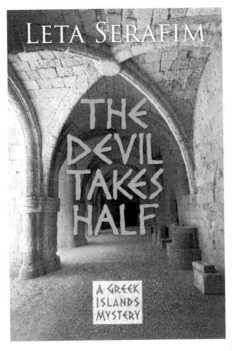

A beautiful archeologist and daughter of a local ship owner is found dead at a dig on the Greek Island of Chios. After the body of her young assistant is also discovered, the chief officer of the local police force, Yiannis Patronas, suspects that the pair turned up something of real value, all evidence to the contrary, and sets out to conquer the evil threatening his formerly peaceful island.

A German tourist is found murdered in the garden of an estate on the Greek Island of Patmos. Chief Yiannis Patronas is called in to investigate, assisted by his top detective, Giorgos Tembelos, and his friend, Papa Michalis. As they probe into the background of the dead man and his family, they uncover terrible secrets from the recent and distant past. But which secret led to murder?

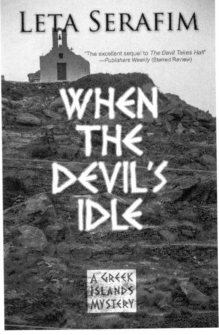

To Look on Death No More

LETA SERAFIM

In autumn of 1943, a Greek village already weakened by civil turmoil and deprivation is beset by the Nazis. An Irishman dropped into the fray by the British devotes himself to their welfare and becomes particularly attached to a young woman named Danae and her brother Stefanos. Although he joins the Greek soldiers to support their cause, what can one man do amid so much carnage?

64990250R00126

Made in the USA
Charleston, SC
12 December 2016